HAITI NOIR 2

HAITI NOIR 2

THE CLASSICS

EDITED BY EDWIDGE DANTICAT

Published by Akashic Books
©2014 Akashic Books
Series concept by Tim McLoughlin and Johnny Temple

Haiti map by Aaron Petrovich
Cover photo by Jerome Handler, "Le Negre Marron" (The Black Maroon), Port-au-Prince, Haiti, 1970; image reference NW0229, as shown on hitchcock.itc.virginia.edu/Slavery/, compiled by Jerome Handler and Michael Tuite and sponsored by the Virginia Foundation for the Humanities and the University of Virginia Library.

ISBN-13: 978-1-61775-193-6
Library of Congress Control Number: 2013938709
First printing

Grateful acknowledgment is made for permission to reprint the stories in this anthology. The Kurt Vonnegut Jr. epigraph is reprinted by permission of The Trust u/w of Kurt Vonnegut, Jr., Donald C. Farber, Trustee; "Praisesong for Port-au-Prince" by Danielle Legros Georges was originally published in *MaComère* 2 (1999), © 1999 by Danielle Legros Georges; "Preface to the Life of a Bureaucrat" by Jacques Roumain was originally published in French as "Préface à la vie d'un bureaucrate" in *Haïti-Journal* on February 19, 20, 21, 22, 24, and 25, 1930, reprinted by permission of Claude Roumain; "A Strange Story" by Ida Faubert was originally published in French as "Une étrange histoire" in *Sous le ciel caraïbe* (Paris: Éditions O.L.B., 1959), © 1959 by Ida Faubert; "The Enchanted Second Lieutenant" by Jacques-Stephen Alexis was originally published in French as "Le sous-lieutenant enchanté" in *Romancéro aux étoiles* (Paris: Éditions Gallimard, 1960), reprinted by permission of Éditions Gallimard, © Éditions Gallimard, 1960, renewed in 1968, published in English in *Callaloo* 20, no. 3 (Summer 1997), trans. Sharon Masingale Bell, © 1998 by Charles H. Rowell, reprinted with permission of Johns Hopkins University Press; "A White House with Pink Curtains in the Downstairs Windows" by Jan J. Dominique was originally published in French as "Une maison blanche avec des rideaux roses aux fenêtres du rez-de-chaussée" in *Évasion: nouvelles* (Port-au-Prince: Éditions des Antilles, 1996), © 1996 by Jan J. Dominique; "Oresca" by Paulette Poujol Oriol was originally published in French in *Boutures* 1, no. 4 (March–August 2001), © 2001 by Paulette Poujol Oriol; "Children of Heroes" (excerpt) by Lyonel Trouillot was originally published in French as *Les enfants des héros* (Paris: Actes Sud, 2002), reprinted from *Children of Heroes* by Lyonel Trouillot, translated by Linda Coverdale, by permission of the University of Nebraska Press, © 2002 by Actes Sud, English translation © 2008 by the Board of Regents of the University of Nebraska; "Remember One Day" by Emmelie Prophète was originally published in French as "Un jour rappelle-toi" in *Boutures* 1, no. 1 (July 1999), © 1999 by Emmelie Prophète; "Rêve Haitien" by Ben Fountain was originally published in *Harper's* magazine, January 2000, © 2000 by Ben Fountain; "Heading South" by Dany Laferrière was originally published in French as *Vers le sud* (Montréal: Éditions du Boréal, 2006), licensed here from the book *Heading South*, by Dany Laferrière, published in 2009 by Douglas & McIntyre: an imprint of D&M Publishers Inc., reprinted by permission from the publisher and Éditions Grasset et Fasquelle (France), © 2006 by Éditions Grasset et Fasquelle; "Three Letters You Will Never Read" by Georges Anglade was originally published in French as "Trois lettres que vous ne lirez jamais" in *Rire haïtien: les lodyans de Georges Anglade (Haitian Laughter: A Mosaic of Ninety Miniatures in French and English)* by Georges Anglade, trans. Anne Pease McConnell (Coconut Creek, FL: Educa Vision Inc., 2006), © 2006 by Georges Anglade; "The Port-au-Prince Marriage Special" by Edwidge Danticat was originally published in *Conjunctions* 50 (Spring 2008), © 2008 by Edwidge Danticat; "True Life" by Michèle Voltaire Marcelin was originally published in French as "La vraie vie" in *Le Cahier de la RAL,M*, no. 8 (2008), © 2008 by Michèle Voltaire Marcelin; "I Just Lost My Way" by Ezili Dantò was originally part of *The Red, Black & Moonlight* monologue series, based on *Kenbe La! Crossings of a Vodun-Roots Woman* by Ezili Dantò, © 1997 by Ezili Dantò/Marguerite Laurent; "The Mission" by Marie-Hélène Laforest was originally published in *Foreign Shores* (Montréal: Éditions du CIDIHCA, 2002), © 2002 by Marie-Hélène Laforest; "Barbancourt Blues" (excerpt) by Nick Stone was originally published in *Mr. Clarinet* (New York: HarperCollins, 2007), © 2007 by Nick Stone; "Dame Marie" by Marilène Phipps-Kettlewell was originally published in *Callaloo* 30, no. 3 (Spring 2007), © 2007 by Marilène Phipps-Kettlewell, reprinted by permission of University of Iowa Press; "Surrender," excerpted from *The Loneliness of Angels* by Myriam J. A. Chancy (Leeds: Peepal Tree Press, 2010), appears here with minor editorial changes by permission of the author, © 2010 by Myriam J.A. Chancy; "Things I Know About Fairy Tales" by Roxane Gay was originally published in *Necessary Fiction* (blog), May 13, 2009, http://necessaryfiction.com/stories/RoxaneGayThingsIKnowAboutFairyTales, © 2009 by Roxane Gay.

Akashic Books
PO Box 1456, New York, NY 10009
info@akashicbooks.com
www.akashicbooks.com

ALSO IN THE AKASHIC NOIR SERIES

PORT-AU-PRINCE

Cité Soleil

Boulevard Jean-
Jacques Dessalines

Rue des Miracles

Port-au-Prince
Central Prison

Place des Héros

Delmas

Pacot

Turgeau

Bolosse

CANAL DE
LA TORTUE

GOLFE DE
LA GONÂVE

BAIE DE
GONAÎVES

HAITI

BASSINS-COQUILLEAUX

CANAL DE
SAINT-MARC

KALIKO BEACH

CANAL
DE SUD

DAME MARIE   BONAIR

PORT-AU-PRINCE

QUINA

KENSCOFF

HAITI

DOMINICAN REPUBLIC

CARIBBEAN SEA

SOURCE DIQUINI

ANBA DLO, LAN GINEN

PÉTIONVILLE SQUARE

TABLE OF CONTENTS

Haitians speak Creole . . . which has only a present tense. I have lived in Haiti with my brother for the past six months, so I can speak it some. Felix and I are innkeepers now. We have bought the Grand Hotel Oloffson, a gingerbread palace at the base of a cliff in Port-au-Prince. Imagine a language with only a present tense. Our headwaiter, Hippolyte Paul De Mille, who claims to be eighty and have fifty-nine descendants, asked me about my father.

"He is dead?" he said in Creole.

"He is dead," I agreed. There could be no argument about that.

"What does he do?" he said.

"He paints," I said.

"I like him," he said.

—from *Deadeye Dick* by Kurt Vonnegut

INTRODUCTION
NOIR DEUX

How often are you asked to put together an amazing literary party? In my case, a mind-blowing two times. The lit party of my dreams has been *Haiti Noir,* and lo and behold, I get asked to do it again.

As you can imagine, I wanted everybody to be here. The noir genre, or elements thereof—however stretched—narrowed that a bit. The contributions had to be, well, "noir" and they had to not only be about Haiti, but be set there as well. It also helped if they could be pinned down to a particular neighborhood—real or imagined—so that we could make a map. (All the books in Akashic Books' award-winning Noir Series have maps.)

Like all parties, this one began with a dream list, and the narrowing of it. Because there was still so much ground left to cover after the January 2011 publication of the original *Haiti Noir*—which comprised brand-new stories—those writers who had been in that volume could not be included in this one. Though the term "classics" in this project's subtitle made it seem as if everyone had to be ancient or dead, there was thankfully some wiggle room to allow in contributions which are nearly vintage.

As with the first book, the idea of all these writers—dead or alive, classic or vintage or almost new—being together between these pages thrills me to no end. And I can't help imagine them joking, laughing, as well as arguing about Haitian politics and culture, all while swapping their unique stories.

Like all parties, not everyone we invited could make it. (The cost of reprint rights or the difficulty locating heirs for several writers were insurmountable obstacles.) So we are grateful and celebrate those who could, keeping in our hearts those who cannot be with us. Besides, a book like this is meant to be a sampler anyway, something to give you a desire, a yearning for more. So for every writer here you should seek out at least ten more, noir or otherwise, in the cannon of Haitian literature. This is especially important for a country that is unfairly known more for its natural and political disasters than its exciting and vibrant literature.

After the first *Haiti Noir* was published, people kept asking if I wasn't contributing to a negative image of the country by editing a book filled with so many "dark" stories about Haiti. My answer was, and remains, that showing the brilliance of our writers and their ability to address Haiti's difficulties through their art can only contribute to a more nuanced and complex presentation of Haitian lives. After all, the writers here are not Haiti virgins, to paraphrase from "Heading South," Dany Laferrière's story, included here, of sex tourism gone wrong. They are all old hats, either by blood or their deep love for Haiti. Also, the beauty of using, unlike the last time, previously published writings, is that they have been tried and tested and have already traveled their own paths in the world. For this is not just a party, folks, but also a costume party, a noir party. The author of each story, poem, or novel excerpt has shed his or her skin and has sunk into the deepest and most revealing places of the human heart.

Most of these works remain timeless and one imagines might be written the same way today as they were seventy, fifty, or even just three years ago. Others display their visions of their time, especially when it comes to Vodou. While some of the older writers handle the subject of Vodou in the same way that an outsider might, there is still an attempt to adjust their initial approach and show its misuse rather than blame it. And though the police procedural is hinted at in a few of the stories—Jan J. Dominique's "A White House with Pink Curtains in the Downstairs Windows," for example—most of the time when crimes are solved, this is done by individuals, either through confession, personal endeavors, or communal action.

Recently, Haiti saw its own "you can't make this up" high-profile crime stories explode then fizzle, in a way that might intrigue then disappoint any noir reader. The son of a very rich family was revealed to be part of a massive kidnapping ring. He had abducted the son and daughter of another rich family, with whom his family was feuding. He was arrested then forced to lead an elite police team to the house where his victims were being held. The kidnapping victims' rescue and subsequent reunion with their families was all captured on tape and later aired on a *Cops*-like television program called *Alo Lapolis (Hello Police)*. Aside from a single brief court appearance, the kidnapping ringleader, as of this writing, was never heard from again. He had supposedly been taken to a brand-new American prison, where he and his comrades were the sole inmates.

Then, in another case, a judge died while investigating the first family. His doctors said he suffered a stroke, but many, including members of the judge's family, believed that he was poisoned via a glass of whiskey. Several weeks later, the man who had filed the corruption complaint against the first family was arrested for an unsolved murder from a few years earlier. His future, as of now, is unclear.

These events could inspire several noir novels. Yet beyond the realm of fiction, they might never be resolved. That elusive justice might never come. Which makes the noir genre rather redemptive in Haiti. At least justice can be found in our writers' imaginations. At least justice can be found in art. Children who suffer abuse can find revenge. Nature can join the fight against invaders and occupiers with surprising results. Choices can be made, good or bad, in marital beds, hotel rooms, and prison cells. Dreams, though perhaps not the dreams one expects, can still be had. We lose our way, but not all in the same manner. We are haunted and hunted by ghosts as real as kidnappers and as imaginary as fairy tales. But as Jacques Roumain's novelist-protagonist soon discovers in "Preface to the Life of a Bureaucrat," sometimes art creeps into life and sometimes life creeps into art.

This is why we open each of the sections of *Haiti Noir 2: The Classics* with a poem to set the mood. I am grateful to Danielle Legros George, Emmelie Prophète, and Èzili Dantò for allowing us to include their work. Their poetry definitely adds a special element to this book.

Some years ago, when I met the late American writer Kurt Vonnegut through his wife Jill Krementz, he mentioned in passing that he had been to Haiti and had incorporated some of his experiences there in a book called *Deadeye Dick* in which, as he explains in the preface, the country becomes New York City. I chose a scene from *Deadeye Dick* as an epigraph at the front of this book not so much because of his notion that Creole has no past tense—it does—but because I like the idea that a dead man can paint. I am also grateful for the prerogative that is offered the editors of the Akashic Noir Series to also contribute a story when possible. I am the only repeat offender here. My story "The Port-au-Prince Marriage

Special," though set in a hotel, doesn't take place at Vonnegut's or anyone else's version of the Oloffson Hotel, which appears in various noir and ghost stories, including a most famous novel by Graham Greene called *The Comedians*.

Once again, as the humble hostess, I am happy and proud to introduce you to this book filled with both my literary ancestors and my contemporary peers. It is wonderful to have them here—and it is wonderful to have you here with us—from the oldest, Ida Faubert, one of Haiti's first published female writers, to Roxane Gay, a rising literary star on the verge of publishing her first novel, *An Untamed State*, which grew out of "Things I Know About Fairy Tales," her story in this anthology. I imagine Ida and Roxane, and many of the other contributors, being very happy to meet at my little party and kissing one another on both cheeks as a roomful of other illustrious literary lights look on. And while some konpa or rasin music and even some blues is playing in the background, I am still bringing out the salt cod–filled chiktay and the Barbancourt rum, and putting the finishing touches on my welcoming address. And it would be rather brief, my welcoming address. It would begin with "How often are you asked to put together an amazing literary party?" and end with a traditional welcome.

"Onè," I would say. Honor.

Then "Respè." Respect.

Much respect indeed.

Edwidge Danticat
October 2013

PART I

HUNTED/HAUNTED

PRAISESONG
FOR PORT-AU-PRINCE

BY Danielle Legros Georges

Port-au-Prince

(Originally published in 1999)

Cold kills slowly.
One moves and keeps
moving until suddenly
an arm grows dead
then a foot falls off
and the torso freezes
as if submerged in chilled water,
ice and swimmer
forming a block.

It's a slow death,
never red or yellow
with guts hanging out
and decay that spreads
its blanket and birds
that descend with feathers
and beaks,
and finally peace:
efficient, spectacular.

You, city of the fast death,
of the bloody coup,
I bow to you.
For you I cut flowers
to put into a blue vase
of cold, clear water.

PREFACE TO THE LIFE OF A BUREAUCRAT

BY Jacques Roumain

Bolosse

(Originally published in 1930)

Translated by George Lang

I

Waking, Michel Rey watched the dirty day slipping in through the blinds. He smiled his own special smile—a sorrowful slit that drew his lips aside with two diagonal wrinkles—and faced the usual question: why smile at that dead light, at that room whose shabby furniture was his wife's pride and where there floated traces of strong perfume and the acrid rubber smell of his raincoat drenched in the shower that had caught him coming home at dawn, and which was still sweating the occasional drop of humidity . . .

Seeing the little half-evaporated puddle dark on the floor, Michel smiled again. This time he knew why.

Five years ago . . . he remembered the day he had returned to Haiti. The noonday sun beat down on a silent sea of smooth and crestless swells. He was filled with joy: in the anonymous crowd pushing and shoving up toward the bridge, in the visitors and porters, he recognized himself at last. He was a happy echo of this Black world, and he felt melting within him the ice shored up in Europe. What he bitterly called "The Great White Silence" (that racial gulf which friendship, loves, and contacts had never been able to bridge) began to disappear. Now he was among friends, his own people. He felt like kneeling to kiss that cherished soil.

The port danced before him in a mist of tears. His parents harassed him with questions as they carried him off toward town. He wanted to answer, but felt even more like escaping to walk alone in solemn ecstasy, like embracing the passing mango vendor: her fruit a queen's crown on her head, her back arched, her step certain, the ripe purple grapes of her breasts straining against the blue cloth of her coarse dress. Yes, he wanted to hold her tightly and say, "Sister." He wanted to take the tattered child holding out his hand to an American tourist, to draw him near: "Brother, little brother . . ."

But a clock struck somewhere, and Michel returned to the present. It must have been late; his wife was already up and about. Weary, he rose slowly and began moving about the room, dressing and thinking of his past: I embraced life too strongly. I took it by the throat, strangled it . . .

As he was finishing, someone knocked at the door. The servant entered, barefoot, eyes lowered; and with the respectable look of those who do make it to four o'clock Mass, announced that Mme. Ballin was downstairs waiting, yes.

The Widow Ballin is Michel's mother-in-law. He hates this woman swathed in yellow fat like rancid lard, in her funereal dresses that not even enormous cameos can brighten. Her tiny bony head, out of all proportion with her bulky body, and her wide thin mouth chopping out words like a butcher knife repulse him in a way the Widow Ballin would never understand. She is proud of her sharp face. When she refers to it, she has a droll but haughty way of saying, "I have overcome atavism." By this she means her features are no longer recognizably African. She is indeed the daughter of Mme. Ochsle, a brown-skin woman who married a German of poor extraction but of great recent wealth, and thereafter never stopped referring to "German ladies like ourselves . . ."

Michel cannot stand the woman, but is moved at the same time by a vague tenderness toward her. He cannot get along without her. She is his revenge on that corrupt, hypocritical, stupidly bourgeois Port-au-Prince society which has ruined him, and of which she is an excellent example. He takes a malicious, exalting pleasure in wounding her, and can easily do so since the Widow Ballin—as superficial as they come—lends herself to it.

He knows his remarks are repeated in drawing rooms where the "Fates" of Turgeau and Bois Verna, assembly-line stiff in their 1880 corsets and blasted by bile, hold forth on the future of a young couple or the reputation of an honest man. And just knowing that his gibes are transmitted to all by the astonishing technique Haitians call *télégueule* makes him very happy indeed.

Michel Rey's hatred for his mother-in-law is perhaps the only feeling he has left to make his life bearable. He clings to it like a drowning man to a floating log; and if somehow the Widow Ballin were one day to die, he knows without a doubt that he would weep at her funeral.

Michel goes down to the drawing room without his jacket, wearing large old sandals. (His mother-in-law had proclaimed one day that it was "unaesthetic" to appear in shirt sleeves. She loved all words ending in "ic" and "ism"—words she was incapable of understanding, but which she thought distinguished.) She would be furious with him.

This in turn pleases him, because he still retains a touch of childishness, which is not a sign of innocence, but a holdover from a boyhood whose candor has long since passed. Basically, he is like those mistreated and battered kids, kept mischievous and lively by their youth, but whose sole pleasure consists of the dirty tricks which feed their bitterness.

The Widow Ballin spills over both sides of her chair. She has slipped her glasses up from her nose to her wide, low forehead. Michel, who has wished her good day, listens to her trivialities and examines her in detail. He feels she assesses the forces of each venomous phrase like a huge snake with glasses, coiled back upon herself waiting to strike.

"Jeanne isn't here?"

"No."

"You don't look at all well. You're working hard, aren't you? That's what they all say."

"My God, if they all say so, then there's no reason not to believe it."

"That's right. Everyone's waiting for your novel. It's supposed to be a masterpiece. You're working so hard on the documentation."

Michel keeps his silence.

"You've become more polite since, under the pretext of studying the Haitian soul, you began to visit the slums."

Her calls at Michel's are usually short. It is as if this fat woman comes to see him from time to time just to feel insulted by remarks which sting, but which she herself provokes.

"You're wrong on that count. It's not what I'm up to at all. I've been going there ever since that reception given by Monsieur and Madame Couloute, the uppercrust of Port-au-Prince elite. The straightforward seaminess of the slums compensates me for the rotten hypocrisy of those two."

"My son, this is really too—"

"Leave me alone!" Michel interrupts her. "You make me sick, all of you! I know what's beneath your slick surface, your aristocracy, etc., etc. The luxurious dress that hides the putrid flesh of the whore! I tell you I've had enough of your life. Your worldly whirl doesn't attract me. I haven't the least desire to live in a vacuum."

"Ah, it's easy enough to guess where you got those ideas! And to think I entrusted my poor daughter to such a creature."

"It would have been a better show, perhaps, to have married her off to one of those oh-so-fascinating well-bred gentlemen, guaranteed against any excess by a Tartuffe-brand safety valve. The ones I've had the dubious pleasure to come across in your drawing room: so seriously interested in charity and in the general progress of mankind, their hands folded in their laps with that touching gesture foreshadowing the day when they'll have become sector chiefs or members of the board and will only have to shift their arms a bit to twiddle their thumbs upon well-earned little paunches adorned by gold watch chains . . . Yes, my dear Widow Ballin, why in fact didn't you choose such an exemplar—the dream of every Haitian mother—for your poor daughter?"

"They're a thousand times better than you!" she cries.

Her face, green with anger, sweats out an oily film. Michel looks at her curiously, wondering how such a dried-up face can secrete all that grease. "Well, then, they're not worth much, are they?" He gets up, pleased to have provoked such fury.

At loose ends, his mother-in-law shouts: "You have no respect at all! You are cursed!" And louder, like a prophet: "You will go to Hell!"

"Shit!" replies Michel heartily, and goes back to his room. But as other cutting remarks come to mind, he is sorry to have left so quickly. He decides to make up for it by going the very next day to the shopping district where his elegant mother-in-law has a flourishing hardware business.

II

He knots his tie, leaning at the window as before a mirror. Beneath this Bolosse cottage, the sea is spread out gray and dirty like a corrugated roof beyond the palm trees, those feather dusters that sweep away the rain.

This ocean view has for a long time left him unmoved. He now looks toward the sea with the eyes of a fisherman who regrets having run out of line. Something has snapped within him. Without it, how can he go in quest of that rare prey: enthusiasm?

Michel Rey thinks that from now on his life will be like that bitter, monotonous, watery to-and-fro. No great storms. He is sinking deeper and no longer has the strength to rise to the surface. His descent will continue slowly until the day when, stretched out on the bottom, human waves will stir him no more.

All that remains to while away his time until this final peace is insulting his mother-in-law, making his wife unhappy, and downing a rainbow of cocktails.

"Well, let us carry on with this absorbing day," he sighs, "by having a drink at Horatio Basile's."

The bearer of this Shakespearean name is a "young man from a good family" back in Haiti several months now from a stay in France, where he studied law. With five thousand francs a month, it is easy to flunk your finals. Horatio Basile failed the first time around and, a persistent sort, went on to fail again. Bréville Basile, a coffee speculator and a man of solid common sense, sent his son a check without the usual row of zeros, accompanied by an order to hop the first boat back home. Horatio tore himself from the arms of his girlfriend and took his leave (like a good Haitian) with several off-the-rack suits and a suggestive one-piece outfit as souvenirs. But he had hardly reached the Azores when the elder Monsieur Basile, showing a kindly spirit of which none would have thought him capable, passed away leaving his son thirty houses and around two hundred and twenty-five thousand dollars earned in commodities and customs deals at Petit-Goâve.

The process of selling off several huge coffee plantations keeps the latter here—far from Place Pigalle—under our tropical sky, where he lives an idle, scandalous, and aristocratic life.

Physically, he exemplifies perfectly that sort of *grimo* Haitians call an "exaggerated mulatto": tall, thin, with a tapered face the color of our red water jugs and that always seem to be in profile, dominated by a low forehead and unruly red fuzzy hair. He has a neck like a bottle, along which rises and falls his large and pointed Adam's apple. Unbalanced and jerky, his hesitating walk and oversized feet which are too slow for the rapid movement of his arms make one think of a huge crustacean.

He has three passions: cars, record players, and Michel, whom he insisted on meeting after reading a manifesto of his—"Lamartine, Crocodile Poetry, and the New Afro-Haitian Literature"—in a review called *The Assassinated Crocodile*.

Michel amused himself immensely at their encounter, during which Horatio had said to him: "I understand you well, my good sir. We must destroy our weeping willows, the palm trees. We must from now on bear this scenery within us. Palm trees must no longer merely set the scene which makes us native. We must plant them, so to speak, in our very soul."

"Precisely," Michel replied, deadly serious. "But we must

never overlook the African drum which is made, as you know, from the skin of asses."

Then, having charmed the heir of Bréville Basile, he passed by every day at noon for cocktails *chez* Horatio and, toward the end of each month, borrowed rather considerable sums of money from him.

III

"Hello there, Horatio."

"Hullo."

When Michel came in, Horatio was dancing about among a buffet well-stocked with flasks and cocktail shakers, a huge divan, and nine different gramophones all arranged in a row by size, like children in family pictures.

He was very drunk. His nose was shiny. In his eyes a flame flickered uncertainly, a fire the dampness of alcohol would soon extinguish.

All the gramophones were going at once: coffee mills grinding the black beans of depression.

Michel went from one to the next and, with the quick gestures of a father meting out discipline, stopped each one. They went silent, like good children.

"Idiot!" he says, pouring a tumbler full of Manhattans and smiling contemptuously.

Horatio tries to fix his eyes on the confused and staggering world within which Michel alone stands upright, preparing a second drink in the midst of that new miracle: the multiplication of gramophones.

His tongue has the greatest trouble unsticking itself; but finally, with an overwhelming English accent, he says: "Whyyyyy?"

His eyes half-closed, Michel drinks: each swallow is like

a spider jumping toward his brain and drawing in the tangled threads of his thought.

His glass empty for the fourth time, he speaks: "Have you ever seen a peasant girl come down the wine-red zigzag paths of our hillsides? She passes among leaning banana trees torn by the wind, musky mango trees heavy with the honey of their fruit, baobabs through whose branches stir garlands of parasites, and the sacred mapous with their tentacular roots. She moves like a tightrope dancer, her bust high and her arms swinging, her wide hips swaying *dolce armonioso*. Sometimes her hard foot strikes a stone, and it skips down the slope *decrescendo*. Music! Music! Music!

"In front of a hut, I saw a brute beating his wife with a stick in a measured drummer's rhythm; and his victim kept time and danced and sang and shouted out in her pain.

"In Amsterdam I saw two Black acrobats, naked savages really, hanging from a trapeze like a sixteenth note. The music stopped, powerless. Their bodies wet with sweat, their nervous legs and the solid arms where the ropes of their muscles tightened were already a magnificent and insolent psalm to life.

"When they came down from their heights and smiled, their native souls played on the keyboard of their shining teeth.

"But you, Basile, are an idiot, an insensitive ass . . ."

He stops. What giant droning insect zigzags through the sudden silence? Horatio, stretched out on the sofa, is sleeping with his legs apart. His wet lips open and close, trapping and freeing the buzzing bees of his snore.

IV

Jeanne was waiting in the modest dining room. He saw her dark, sad eyes.

"Mother told me . . . oh, why, Michel?"

She is soft and plaintive. He caresses her hair. Will she ever understand, my God, the horrible self-hatred which makes me torture the ones I love?

"Oh Michel, Michel, how unhappy you are."

He rocks her.

"My little one, my little one."

"Michel, listen . . ."

He calms her with a gentle touch. His two children seated on a palm-straw mat play at cutting out pictures from a mail-order catalog. They do not look alike. What strangers they seem! When he tries to take them in his arms, they cry.

This is his prison: this sad house. And the bars of his cell: his wife who cannot understand, his children who fear and refuse to love him.

The whole of his future life rises up before him like a narrow horizon, like a thick screen behind which life—real and vibrant life—lies hidden beyond his reach.

Ah, is it possible that this could be his irremediable fate: to grow old and gray, broken in body and soul, sitting in this cheap and ugly room by a steaming kettle and an old and fattened mate?

Inside, a sharp taunt tears at him: "The whole future, waiting for rheumatism."

This time it is she who consoles him with a luke-warm embrace.

He leans against her shoulder, almost won over, and lets tender persuasion take the upper hand.

He gives himself over to a cowardly voice which repeats: Yield, yield. Yield to that calm current. Those who win out are the ones who know how to cultivate the cold and unfeeling patience of flotsam. Do not be ashamed to fail: it will lead to a normal sort of happiness. Besides, is it not absurd to pit your tiny flame against the infinite flood of life? You remind me of the madman who tried to ignite the sea with a match. Who are you, anyway, to want to win? Just look around you, and disgust will overwhelm your faint heart. For a while you were drawn to politics, but you were never more than a puerile demagogue. You thought you were a man of letters, and still do: you've written manifestoes, poems, and one book that no one reads. You're a pitiful petit bourgeois, only too aware of your ugliness and your impotence. This clear picture you have of yourself is your only merit. The day your fellows stop deluding themselves, they too will revolt; and the world will suddenly be filled with herds of superb and bitter malcontents who take themselves for unrecognized geniuses.

Come on. Straighten out. You're what they call someone with everything it takes to succeed: a respectable family, no rent to pay, an opening in the Department of Internal Affairs. Accept it. With a hundred and twenty-five dollars a month, your debts will be paid and your household will be in the black. Your children will be happy. You'll renew old friendships, make up with your family. Happiness and life will open up before you.

You fought. You desired. But no more. Why struggle when you know you're bound to lose?

And then his wife spoke: "Listen, Michel, I saw Mother. She said she talked with Pralier . . . you know, Pralier, the minister's friend. Just like that, the minister said to him: 'Tell Madame Ballin that we are very well disposed to welcome her son-in-law. Tell him to write a proper letter.' Michel, think of your wife, your children, of our lives." And with a surge of anger: "All my friends live better than I do! Take it, Michel! It means so little to you. You'll be as free as before, and nothing can stop you from thinking what you want. But you see, I'm still young. I love life. And here I live like a beggar-woman. Please, I implore you, accept it!"

She goes on and on, and he sinks deeper into an ignominious lassitude.

For God's sake, if she would just shut up. He's beaten, yes, and broken. But if only this woman would stop trying to bargain for her own happiness with his principles.

He shoves her away, gets up.

"Michel . . ."

"Shut up!"

His voice has lost its force. The sorrow which strangely hollows out his face reveals the depths of despair in his eyes.

And he leaves, ridiculously stiff, like a drunk trying not to stumble.

V

A dingy study welcomes his distress. It is cluttered with books, his final companions. But they too have been put aside, and are covered with a thin layer of dust which his movements stir up into golden specks in a shaft of sun.

Blank pages are piled on the table. Others are filled with his writing, yellowed by time, the ink already faded.

All his wasted life is here.

His head between his hands, he goes over it all once again.

Am I limited by my weakness? Or are my desires inhuman, far beyond the bounds of what I really want, more than I can honestly accept?

Maybe it's really sour grapes. I convince myself I have contempt for all the things I'm incapable of leaping up to take.

Yes, it really is clear. I'm a failure, my teeth set on edge by life, by the sour grapes I cannot bite into.

But why all this awful questioning? That final question—

Why?—can never be answered. And any truth achieved through struggle carries ridiculously within itself the simplicity of its own explanation.

Or else, everything comes down to: "What for?"

But "What for?" to be exact, is not a question. It is an answer.

And isn't this very analysis the ultimate proof of my weakness, of my emptiness? The vain incompetent digs within his empty self, possessed by a wild (and all the more cruel, because he knows it is all so futile) hope of finding some unknown virtue. I agree with Carlyle, who said that a strong man—who knows what little one can know of oneself—never torments himself, but puts himself to the test. "Whatever you do, do it like Hercules." Alas, I have never had that kind of pride. My pride was nothing but bitterness against myself, bile projected toward others.

Having come finally to these moments of total and painful sincerity, Michel felt lighter and freer; but his relief did not last, and soon the poison began to spread again . . . to suffocate him. He was a vessel which fills and empties inevitably with agony.

He remained immobile, his forehead in his hands.

"Ah, to bring it all to an end, to get it over with!"

He opened the drawer. The weapon was turned toward him. He stared at its black and shiny muzzle.

One movement, a mere pressure of the finger, and I put a big red full stop at my temple, in my life, to all my pains.

But cowardice welled up inside.

He did not shut the drawer, but suddenly took up a blank page and began to write slowly and ponderously:

My Dear Mr. Secretary of State, I am honored to . . .

A STRANGE STORY

BY IDA FAUBERT

Turgeau

(Originally published in 1959)

Translated by Nicole Ball

O dead woman, half-buried . . .
—Sully Prudhomme

T he sick woman was getting weaker, yet she was hanging on to life with superhuman strength. Her eyes were still sparkling in her mournful face and she kept staring at the door, as if waiting for something.

Jeanne Marais didn't want to die without seeing her daughter. Aunt Brigitte had quickly sent for the young woman, who'd gone to Port-Vent to collect an oxygen pump in case one was needed.

Outside, the tropical sun engulfed everything. The slatted doors that led to the wide, jasmine-covered balcony were closed, giving the room a welcome shade.

Since no one was napping, the siesta hour dragged on. In fact, the house was in a state of alert, brought on by an unusual series of events.

That morning, when the doctor left his patient, he'd shrugged his shoulders in defeat. He felt he could no longer keep Jeanne's exhausted body alive. He had told Brigitte in the frank but sensitive language of an old family friend: "Your sister won't live through the day. I must say she has amazing courage and lucidity, but don't be fooled by it, it's the end. She can't fight it anymore. Go tell Lélia."

Although Dr. Poytevin had lived on the island for a very long time, he knew nothing of the darker forces of the country. Some cases were still beyond his realm of knowledge. He couldn't understand the nature of the illness that had suddenly taken hold of Jeanne Marais and had consumed her, little by little.

He had entertained all kinds of speculation. Strangely, the widow had always kept quiet. She seemed to be carrying a secret sorrow inside her. Remorse, maybe?

No, Poytevin could not understand. No more than he had been able to get to the bottom of Mina Valpont's death a few years earlier. She had succumbed to some mysterious illness in just forty-eight hours, and in this very same house!

The death of that ten-year-old girl had taken everybody by surprise. The odd fact that the child's body kept sweating profusely the day after she died was much talked about.

It was bizarre, to say the least.

The door creaked and Aunt Brigitte turned around. Lélia Marais ran in and found her mother in a state of great distress.

When Madame Marais saw her daughter come in, her dark eyes gleamed and she whispered, "Come here, dear girl, I want to talk to you alone."

Aunt Brigitte slipped away without saying a word and Lélia sat down on the edge of the bed.

"Darling, don't cry like that, we'll meet again," Jeanne Marais said as her daughter sobbed. "You were always gentle and kind, and I loved you more than anything. Now, I have to tell you a secret that has weighed on me so much it's killing me—"

"You'll get better, Maman, I know it," Lélia said, trying to control herself. "Don't be afraid to tell me, but believe me, this is only a bad dream."

Jeanne knew very well that wasn't true. She waited a moment, then said, "You remember Mina Valpont, your father's godchild, who used to live with us?"

"How could I forget her? She was my friend. She would be twenty years old by now. Poor Mina!"

"Well, dear, Mina isn't dead."

"Not dead? What do you mean, not dead?" Lélia was staring intently at her mother, trying to make sure that the unfortunate woman still had her wits about her.

"Don't think I'm crazy. Come closer. Quickly." Jeanne Marais's voice was fading. "Mina must be delivered. You'll ask her to forgive me. Promise me."

Lélia nodded weakly. Her heart was racing. She was losing track of where she was.

"Come closer. Listen. Our old Zanoute will tell you."

Lélia couldn't hear the rest. The shock was too strong for her nerves. She collapsed, unconscious, on top of her dying mother.

Some light was filtering through the lowered blinds when Lélia opened her eyes. She was not immediately aware of what was happening. She was totally numb, had no strength left. She saw herself stretched out on her bed with her clothes unbuttoned. She barely recognized her room.

Aunt Brigitte was putting cool, wet compresses on her forehead and someone was taking her pulse. Someone? Dr. Poytevin, certainly.

Lélia suddenly stood up: "Maman, maman!" she cried. She rushed toward the door. Some arms tried to stop her.

"Easy, girl," the doctor said in an affectionate tone. "You'll see your maman a little later. You fainted while she was talking to you. You must rest."

"How is she?"

"Unfortunately, not better, dear."

Poytevin did not tell Lélia that her mother had died half an hour earlier, when the girl had fainted on her. He'd had to unclasp the mother's arms to carry the daughter away. Since Lélia had just then regained consciousness, everyone thought it best to keep the truth from her for now.

After the funeral and the usual exhausting series of condolences, everyone had gone home. Lélia was waiting for Zanoute, who, overwhelmed by the grim ceremony, was resting.

The old woman was practically family. She'd been with the Maraises for over twenty years, serving them with great devotion. Then she had to go back to the mountains where she came from, to care for her parents who were too old to do without her. Zanoute never came to the city unless she absolutely had to. Still, she had been looking forward to attending Lélia's wedding one day. She loved her like her own child. Instead, they had invited her to a funeral.

The poor woman couldn't stop moaning and crying.

On the way back from the cemetery, Lélia had said to her, "Stay with me, Zanoute. I have to talk to you about something very serious."

Something very serious? What could it be? Zanoute was worried.

Later, on the terrace, the two women pulled their chairs close. The air was humid. From time to time, lightning flashed silently through the sky. All they could hear were the flapping wings of frightened birds fleeing the looming thunderstorm. Sorrow, fatigue, the crushing heat of that mournful day all seemed to come together to create an unbearable atmosphere.

"Zanoute, what became of Mina?" Lélia finally decided to ask.

The old woman seemed stunned. She looked around fearfully. "Shhh. What if someone hears us?"

"Tell me what happened. Maman wanted you to tell me."

"You don't know anything?"

"No, I swear. You have to tell me what happened to Mina. I promised to go see her."

"See her? How? She's in France—"

"In France?"

The servant realized she owed this anguished soul the whole truth. "My poor child, your mother was a martyr. She died eaten away by sorrow and fear. May God forgive her silence." Just as Lélia was about to ask another question, Zanoute lowered her voice and added, "Don't interrupt me, I need courage to explain it all."

It was so dark you'd think you were at the bottom of a pit. They couldn't discern anything around them, but Zanoute bravely made up her mind. She had to reveal the unspeakable.

"Since you insist, here's the story: Your father secretly possessed a temple. He practiced Vodou there, even though no one thought he would be involved. He was too bourgeois. He had the airs of a good, upstanding Catholic. For his temple, he chose beautiful women who became priestesses as well as his mistresses. He took them younger and younger. That's how he cast his eyes on little Mina, his pretty orphan godchild who lived in his house. Ten years old! She was only ten! But she would soon be a woman. How could he reserve her for himself? So, this demon—excuse me, but he was the devil incarnate—resorted to spells to put the child to sleep, simulate her death, and turn her into a zombie!"

"Stop, stop it, Zanoute, this is awful!" Lélia felt her heart bursting with pity and shame. There was a long silence, which the young woman finally broke, apprehensively: "Go on. And then?"

"And then Mina grew up with the others in the temple and received the title of guardian. No one knows how, but it so happened that your mother found out about these sinister schemes. She nearly died of indignation and wanted to step in and denounce her husband. But he terrorized her and swore she would have the same fate as Mina if she betrayed him. Racked with fear, the wretched woman kept quiet. Soon she began to wither away. No one knew why.

"One day, you remember, there was that accident. As he was walking up the ravine, your father slipped and smashed his skull against a rock. He was brought back to the house, lifeless. Madame Marais thought she was saved. That's when she confided these sad things to me. I had never suspected something so horrible. I was ready to do anything I could to help your mother. We had only one thing on our minds—to take Mina back.

"On an evening much like this one, sitting on this same terrace, we were trying to find a way to reach the girl without creating a scandal, when an old man suddenly popped up in front of us—where could he have come from?—and came so close to Madame Marais that she felt his breath on her face. He told her, hammering out his words: 'You know too much! I am Marais's successor. Woe to you and yours if you talk.' I had to help your mother. She was feeling terrible."

Overwhelmed with all this information, Lélia's breathing became shallow, though she still managed to keep pushing Zanoute for more information. "But you said Mina was in France."

"Shhh! Shhh!" Zanoute looked terrified as she peered into the darkness around her. "Without your mother's knowledge," she continued in a very soft voice, "I went to see the priest of Port-Vent and told him the story at confession. The good father was appalled. He was so upset that he did all he could to find Mina. After much searching, he discovered the temple and waited for the right moment to get inside. He found himself in the presence of the poor girl, Mina, who had become a complete idiot. She followed him to the presbytery where she was immediately treated by someone familiar with antidotes. Was there any hope for a cure? So many years had passed.

"The next day, at dawn—time was of the essence—Mina, dressed as a nun, boarded a ship for France with her savior. How did our good priest do this? Who had helped him? These things were so serious he couldn't reveal them to me. He had told me enough already, and he made me promise to keep it all secret. In short, Mina is now in Paris, in the Convent of the Holy Sacrament. She's a novice, under the name of 'Sister Louise.' I'm throwing all caution to the wind to obey the wishes of a dead woman. I'm taking a great risk."

Lélia was crying uncontrollably. Nonetheless, she regained her courage. "Thank you, Zanoute. I will see Mina again. I promised my mother," she said in a firm voice, while the storm they had been expecting began raging over the land.

"Sister, I would like to see Sister Louise of the Holy Sacrament. Is this possible?" Lélia asked at the convent in Paris.

"Whom should I announce, mademoiselle?"

A second of hesitation, then she said, "Sister Louise won't

remember my name. I'm just a fellow Haitian passing through Paris and I would really like to say hello to her before I leave."

"Please wait here, mademoiselle, I will inquire."

Lélia Marais stood there in the parlor for a while without looking at anything around her. Not the gleaming waxed floor, nor the chairs neatly lined up against the wall, nor, on the ebony cross, the great ivory Christ whose emaciated face reflected all the sorrow of the world. She saw none of these things. She just stood there, waiting.

And then the door opened. Very slight in her black novice's robe, a woman moved toward her. A young woman? No. A strange form of a woman. A livid, ravaged face hardened by a white headdress, her sunken eyes lifeless, that mouth with a frightening grin, and that walk, the walk of an automaton—could all this belong to a living being? The girl of twenty had no age.

Miraculously dragged from her torpor, she had awakened, but did she even belong to this earth? Where was she coming from? What had she seen? What did she really know? Was her body still the prisoner of unknown forces or had it recaptured its soul?

Stunned, Lélia stared at her childhood friend. Mina didn't seem to recognize her. Lélia held her arms out to her, then, shaking and sobbing, fell to her knees and grabbed both of Mina's hands, pulling them to her lips.

"Forgive us, Mina," she said. "Please forgive all of us. Maman. All of us."

Mina briefly leaned over her. When Lélia looked up, she met two eyes that bored right into her, then, like two flashes of lightning, immediately went out again. And already the door was opening, and Sister Louise was walking away, her steps as stiff and as slow as when she had arrived.

THE ENCHANTED SECOND LIEUTENANT

BY JACQUES-STEPHEN ALEXIS

Bassins-Coquilleaux

(Originally published in 1960)

Translated by Sharon Masingale Bell

I couldn't have known Second Lieutenant Wheelbarrow—
but on the other hand, I wouldn't swear that I never met
him. I can almost see his changeable, rather blue-green
eyes, bitter and bloodshot, and his humped nose, curved and
worried and aimed at his too-thin lips and undershot chin.
And his hair—I see it like a reddish brush, abundant and
curly, floating like a halo above a lanky body. Maybe that's
simply the image of some other Yankee soldier encountered
some morning of my vagabond childhood; but anyway, I see
Lieutenant Wheelbarrow. Arcane mysteries of childhood!
Imagination! Fancy! Alluvions and illusions! Memory, that
incredible sculptor that gives dimension, form, colors, and life
to the entire virtual little world where we frolicked, stretched,
and played so long ago!

But don't conclude from this that Second Lieutenant
Wheelbarrow never existed. Everyone knows how close I was
to Maréchal Célomme, God rest his soul, and how he loved
me. For this old fellow, a bit scolding and fatherly, a pious,
severe *papa lwa*, was actually a great friend of plants, animals,
and small children. It was he who entrusted me, long, long
ago, with the few yellowed pages where the second lieutenant

told his strange, brief story. Maréchal Célomme even showed me the little tomb crowned with basil where the second lieutenant lies, a few steps from the famous La Voûte grotto in the St. Marc highlands—a small sepulchre of bricks, ashes, and conch shell whitening next to the verdant little trail. Considered alone, the manuscript is nothing but the disturbing notation of an inner dream; and without Maréchal Célomme's narrative—he was a marshal in the rural police force—I would never have been able to reconstruct the harsh poetry, the strange love that enflamed a brief but enchanted life like a Bengal light in the violet, violent mountains of the Bassins-Coquilleaux.

The story takes place around 1913 or 1914, when Earl Wheelbarrow was a noncommissioned cavalry officer in the United States Army. Born in Kentucky, an orphan, poor, and unsure of what could be done with a human life, Earl had vegetated up to that time like mildew without ever truly plumbing the depths of his own heart. Once he'd graduated from the high school where his uncle, a major in the Marines, had had him sent after his parents' deaths, the youth was very much at a loss. He had no desire to go into the only large business in town—Chattanooga, a typical small Southern town, where he'd always lived. As a matter of fact, it was the metal works where his father had been killed by falling into a rolling mill. Earl wasn't very good at math, so he couldn't have made it in a small business or in sales. Being a bookmaker didn't interest him. Becoming a gangster, a Tennessee terror, didn't attract him either because it took too much energy; besides, he'd've had to recruit his own gang, there being very few racketeers and killers about town. At one point he'd thought of becoming a preacher and founding a new religion, but the Bible bored him. Leave, then? . . . Yes, but . . . He'd had no real friends, no real joys but ice cream sodas, the few parties to which nameless buddies would take him sometimes, Thanksgiving Days, a few deplorable lynchings of Negroes who'd had lustful eyes, and other obscene gesticulations that shook his native Chattanooga. So a carefully thought-out choice was no easy thing for this young man as tall as three days without bread are long. He operated for a while as a campaigner for a Dixiecrat candidate for governor; he tried baseball, joined the Salvation Army, worked on the local paper, pumped gas; nothing worked out. In the end, since his uncle (whom he'd known only through his letters) had often said that the army was a good old gal who relieved a man of the bother of having to think, he let himself be recruited. Not long afterward, without his knowing exactly how, he was promoted to second lieutenant.

In Earl Wheelbarrow's life there were Rosasharn, Dorothy, and Eleanor, true enough, but he had never been able to make himself choose among them, nor had he let himself fall in love with any one of these Three Graces, so inseparable in his heart, one as essential as the other to the tranquil order of his habits. Between him and Rosasharn, a classmate's sister, there did exist the seed of adolescent love, but it had never grown and flowered, never even germinated; it had barely put out a shoot, a hesitant, romantic camaraderie. As she grew up, Rosasharn had become a thoroughly sophisticated girl. In their external relationships, in public, Earl liked that, as long as Rosasharn became her old self again in private. However, Earl wouldn't have wanted a real relationship with this girl for anything on earth. Alone, she'd have been incapable of fulfilling him, for without really knowing it himself, he was a puritan, as monogamous as he was lustful.

He'd made Dorothy his sweetheart. He liked to caress

her the way one pets a pretty little animal, bite her cherry-red mouth in movie theaters, snuggle her cat's body against his while dancing, listen to her insipid babbling, or watch her stuff herself with sweets, but that was all. This Dorothy, daughter of a local businessman, was delightfully stupid, marvelously lovely, shapely, ample of bosom, flat-bottomed, slim-hipped, long and lean of line—in short, a perfect example of the Yankee Venus. Earl couldn't imagine that their relations could become anything other than what they were. Finally, Eleanor was a deceptive, elusive girl who sought out and fled from the pale officer at the same time. Sometimes she would court him with passionate, gothic novel phrases; other times, with no warning, she'd send him packing, dropping him cold without so much as a by-your-leave for the first man she saw. She would always come back to him, however, without the least embarrassment, like a chronic illness. This child-woman couldn't stand the idea of anything tying her down and would give herself proof to the contrary as soon as she imagined it. And then, she liked to dabble, tasting everything, for the pleasures of love left her a strange taste of death. It was delightful. Life is short . . .

When his uncle died of apoplexy in Port-au-Prince, where he was something or other in the offices of the military attaché of Uncle Sam's legation, Earl Wheelbarrow received, as expected, a meager inheritance, but also a letter in which the major said that he was on the trail of a stupendous treasure. He'd been preparing for the expedition when death struck him. Nevertheless, he'd thought of all contingencies and had included in the sheet addressed to his nephew in case of his death papers indicating the probable location of the treasure. It was supposed to be somewhere in the region of the Bassins-Coquilleaux, in the St. Marc highlands. An unaccustomed energy took hold of the second lieutenant. Since he had no money but his salary, he racked his brain to find funds to complement the small sum his uncle had left him. He had to plan for a systematic search that might last a long time. When he was just about ready to give up, Dorothy, as a last resort, offered to act as Earl's go-between and ask her father for a loan. This ape doubted the seriousness of the proposition, but he was a betting man. He grumbled, stormed, and thought about it, but as he never refused his daughter anything, he wound up giving in. Anyway, it wasn't a fabulous sum; Earl was honest and would pay him back out of his salary if need be. And then—you can never tell—suppose Earl came back a multimillionaire?

The *Muslin*, a small freight and passenger vessel of three thousand tons, danced in the port of St. Marc. In the smoking room, Second Lieutenant Wheelbarrow stood at the portholes studying the foam-crinkled sea and the lofty mountains that form a bucolic crown around the little town. Along with two or three other passengers, Earl was waiting for the authorities who were expected for the customs formalities, which amounted to very little at that time. Earl looked at the titanic, voracious jaws of this bay, with little beaches of golden sand as teeth, and its immense blue tongue, the sea, greedily licking the shore. Earl let his eyes wander here and there, curious, preoccupied, and pensive at the same time.

He had embarked full of apprehension, wondering if it were possible for him to get used to the unthinkable: a country ruled by Negroes. Earl Wheelbarrow had no malice in his heart, but naturally, his young Southern ego, brought up in racism and imbued with the concepts of *apartheid*, recoiled at this idea. Up until then, Earl, unlike some others, hadn't had even the slightest chance at real contact with the Negroes of Chattanooga or of the neighboring plantations. Naïve in his assumptions, ingenuous in his implacable mental cruelty, Earl Wheelbarrow remained indulgent with these bastards of the human race in spite of everything. Strange "happy-go-lucky" creatures whose souls he was sure he knew by dint of having crossed some of them in the street, or from having seen the white eyes and the lips turned back from the pink gums of niggers being stoned or made to dance from the end of a rope. Legitimate son of Jim Crow, contradictory, idealistic, generous, and yet capable of the worst frenzies of crime—what reflexes, what vivid inner sensations Earl Wheelbarrow would have to keep in check, to repulse, to hide, to bury deep inside himself during the time he expected to spend in this country! People said that these Haitian Negroes were unconscious of their innate inferiority, even proud of their race and their legendary past, sensitive to the slightest allusion, subject to take umbrage at the lightest prick, violent, and so familiar!

Small sailboats, white, triangular birds, run over the waves. At the river's mouth, washerwomen and half-nude bathers with cloths draped below their navels sing and play. Black little children bawl and give each other great kicks in the water. The sky is dotted with small, cottony clouds. Bronzed dockers bustle about on the wharf. Splashed with sun, laughter, and sweat, they shout in chorus, and their walk is drunken, bent over, waltzing beneath the sacks of coffee and the bales of cotton. A veritable dance-song, a kind of worker's ragtime. The ship is surrounded by a string of small boats where market women offer fruit on large wooden trays and hold out coconuts, which, decapitated with one brusque machete chop, laugh and cry before reaching the lips of the sailors leaning on their elbows on the bulwarks. Below, ten o'clock peals from the bell tower that lifts its sharp finger above the foliage and the flame trees. Here, just beyond Customs on the little parade ground, a stream of military music suddenly unfurls. A general as black as jet in his bottle-green uniform trimmed in gold braid prances on a white charger amid the blare of the war music, cannon salvos, and bursts of gunfire. He shouts orders and maneuvers an army of *cacos-plaqués*, cuirassiers in uncured, hairy leather vests. Second Lieutenant Earl Wheelbarrow, his eyes beckoned from every side, is still thinking of his native Chattanooga, of the frame houses on his street, of the Negroes of his town; and the three faces of Rosasharn, Dorothy, and Eleanor jumble together in his mind.

The smoking room is full of people. The first to be called on, Earl answers the questions of the officer, a *grimo* with a pockmarked face, his lips barred by a bristling mustache. Purpose of trip . . . Length of stay . . . The arrival of a fat man in a black alpaca coat and cream tussor pants brings the questioning to an end. The supercilious Maître Desagneaux extends a moist, pudgy, spatulate hand to Second Lieutenant Wheelbarrow, who quickly seizes the black paw.

"Lieutenant Wheelbarrow? Maître Desagneaux, Anténor Desagneaux, your uncle's business manager."

In his speciously courteous hurry, the second lieutenant almost sweeps the immigration officer's documents off the little table. He apologizes. Maître Desagneaux pulls the immigration officer aside and speaks to him.

"Everything is in order, lieutenant; we can leave . . ."

Earl Wheelbarrow feels an arm slip around his shoulders like a familiar serpent and a hand pat his left deltoid. He trembles with horror, smiles, and lets himself be taken in tow, pressed against the shoulder of Maître Desagneaux.

* * *

Under a driving rain, the horses were scaling the rugged slopes of the mountains that surround St. Marc. Until further notice, the lieutenant is an archaeologist obsessed with pre-Columbian relics. Once landed, he'd had only one thing on his mind—to climb the foothills standing before him. The pretext of archaeological research had worked wonders against all suspicion, even that of his uncle's former business manager, Maître Anténor Desagneaux. In this little town, provincial if ever there was, the wooden shutters had clattered ceaselessly as the second lieutenant passed. The parish festival had been somewhat eclipsed by his arrival. Everyone had kept up with all the comings and goings of the white man, and his haste to climb into the mountains despite all advice had caused a sensation and testified to the finest scientific spirit. Indeed, in these troubled times, the fearless climb toward the uncertain heights, where the streams were said to be wild and the torrents raging, at the very moment when people talked of hordes of *cacos* commanded by a glory-hunting braggart swarming all over the mountains and ready to fall on the city—in such times, the climb was an act of courage. Such intrepidness was bound to inspire good will.

The white man made his way alone, then, accompanied by a guide and three mules loaded to the breaking point. They hurried through cloudbursts, their clothes clinging to their bodies, their waterlogged eyes fixed on the precipices. At all costs they had to make La Voûte; this grotto would be the best shelter against the downpour. And the guide was showing plenty of signs of impatience. He was afraid of running into *cacos*, who were likely to give him hell if they mistook him for a spy: cut off his ears, beat him within an inch of his life with the flat of a machete, or leave him tied up in a ravine. They forced their animals so insistently that they soon arrived despite the opposition of branches and foliage allied with the rain.

Wheelbarrow was snoring in the grotto, making loud noises reverberated by the echoes. The guide had left in the middle of the night in spite of the raging rainstorm, declaring that he'd rather spend the night with some peasant before returning to town. He had left the second lieutenant somewhat disturbed by the wild ups and downs of this grotto, as high as a gothic cathedral and hairy with vines that fell from all over the ceiling like frolicking snakes . . . So the lieutenant was sleeping when a slight form slipped cautiously into the grotto and headed toward the cot where he was lying. He opened an eye at a rustling sound but pretended to continue his snoring, a flashlight in one hand and his Browning in the other. The form was very close to him; it was leaning over the bed.

Suddenly, the lieutenant sprang up and ran his flashlight over the visitor's face. The figure screamed and threw itself backward. It was a woman with a curvilinear face, reddish, with round features haloed by a cascade of black hair. She was as tall as a logwood beam. They rolled on the ground, she furiously defending herself, he gripping her. Three times the lieutenant rose up above her, grasping her wrists in a vise-like grip; three times she threw him. The fourth time she finished his fall with a head butt straight to his face. He let go, stunned. She fled. His finger on the trigger of the pistol, the lieutenant followed her with his eyes. He didn't fire.

Covered with sweat, Lieutenant Wheelbarrow spent the rest of the night wide awake. Dawn found him sitting with his pistol in his hand, surrounded by empty whiskey bottles, haggard-eyed.

Some time later, the lieutenant had settled in at Bassins-

Coquilleaux on the small mountainside domain his uncle had left him, which overlooked the seven circular, azure-watered basins that open toward the sky like human eyes. They rise like the steps of some mysterious staircase to the plateau—a mystery so old that no one can say whether man or nature had placed these wonders in such a remote place.

Initial contacts with the peasants had proven disappointing. The first time a peasant had approached the lieutenant, holding out a bit of flint, Wheelbarrow had asked him curtly, "How much?"

The man hadn't answered, but he'd taken the bill he was offered. That night, a hail of stones beat against the lieutenant's cabin. They came from every direction, seeming to fall from the sky itself. This left Earl stupefied for several days. Without his knowing why, the hostility spread. Men would turn their heads and spit as he passed. Women would whisper to each other when they saw him and burst into ringing, scornful laughter. Even the children would follow him at a distance sometimes, innocent-looking, beating a hellish din on old cooking pots, a nettling, provocative *chalbarique*: "There's the seditty white man!"

After a heroic struggle with his conscience, Earl descended toward the hamlet on the little plateau at the place where the foaming river, as white as the pebbles it sweeps crazily along, hums its centuries-old song. He walked straight up to a cabin in front of which an old man was sleeping and, speaking gibberish, asked for a light for his pipe. He was invited in and offered coffee, served by girls who accompanied their offering with a curtsy. Still, peace was not restored, nor did the stones stop falling, until he had visited all the men of the area, had slapped them on the back and let them slap his, and had drunk with them, chatting about the seasons and harvests.

All these things had plunged the lieutenant into a bottomless reverie. In the town, where he went for supplies, he hadn't dared discuss it with anyone, not even Maître Anténor Desagneaux, who collected his mail. So the men of these mountains had forced him to capitulate! Actually, he was surprised to find that he was not displeased. And from the day a little girl offered him a bouquet of field flowers beside a path, he was no longer the only one to go visiting. He was visited in turn. The peasants brought him splinters of flint, pre-Columbian axes, pieces of quartz, fruit . . . He was accepted as a maniac for vestiges of the past, and if he'd consented to go and dance the Martinique, the calinda, or the mahi under their *tonnelles*, the people would have ceased to notice that he was white and would have considered him a *natif-natal* Negro, a dyed-in-the-wool Thomas of Haiti. He was playing his cards right; soon he could start digging without arousing suspicion.

Earl had questioned the people in vain about the existence of a woman with a complexion the color of apricots and tumultuous black hair. They had looked at him, but had not answered.

One night, however, Earl thought he could see the woman on the bank of the third basin. He was convinced it was she; he'd have staked his very life on it. She was sitting down, feet in the water, combing her hair with a glittering comb, singing to a strange rhythm that he'd never heard in the region. Earl tore down the slope like a madman. When he was a few steps from her, the woman turned around, stood up, and burst into a crazy, cascading laugh. Her only covering was a palm leaf that crossed her chest at an angle. She took off running under the moon, sowing her gay goat's laughter, and disappeared into the bushes.

When the second lieutenant went back into his cabin, where the mosquitoes were already buzzing, he lay down. The fever took hold of him not long afterward, a cold fever that bathed his body in thick sweat . . . For days Second Lieutenant Wheelbarrow stayed in his cabin with chills and fever, swallowing handfuls of quinine and glassfuls of whiskey that would have stunned an ox. One night, while he was in the grip of the fever, the alcohol, and his waking dreams, grumbling and arguing with himself half-naked on his bed, two visitors walked in. Suddenly seized with terror, the sick man sat up and bellowed like an animal. The visitors fled. The strangest tales began to circulate about the white man who lived near the basins. People said that he was a fiend and that they had caught him in his cabin, naked as an earthworm, offering satanic worship to the spirits below, grumbling strange words and howling like a wild man. They gave him a wide berth, and people no longer ventured out to visit him.

When he began to feel better, he went out. People turned away as he passed. He wanted to go visiting, but he never found anyone at home. Weak, his mind still dimmed by the fever, Earl realized that he would have to act quickly to find his treasure. The climate in these mountains was killing him. He had become convinced that the treasure was at the foot of the last basin, where he'd seen the mysterious woman again. This concurred with the directions his uncle had left, based on an old sketch found in the papers of a Frenchman from the colonial era. Thin, a mere shadow of his former self, Earl Wheelbarrow was the victim of strange mirages after that; he dreamed of Spanish doubloons, of animals, and of an enchantingly beautiful woman with a crazy laugh.

One night, the lieutenant began to dig. He had chosen a very dark night, thick as *kalalou djon-djon*. After working for several hours by the light of his flashlights, he had dug a hole at least three meters deep. Water spouted. An underground pocket of water as pure as crystal had burst open. The water began to fill the hole. Animated by anger that was tied to a penetrating fear, his nerves set on edge by fatigue, Earl grabbed the pick again after a minute's hesitation. He began to dig a drain-off pit to empty the trench. After two hours of back-breaking work in water that already reached his belt, he emptied the hole. The water was coming through the opening now only in spurts; it was draining out quickly. Earl began digging again. After he wore himself out getting through a rocky layer, his pick met a crumbly subsoil. Once in a while Earl replaced the pick with the shovel, digging without stopping, his body flooded with torrents of sweat.

Suddenly, the lieutenant turned around and froze where he was, terrified. There was an enormous snake in the pit! Then a burst of laughter rang out above his head. He looked. It was the woman, watching him, the same woman he had surprised in the grotto and whom he had seen again near the third blue-watered basin. He turned a flashlight on her. She didn't flinch. She stood there like an antique statue from ancient days, priest-like, haloed by a full-blown beauty, dressed in a simple cloth draped around her hips.

"You're mighty daring to touch the Vien-Vien mountain!" she declared slowly, as if letting the words fall drop by drop.

"You're mighty daring!" she said again after a silence.

"Mighty daring!" she threw out one more time.

Then she disappeared. The snake which had been in the pit a minute ago too!

Furiously, Earl climbed the walls of the deep trench. Dawn was whitening the sky now and was lighting up the horizon with pink and orange miracles. The lieutenant tore off his clothes and dived into the water near the last basin to clear his mind. He was wide awake. He came out immediately and ran like a madman toward his cabin. He brought out a few pre-Columbian axes and all the pottery he had collected up to then. Was he the victim of one of those mirages that seemed to emanate from this country whose very earth seemed magic? He thought he could still hear the woman's voice in the distance shouting, "Come! Come!"

After three days of a raging fever, Wheelbarrow was feeling better. As soon as he was up, he tore up all the letters he'd gotten from Rosasharn, Dorothy, and Eleanor, as well as all his identification papers—in a word, everything that tied him to Chattanooga and the star-spangled republic. From now on he would live in this country. He would get to the bottom of its mystery. He would have that woman if it killed him!

He reflected a long time. Then he remembered having heard of Maréchal Célomme, a former rural sheriff, a patriarch, a *papa lwa* above reproach, who lived still farther up in the mountains in the area around Gouyaviers. There was no mystery of the heart of man, no mystery of the lily-like bodies of the Invisible Ones, that was unknown to Maréchal Célomme, the peasants said. He had "the gift of eyes," clairvoyance. He even knew what only the knife learns as it penetrates the heart of the yam, they said. Life is a yam . . . So Wheelbarrow made the decision to climb up the pathway that tirelessly winds itself around the summits to go and consult the high priest, servant of Heaven and of the Eloahs.

I can remember the very sound of Maréchal Célomme's voice as he told me this story. In fact, the old man recounted his interview with Lieutenant Wheelbarrow so many times that the very words he used are engraved in my memory. I don't think the old sage would have added to the facts. Not only was he incapable of lying, but, more than that, he never varied a single detail. I've often met *papa lwas* who respected the orthodoxy of their venerable religion; I've had long discussions on occasion with honest Servants burning with faith in Vodou and the Eloahs of their fathers; but never have I met a man who was purer, more righteous, more humane, or more selfless than Maréchal Célomme, in spite of his credulity and ignorance. This is the way he related his interview with Second Lieutenant Wheelbarrow to me.

When Earl arrived at Gouyaviers, whose peaks dominate the Bassins-Coquilleaux and all the surrounding area, he got off his exhausted mule and inquired for the *papaloa's* dwelling. Maréchal Célomme was waiting for him, standing before the door of the sanctuary. He summoned Earl with these words as he advanced toward him: "I was expecting you, my son!"

They greeted each other. The lieutenant gave him his hand and told him he had come to penetrate the mystery of an apricot-colored girl who haunted the blue basins on moonlit nights. The *papaloa* bade him enter the sanctuary and led him to the room where stands the *badgi*, over which the great soursop tree sways its fruit, pimply green breasts, above the golden roof thatch. Watching Maréchal Célomme exercise the powers that the highest stage of Vodou initiation confers, the taking of the eyes, was an unforgettable thing. After a short prayer before the *badgi*, Maréchal Célomme gravely took in his left hand "the eye of Heaven," a small Indian ax of blue stone, the product of the fusion of maroon Blacks, of Zambos, and of independent Indians under the great Cacique Henri. He took a fistful of ashes, which he let sift slowly between his withered fingers.

"Whoever dares to touch the treasure of the mountain will die . . . But man can attain the treasure of life . . . I see a red woman, the beautiful mistress of the waters, calling you . . . Walk toward her without fear and without haste; it is the treasure of life that awaits you . . . Each gold coin costs a drop of blood!"

"I don't want the treasure of the mountain anymore," said the lieutenant forcefully.

"Do you love this land and the men of this land? Can you sacrifice yourself to them, sacrifice everything?"

"I no longer know anything but this land and the men of this land," the lieutenant affirmed.

"Then, if your heart knows no fear, if your blood is as un-sullied as dew, if your soul is as serene as the eyes of children, cross the threshold; if not, do not defy the gods of this land . . . Make your way, and quickly!"

What happened after that in Maréchal Célomme's *houn-fort*, I have no way of knowing; the old man has always been reticent about it. The lieutenant's manuscript is also silent on this point. No one will ever really know. What I do know is that Lieutenant Wheelbarrow met the woman on a moonlit night. Woman or Simbi of the waters, siren or mermaid, Vien-Vien or goddess, he saw her. We name things with our hearts, and everything is real if we hold the keys. Second Lieutenant Wheelbarrow was enchanted from then on, and his eyes could see what he thought he had distinguished in his fevers. To each his own task on earth, believer and nonbeliever alike; the one describes, the other explains, the marvels of life.

The blue basins sparkled like shimmering mirrors. The dazzling beauty, fed by the primeval splendors of the Haitian land, held no more secrets for Earl Wheelbarrow. He had cast off his dross; the old man had died in him; the old rancor and the rags . . . She was waiting for him on the banks of the waters. She was a slender woman whose figure and features remained Indian in spite of the visible warmth of the blood of Ham. She was waiting for him, motionless . . .

"Come! Come!" she said to him.

He came closer.

"I am the guardian of these mountains and these waters," she told him. "Look at my green flocks jostling along as far as the eye can see; look at my blue waters mounting up to the largest blue basin of all, the azure of the sky. They're sleeping quietly with all my treasures. It's not yet time for the men of this land to take the buried treasures for themselves . . . I was waiting for you . . ."

He came very close to her. She held out her hands to him. He took them.

"One day the earth will open to give its treasures to all the sons of this land. For now I must watch over them . . . Will you help me watch over them? . . . If you betray the secrets of the earth, the earth will devour you alive, before you've even finished conceiving the idea!"

"The earth will devour me!" repeated Earl Wheelbarrow.

"To possess the land, to share the guardianship of the treasures, you have to defeat me in combat. Can you bend my back to the ground?"

He seized her, and the combat began. They fought under the moon on the banks of the basins; they fought on the damp cress; they fought on the cool soil; they fought in the waters. It was at the last basin that they embraced . . .

After that, no one ever saw Second Lieutenant Wheelbarrow again in his cabin at Bassins-Coquilleaux. His manuscript is quite fragmentary, quite obscure, but in it he speaks with such an accent of joy and fulfillment that he may truly have known happiness. If the scraps of his journal that have come down to me are the work of a madman, then I don't think the happiness all of us look for is far removed from madness. Perhaps his notes are somewhat incoherent, but then I distrust reason that's too cold and rational.

When she wants to taste a guava, wrote Lieutenant Wheelbarrow, *I immediately feel two cold acid streams flowing along my jaws. She doesn't need to speak. Our eyes meet, our hands clasp, and we rush out to the countryside . . .*

It seems that they never rested, and that every night they ran through the mountains. Earl wrote in his journal:

I hurt myself falling into a deep ravine. She picked me up and carried me into the grotto. My calf is half torn off, but I'm not suffering. She gathers fresh dew to bathe my wound; that's all. She takes care of me, and if by chance she sees a shadow of pain in my eyes, she simply puts her mouth to my wound, and immediately the pain is gone.

Earl Wheelbarrow must have reached the point of human knowledge where one participates in every breath, every vibration, of living matter. He notes:

Yesterday she told me that she would teach me to laugh like the flowers. For hours she directed my lessons. Then I felt a great peace and our bodies merged . . .

He relates further:

Now I can stay for long minutes underwater . . . The fish come and go around us, come close, look at us, rub against us, and leave again with slow strokes . . . I can't make them snuggle into my hand yet the way she can . . .

Then:

Last night it was cold. I felt chilled. Then she beckoned. I slid behind her into the narrow fault in the grotto that descends almost straight down. We went down into the heart of the earth for perhaps an hour. At a point where the space widened, we stopped and settled in a crevice. There was a soft warmth everywhere. I felt the radiant life of the depths vibrating against my body and the trembling of the great thermal waters dancing under the earth's flesh. Some kind of little golden flies flitted around us. I penetrated her and we slept . . . We went back up when day broke . . .

If the manuscript is to be believed, life is a brotherhood among the Vien-Viens:

Life is sometimes hard in the mountains, and it may happen that we're hungry. If I've picked a fruit, a bittersweet root, a sugary stalk, she won't eat if I won't bite our find with her, turn by turn . . . Then her eyes are the most loving color I've ever seen.

Never was there a more intimate union than that of Earl Wheelbarrow and the survivor of the gentle Xemi people. I read in his pages:

The other day, for just a few seconds my spirit wandered far, very far away. She knew it immediately. So she took the musician-bird that lives with us and closed my fingers around this bouquet of living feathers. At that moment, I

felt all the vibrancy of her love, her love as large as life,
pass through me . . .

I decipher from another fragment:

She takes my hands, rests her head against my chest, and
stays there for long hours listening to my heartbeat. I am
merged with her . . . Often we play: she's the waterfall,
and I bathe in the mad tumble of her blueblack hair . . .

Earl Wheelbarrow was still young, yet he was constantly
anxious about the passage of ever-fleeing time. I can make out
these sentences:

I have no impression of aging or using myself up. I feel
sure that I'll go out like a candle some far-off day. May it
be as far-off as possible, for she doesn't know what it is to
cry! . . . She would tie herself to my remains and hold me
tightly against her until death came for her too. She would
let herself starve to death, but she would never let me
go . . . That was, she told me, what the wives of the great
Caciques did in the olden days: they accompanied their
mates into the tomb . . .

Perhaps the enchanted second lieutenant learned all the
secrets of the Xemi people, the secrets we would like so much
to know. In any case, it seems that several times he was in
contact with other Vien-Viens. He relates:

I saw the great red xemès-god in the immense underground
chasm . . . She told me the great samba of the Xemi people
and taught me the words of the great, ancient areytos.

I managed to read still more of the old, worn, tattered, ragged document whose letters are often faded by the water of heavy rains and by the sun's burning heat:

With the rainy season, the great festivals of the sambas arrive. We blow three modulated notes into great conch shells, and our brothers and sisters on the mountains answer us from far away . . . Then we come together, we sing, we dance until the end of the rains . . . The music turns me into a wretched, torn-up thing; even my tearing is melodious and participates in hers . . .

That's all I can say about the life of the enchanted second lieutenant, about the bitter poetry, the strange love that made it flare up like a Bengal light in the violet, violent mountains of the St. Marc highlands. He would run by night like an elf, drunk with the splendors of the mountains. He would run every night with his companion in the greening of the earth, in the mouth of the wind, in the shimmering of the waters. During the day he lived in the grottoes where lay the treasures amassed by the Cacique of the House of Gold, the formidable Caonabo. He knew all the ancient spells, all the songs, all the dances of Queen Anacaona the Great, the Golden Flower, those songs and those dances that the mistresses-of-the-waters and the mistresses-of-the-mountains keep alive on moonlit nights.

Some say that the Vien-Viens, the last descendants of the Xemis of Haiti, the guardians of tomorrow's riches, who live hidden out of reach in the high, steep, inaccessible mountains, do not exist. More power to them . . . As for me, I know that in his manuscript, Second Lieutenant Wheelbarrow affirmed having shared the life of the last of the Vien-Viens. I have no reason to doubt it. Neither whiskey nor madness seem decisive enough arguments to me after reading his staggering testimony.

Maréchal Célomme, my friend, told me finally that one night, at the time the fighting was at its height between the armed patriots—Charlemagne Péralte's *cacos*—and the American invaders, Second Lieutenant Wheelbarrow was captured by the Yankee marines. Several of the old peasants of the area have told me that they saw the lieutenant bound and tied to his companion; that he was judged and executed on the spot, accused of high treason and complicity with the enemy. The two bodies were gathered by the peasants and piously buried in the little tomb whitening near the La Voûte grotto . . .

They're dead, and yet it's said that in this area people still see a mistress-of-the-water on moonlit nights, tirelessly combing the black silk of her tumultuous hair on the banks of the blue basins that climb up the mountain. Could Lieutenant Wheelbarrow and his companion have left children? . . . Whatever the case, it's a great and beautiful thing for a people to keep its legends alive!

A WHITE HOUSE WITH PINK CURTAINS IN THE DOWNSTAIRS WINDOWS

BY JAN J. DOMINIQUE

Kenscoff

(Originally published in 1996)

Translated by David Ball and Nicole Ball

Contrary to all common sense, despite the absence of evidence—and besides, what evidence could a reasonably sane person demand when hearing stories like that?—everybody agreed that the house deserved its reputation, or at any rate the people of Kenscoff unanimously agreed that it was inhabited by devils. With the type of seriousness appropriate to the situation, they acknowledged that it was cursed and that nobody should go near the little path that led to it after sunset, or even before that, just to be on the safe side.

To establish his influence, the old *ougan* had announced to the mountain wind that he would take it over, making sure that on its way down the hill, the wind would carry his voice all the way to the marketplace where the villagers were gathered that Tuesday. He admitted, however, that his gentle or violent *lwas*, his holy waters and prayers, hadn't had any effect on the house, and he gave up, even more frightened than the others.

He had seen everything. Exactly what, he refused to say, not wishing to give up his secret, despite his concern about protecting those who were curious about the house. And neither promises nor coaxing could get him to speak.

The man had his mystery. He guarded it closely. He was the only one who'd been in the house since the tragedy and he did not want that to change.

All right, I'll tell you . . .

The house was about ten years old. Its owners had disappeared without a trace one day or one night, except for a few tire marks that no one could even identify with certainty as being from their car. A few weeks later, the masons and carpenters who'd been hired to build the house—all residents of Kenscoff or the surrounding area—died of the same bad fever a few weeks apart from each other. That's when the rumors started. When Joseph—Marilia the priest's cook, Joseph— was found lying on the little path where he'd fainted, and after a rubdown, medicinal tea, and some coaxing, was unable to explain what had happened to him, rumors turned into anxious conversations. And then there was the disappearance of Félicien's black pig. So the priest and a few wealthy parishioners chipped in to build a large wooden fence to cut off the entrance from the little road. Félicien, the best carpenter between Pétionville and Kenscoff, refused to build the fence. It was built by an outsider who came from Port-au-Prince to do the job. It was said that Marilia grew fond of him. He promised to return, but was never seen again in the area. Then a silence fell over the town. Everyone understood that devils, or something else, had taken possession of the house. Not one girl from around Kenscoff would have dared to ask her lover to spend a night in that place as a proof of his love for her. Otherwise she would have been haunted all her life by the echo of his tender words whispered in another girl's ear.

And yet I liked that house, with its tin roof painted red,

its white walls and pink windows. It had caught my attention for a long time, and whenever I looked at it, I had a strange feeling of being summoned, as if that empty house, that garden of zinnias and the path lined with pine trees, was holding out its arms to me. I wanted it. I would often walk up to the end of the path. Accompanied by the old *ougan*, whom I had persuaded to come along to protect me, I would prowl around the house, inhaling its scent as one smells the sea, standing there silently, hardly moving, and at times I thought I could hear the pines and the flowers whispering sad, painful words to me. Then the old man would cross himself, spit three times, and, taking me by the arm, drag me back to the road, to the reassuring streetlamps with their single bulbs looking over the misty night. He would answer none of my questions and it was impossible to know what that old *ougan* had learned. The thing that had shocked him on that November night, he simply couldn't forget. Even those banal words that slipped from him were incomprehensible. In the night, they turned into the strange *"Yo t ap kriye."* They were crying.

Who was crying?

I wanted that house. I didn't care about the legend. I decided to buy it, since the first owners' relatives had announced that they would sell it for a very low price. When I asked for more information, I realized that they were practically giving it away. I even doubted that ten years earlier the construction had cost so little. And I was sure that it was worth ten times as much when compared to other real estate in the region. Everybody thought it was a whim on my part, or worse, that I was losing my mind. But I really wanted it and I bought it.

Things got very busy at work and I couldn't move in as quickly as I wanted to. Then, one day, the mountain winds brought down the smell of red earth, of *ti bonm* mint and white jasmine, and I had to return to the house with the pink curtains.

My absence had allowed some people to sleep more soundly. They were upset, but didn't dare say anything. After all, I was the one who would be living in that supposedly evil house. They should just leave me alone with my devils. A few very brave young men agreed to help me move in, on the absolute condition that they would start working at six in the morning so they could be through before nightfall. When we were done and dusk was still far off, I invited them to dinner. They refused politely so as to leave more quickly, hiding their haste under the false pretext that they wanted to leave me alone at last.

That evening, my first night in the white house, I took an ice-cold shower before going to bed. After a day like that, I needed a good night's sleep. It was a calm night. As I had guessed, the devils did not show up. Could they have been as tired as I was?

The next morning, I woke up with the scorching sun. Everything was truly quiet, since the main road bustle didn't reach my wall of pine trees. The smell of coffee rose from the kitchen, a nice gift from the old *ougan* which was also, I knew, a form of reproach. He must have been furious at my care-free attitude. Sleeping like that with the windows open and the doors unlocked. What carelessness! Yet, I feared no one. If thieves wanted to venture into my house, they wouldn't find anything worth taking. Besides, they wouldn't be brave enough to break in. Funny, a house full of devils was my best watchdog.

Once I got downstairs, a surprise was waiting for me in the living room that I didn't find funny at all. All the curtains, the nice pink curtains, were soaked, and the wooden floor was flooded. What stupid, stupid people had thought it clever to play this trick on me? I almost became angry, but it was too nice and sunny out for me to stay that way. I wasn't going to let myself be pushed around. So I cleaned up everything. Then I put the curtains out in the sun, pinning them down to keep them from blowing away in the wind. Just as I was putting on the clothespins, however, the wind calmed down, then stopped all of a sudden like a door slamming shut, like a mirror breaking apart for no reason. I didn't think much of this then, but now I remember. Now I understand everything. Yes, I tidied up the house a little, watered the flowers, and swept the paths.

Toward the beginning of the afternoon, I mean around two o'clock, I followed the path toward the main road. Yes, at two. The old man was sitting on a pile of stones, his eyes staring into space, with traces of vanished suns on his face. He hadn't heard me come. I stood there for a moment watching him, wondering what could possibly take place behind that brow whose wrinkles reminded me, for some reason, of happy young men and women who'd died at the age of twenty. I did not know how old he was. In his gaze I could also see the naïveté of young children along with the bitterness of those who'd lived too long and seen too much. I didn't know, or even realize, that he'd seen me, but when he finally spoke he asked me if I'd had a good night's sleep. I laughed then asked him if he had eyes in the back of his head. He calmly answered that he had felt me, that the change in the air current could only be due to my approach, and that all beings had a specific presence that he was able to perceive. And when he asked again about my night, I told him to note that I was in a good mood—a sign of a quiet, restful night.

"*Si ou te konnen!*" If you only knew! he said, then closed

his eyes, as if to block out a terror-filled night. Yet nothing bad or inexplicable had happened to me, except . . . But I could no longer bring back the unpleasant sensation I wanted to tell him about. So I didn't ask him anything, certain that he wouldn't have answered. And anyway, I had to go to the market.

My friend Michel was coming over to eat in my new house with a few friends. I hoped that one of these days Michel would finally say something to me that had no connection to our childhood. I suppose that Michel, who used to pull my hair when we were kids, had plenty of reasons for carrying on with another woman these last few months. But I should not even be thinking about that. I left the old man to his dreams and set out for the market.

They ate as if dying from hunger. I could have served them bitter herbs and they would have found them delicious. They loved my house right away. They loved its polished wooden floors and its clean-smelling pink curtains. Actually, the rascals from the night before had forced me to wash the entire house.

Michel's friends left around midnight. He decided he would stay, and go back to town later. I didn't want him to leave. Was it the cool night or the singing pines? As I became more relaxed, my strict and severe nature, which sometimes made me seem too distant, fell away. He said things that made our childhood memories evaporate.

I was happy. We were happy. After he left, I closed my eyes and fell asleep on the living room floor while dreaming about love.

The next day, the bad joke from the previous night was repeated and in spite of my good mood, I had to get angry. I had no intention of spending my life cleaning the floor. When I got outside, I grew still angrier. During the night, all the stones on the path had been thrown on the lawn, on the little flower shoots, on the little balcony, and there were pine branches scattered around the house. This time, it was too much. I lost my patience. No, I didn't want to play this game. Who did they think I was? I had a hard time believing that the old man could be the instigator of such a bad joke. I decided to go talk to him so he could help me find those who were responsible.

To my great surprise, he refused to help me, announcing to me, with that calm I always found so impressive, that the young people in the neighborhood would have never done something like this. They wouldn't have set foot on the yellow path after sunset for anything in the world. I hadn't thought of that. And yet it was true. But in that case, who was responsible? He had no idea, and even eliminated the people from nearby towns, for the house's evil reputation was well publicized. So I had to clear up this business all by myself, the old man warned me, repeating this over and over. He started up again with his spirits and devils. I was becoming exasperated. "Spirits shout," I said, "they howl, pull your toes, bite the tender flesh of newborn babies, but they don't ravage gardens and they don't flood your floors." He did not reply. I was wasting my time. Very well, I would play detective tonight.

That evening, though, I was in town with Michel and his parents, who wanted me to stay over for a few days. Immediately taking charge, Michel did not think it was smart for me to sleep alone in my little house, so I left it, without having cleared up the mystery of the floods. And then I had to go back to work. Somewhere in the city after an exhausting day, I would think back to the way the air smelled there, the feel of the fog on my skin at daybreak, when I had strolled in the little woods and gardens under the mocking but friendly gaze of the peasants. I was hoping that the old *ougan* would take care of everything while I was away and, moreover, that I wouldn't be gone for too long.

Michel had decided that we should get married at the beginning of July. That's when he usually took his vacation, and I was free then too. Michel decided everything. We finally had the big talk I was afraid of. He didn't want to hear about me going on business trips all the time and refused to understand that stocking the store made those trips necessary. He wanted me to stop working, but I couldn't bring myself to do so. After all, there was plenty of time for children. When the children come, I said, we'll see. I was already being somewhat sly. Michel looked at me with his ironic smile. He knew me too well to be fooled. Meanwhile, we had to think about our wedding. I was actually trying to get out of it—well, to be honest, I don't like to organize things. Michel was adamant about spending our first night in the white house though. There was even talk of us living there full time. On this, we agreed. But that argument about my work kept coming back. Michel seemed to have forgotten about our long friendship, and in the name of love, he wanted to run my life. Since he knew I was both patient and stubborn, he must have suspected that eventually I could get him to agree to anything, so he was being proactive. We agreed on one point only: to live in the white house year round.

I continued to travel through the country for two months. I had forgotten Kenscoff. I came back to town just a month before the great beginning—or the great ending, depending on how you see it, but for women, it's well known that it is the beginning, as they will know what real life is like only through marriage, and I must be like all women.

When I got back the craziness began. Michel's mother, like a good future mother-in-law, insisted on preparing the festivities herself while, for her part, my mother took on the role of mother of the bride.

I didn't protest. I let myself get dragged into pastry shops, to the dressmaker's, to the printer's for the wedding invitations (ugly as sin), to all the city stores, where they picked out everything, from shoes to panties. If only I could have given in to my apathy. Michel was on the to-do list. They wanted to teach me how to choose the clothes he liked, explain to me how to organize his books, the secrets for happiness, the best recipes to keep a man home—forgetting or refusing to admit that I wanted a different kind of life and that I had known Michel since first grade. But I let myself go along with it and they were happy.

I would be lying if I said that the month went by quickly. True, I was waiting for July, but I felt nervous, feverish, and the more the days went by, the more I had to control my impatience, and hold back my usual urge to scream. I was waiting for July essentially because I couldn't stand those preparations anymore. I wanted to get it over with as soon as possible. As for Michel, he was calm and he couldn't understand why I was exasperated. Then I would remember my mute adolescent rages during our discussions. When he ran out of arguments, he tried to aggravate me, so he wouldn't look bad. And he would burst out laughing when I would refuse to let myself get angry and flash him an innocent smile that never fooled him. That's how Michel is. He can anticipate my tantrums, figure out when I'm lying, and most of all he knows how to turn my anger to his advantage. Was I happy? I don't know. I didn't ask myself that question. What I really think is that I had put a blindfold over my eyes so as not to go mad with rage.

I only exploded when I discovered, by chance, how much the wedding lunch would cost. I was looking at a caterer's estimate and I couldn't believe my eyes. I even pretended that I was looking at Haitian gourdes instead of the typographic dollar sign that was insulting me with its snakelike face. Our respective parents made it plain that it was none of my business. It was my future husband's business, and Michel was okay with it. When I spoke to him about the lunch, he argued that this was a unique occasion and that we had no choice but to invite all these people this one time. Our parents were the ones paying for it anyway and it made them happy. My whole year's salary—and I knew very well that my salary was high compared to the majority of people. It was none of my business. So I forgot. I even forgot the figure. I swear. I can't remember it anymore. The invitations, the wedding—in reality, I took care of nothing. I merely went along with it. But on the day of the wedding, I couldn't bear the hypocritical good wishes, the allusions to my luck, the smiles produced for the occasion. Who cared about our possible future unhappiness, about those arguments which might destroy our relationship?

Once the ceremony was over, I only wanted to escape to the white house, to a happiness that would have to be built on day by day. And the rest? The rest is my business, Monsieur, the rest is of little importance to you. If you missed the most beautiful, memorable wedding of the year, my mother can show you the twelve albums, not to mention the photographs that haven't been organized yet.

Yes, I will go on, but I don't feel like telling you about those moments of happiness. My love, our happiness . . . At last we were in our white house, alone.

I couldn't sleep. Through the window, I could see the night. I had just spent wonderful moments with Michel. I was lying next to him. I had just been born into our life. I was me. I was him. The night was growing lovelier, sweeter, and I knew I wouldn't sleep. Next to me, Michel had a face I did not know but would learn to love, with those reflected moonbeams in the corners of his eyes. His lips were in another world, too far from me, and I had yet to discover that impermeable face which could disappear at every flutter of his eyelashes. I kept my eyes wide open so as not to miss a minute of his sleep. I wanted to decipher the dreams behind his eyelids, find his gaze under his closed eyes. The moon was making me jealous by throwing light reflections and shadows on his cheeks. I shouldn't wake him. I was hungry. I couldn't fall asleep and I was hungry, so I left the room quietly and went down to the living room, where . . . Oh, leave me alone . . .

In the living room, there was a slight noise that only the silence of the night and the isolation of the little house allowed me to discern: the sound of rain, no, of droplets falling regularly onto the floor. And all of a sudden, clearly, "*Lage n tanpri. Kite n ale!*" Please let us go!

Not tonight! I was sick of it. Who could have known or guessed I would come downstairs? Who could be spying on me in the dark? Perhaps they thought they would frighten me, but I was afraid of nothing. I had no reason to be afraid. Just one cry and Michel would hear me. But I didn't want to wake him. I would deal with this all by myself. I was determined to hurt those nasty people. Armed with a very big, very heavy clay vase, I explored the house. No one. The zinnias were swaying gently in the garden to the same monotonous rhythm as the murmur of the wind in the pines. What was really odd was the way the stones in the path were arranged. You'd think it was Morse code. It was nice out and the moon was lighting up the garden. I was not afraid that no one was there. Just for fun, I tried to decipher the code. Still the same strange plea: "*Lage n tanpri.*" Please let us go.

I was to untie them and let them go. I was curious. I shouldn't have been. Because of the night, perhaps, or the moon? I could sense, because of the sky, that the white house held a secret. Somewhere in the night something was calling me. I was dreaming with my eyes wide open. *Zinnias, pine trees, and stones of the path, what do you want me to do? Is the moon an accomplice? The garden is sad. I mustn't, but I love you. I have no fear. I will help you. Say straight out what you mean. I am a little girl again. I can't understand things easily.* I was singing. I was dancing. I could recreate ancient rites that my body was discovering in the depths of time. I was becoming the most mysterious of all the mysteries of the earth. The stones, in answer, wrote that they could not reveal everything to me. If I was sincere, I had to free the pink curtains and put them in front of the door, then all would be explained to me. The pink curtains. I was in an unreal, marvelous world. I felt relaxed and fearless, and I did what I had been ordered to do.

The curtains rose up and disappeared. Nothing could astonish me anymore. Besides, it all happened so fast. I went on singing melodies awhile longer, melodies forgotten long ago. My childhood was coming back to me. I was dancing. The wind was urging me on; the pines accompanied my melody. The zinnias took up the chorus. I wasn't dreaming. I know I wasn't dreaming. That night they poured out tales for me that no one would ever hear again. Dawn was about to break. The pine trees told me I was expected in the living room.

They were there. Seated, dignified, slightly embarrassed. I couldn't help recoiling. The smaller of the two began to speak and his voice resembled the music of the pines, the rolling of waves in the night when no noise on earth interrupts their melody. I realized that the spell was in my curtains, which had kept these two beings prisoners in the walls of my house, and it was their tears which had been soaking my floor at night. Who they were I do not know, but they were not devils, for they did not harm me in any way. They even thanked me for having freed them, and as they were getting up to leave, the elder asked me if I wanted to make a wish. They would grant me what I wanted most. I said happiness with Michel forever and I could read in their eyes the joy of being able to give me more than money, more than power, the things people would usually ask for.

After the customary salutations, which I politely imitated, they left while the wind was gently dispersing the smells and time was resuming its course. Upstairs, Michel was sleeping. I had to go up to him. I had glimpsed, between those two curtains, a love that I was going to keep. I went back to the bedroom and saw he was no longer in our bed. I thought that he had awakened and, seeing that I was no longer next to him, had gone down to look for me in the rooms of my little house, few as they were. But he was nowhere to be found. He had disappeared. Yes, I swear to you, Michel had disappeared. I beg you to believe me. He was no longer there. No, I'm *not* crazy! This house is mine, isn't it? And my curtains—where are my curtains? I used them to do what? You're sick, all of you! That's not true. He disappeared. And why are the stones of the garden in that order, or rather that disorder? What? Someone could have dragged . . . And who's that "someone"? No, I'm telling you, Michel has disappeared. I want to go find him. Besides, ask the old *ougan*, he'll tell you the house was strange. He saw it too. No, that's another lie. I saw him. I spoke to him yesterday. But leave me alone, can't you understand that I'm in pain?

Michel has disappeared.

ORESCA

BY PAULETTE POUJOL ORIOL

Source Diquini

(Originally published in 2001)

Translated by Nicole Ball

O resca! Oresca! Oresca!

The residents of the Source Diquini district had been calling the man at the top of their lungs for over an hour.

He was a kind of patriarch for the whole area. At least six and a half feet tall, with his broad shoulders, large build, booming voice, and eternal walking stick in hand, he had real influence over the whole neighborhood, mainly because of his healing powers as a *ougan*, which everybody respected. He was also very much feared for his violent fits of anger.

Ordinarily rather calm, he became enraged whenever something was not to his liking or when somebody was rude to him. Then he would fume with rage, launch furious blows right and left with his stick, threatening to beat the culprits and screaming violent curses at them.

His personality was all the more remarkable in that unlike most of our neighbors and in spite of modern trends, he still wore the traditional outfits of our peasants: blue denim pants rolled up over strong calves sparsely covered with thick hair; huge feet in comfortable yellow leather sandals that looked in-destructible; a large overshirt with folds that amplified his size even more; a braided strawhat adorned with pink and green pom-poms hanging at the ends of little strings. His attire was completed with the *koko pòv* pipe planted between two rotten stubs of his chipped dentures and, of course, a multiple-use tumbler tied to his cord belt.

In this outfit, he looked so completely like an authentic peasant of times past that he seemed dressed up for a folk dance.

His shack, built on a large piece of land, stood at the foot of a hill overlooking a small backyard where he raised—not very profitably—pigs, baby goats, and poultry that he only sold to special clients. His eggs were the best in the neighborhood, but Oresca would never agree to sell anything to those fresh youth who dared to defy him and make fun of the way he dressed.

The way he was, huge, loud, violent, he made people tremble and he was undoubtedly the uncontested master of the area.

We lived in the district and had started a small orchard which was blooming, as grapefruits, mangoes, and guavas were already appearing on our well-groomed trees. We checked them every day to follow their progress. They would probably turn out less tasty than the fruit we could have bought at the market but they were our very own creole productions, grown in our own garden, and we insisted on eating them ourselves, or at least having a taste of them from time to time.

Except that the neighborhood kids, free as air and great virtuosos with the slingshot, left us with no chance of ever being able to pick a fruit, even a half-ripe one. So someone talked to Oresca about our problems as novice growers. He came very early one morning, pipe in mouth and angry-eyed, to offer his services against those impertinent youths. We didn't want to give him permission to beat anyone with his imposing punishment stick made of gaiac wood, but he assured us that he knew other methods just as efficient.

He then disappeared from our horizon. We had almost forgotten about him when he showed up one Saturday morning carrying the straw haversack that never left his shoulder, doubled that day with a jute bag. Both of them were loaded with what at first appeared to be coconuts.

Out of that load, he took three dozen small hollowed-out gourds to which he had attached bright red ribbons and he hung them on our healthiest fruit trees. The hanging of those red ribbons and gourds, along with a few incantations, protected our trees more than any squad of vigilantes could have done. Oresca has been gone for a long time now, yet he still watches over our trees even though the gourds and red ribbons are no more.

It's not to reminisce about that flamboyant peasant and how he saved our fruit that we are telling this, but rather for the strange way the story ended.

Oresca oh! Oresca!

Oresca, a man well along in years and a *ougan* to boot, was quick with his stick. He would get easily offended by boys insolent and roguish enough to attack him.

One day when he had fallen asleep under a mango tree after enjoying his dish of ground corn and his little shot of *tranpe*, some young bullies came up to him, broke his pipe, ripped his large strawhat, and stole a couple of chickens and a few eggs.

Oresca's awakening was terrible. Boiling with rage, screaming curses in every direction, he made the whole neighborhood shake with fear and finally, in a threatening voice, he yelled: "I know who did it! I'll get them!"

Did he really know who had wrecked his things and stolen

his hens and eggs? Whether he did or not, two of the area's most mischievous boys suddenly disappeared from their homes. Their parents looked for them in vain for over a week.

The lamentations of their distressed mothers could be heard far and wide. They were sure Oresca had made their sons disappear to take his revenge for what they had done to him.

We couldn't believe this. To do away with ten- to thirteen-year-old boys who would run away at the slightest threat of being beaten with a stick seemed to us completely out of proportion to their initial misdeeds.

Two weeks went by. Lifète and Cinéus, the sons of two sisters, inseparable when it came to troublemaking, were still nowhere to be found. Their parents turned to Dumayric, the police chief, who, completely baffled, alerted the Tonton Macoutes of the time. They descended on the district and after they had rather roughly interrogated the neighbors—whose declarations were somewhat vague and hesitant—they decided to take Oresca away since the public outcry seemed to point to him as the perpetrator of what in the end had to be called a crime.

Arresting the man was more easily said than done. A dozen Macoutes were needed to hold him down. He was kicking and screaming curses, promising the little rascals the wrath of all the *lwas* of Ogou Feray, Damballah, Lwa Zaou, and a few others among the meanest of the Vodou pantheon.

Needless to say, even the worst accusers among the neighbors were not too keen on helping out with the arrest. Not so foolish! What if Oresca identified them during the fight? Recognized them as his accusers and cast a spell on them to make them pay?

The Macoutes had to handle Oresca by themselves and

fight like dogs against an enraged lion. They finally managed to tie him up like a goat and throw him facedown into a small truck they had to drive right near him so they could toss him into it. The wild beast was finally under control.

Two days went by in a kind of passive and expectant wait, for if Oresca was not loved, he was feared, so people were curious about the outcome of the arrest. Would he be tried and sent to jail? The mothers of the vanished children were already sentencing him to the firing squad or life in prison, even though there was no evidence he had done anything wrong.

Suddenly, one evening around midnight, three or four days after Oresca's arrest, people heard a vehicle speeding through the district. It stopped briefly near Oresca's shack, then left as it had come, at top speed again.

Early the next morning, the neighbors, emboldened by the light of day, approached the *ougan*'s place. At first they didn't shout too loudly, but then, without daring to move too near, they grew bolder. And then they all went at it, each yelling louder than the other: "Oresca! Oresca oh!"

One man, less cowardly or more daring, kicked the door open then stepped back, suppressing a cry of horror. Oresca was lying against the back wall, his eyes wide open, his body all purplish, his skull smashed, one ear ripped and dangling, his genitals crushed. He seemed to look at all of them as if in reproach for their accusations and to cast a final spell on them. The neighbors stepped back in terror, the men mute with fear, the women crossing themselves and mumbling prayers while someone less dumfounded went to call on the authorities again. The corpse, which was already stinking, was taken away.

There was never any investigation. Everybody understood that the man who had dared to resist his unfounded arrest had died from the tortures the Macoutes had subjected him to. He had held out for three days, but in the end his strong body gave in and Oresca, who had no friends, no family, who was little known and little loved, had disappeared surreptitiously.

Nobody dared come near Oresca's hut for the next five or six years. Nobody—all the more so as the place was still filled with the objects the departed *ougan* had used for his trade.

Then a young man from the neighborhood who intended to get married soon started to inquire about renting the small plot and cultivating it. This turned out to be easy, as nobody there was too eager to live in a place marked by such tragic events.

The new farmer razed the shack by simply setting it on fire, sending Oresca, his witchcraft, and his memory up in smoke. Then he surveyed the ground to design his own house and plant his poles.

After he had dug three or four holes with his pickaxe, he dropped his tool and screamed with horror. Two skulls, two femurs, and one humerus were buried in the earth that had been packed by the passing years. Lifète? Cinéus? Who will ever know?

CHILDREN OF HEROES (EXCERPT)

BY LYONEL TROUILLOT
Place de Héros
(Originally published in 2002)

Translated by Linda Coverdale

It must have been noon when we began to run. We could have put up with the smell for a lot longer, but when Mariéla saw the mailman coming, a guy who never failed to have a drink with Corazón and reminisce about the legendary greats of boxing, she dumped our savings out of their jar and, warning me not to lose them, slipped the coins into my pocket, then told me to run without stopping until I was out of the slum. If we became separated along the way, she would wait for me in front of old Moses's furniture factory. She led me over to the bed where Joséphine was still sleeping. We looked one last time at that face battered by blows and the passing years. You could see the bones beneath the flesh, and those very bones seemed to be sagging, as if the whole body had cried uncle. With the passing years, she had become a transparent thing. At the last, when Corazón struck her, the blows went right through her. In that image where there had once been a woman, now only a blank remained. Asleep, she seemed even more dead than Corazón, who lay in the middle of the room, his skull split open, his body partly hidden by the chest of drawers and the chairs knocked over when he fell. All the furniture in the house had toppled onto him. The chest. The chairs. The stove and the aluminum plates. The low table where he put his feet while listening to soccer matches on the transistor radio Mam Yvonne gave us, back when she was working in the laundry of that hospital in the Bronx she described to us in her letters as sometimes a paradise and sometimes sheer hell. The kerosene lamp we used when money was tight. The pot of plastic flowers and the big stone ashtray Joséphine had bought as ornamental touches. The four little pink glasses with hearts on them. The décor and all the trimmings. Everything—or almost everything—in the house had been broken over Corazón's big body. The blue of his overalls disappeared in places beneath the debris of incongruous objects. He had lost one of his sneakers and I could see the sole of his foot, as rough as lizard skin. I preferred to look at his foot. Every time my eyes landed on his face, I felt the prickling that comes before tears, and I tried to reassure myself by behaving like Mariéla. She is the strongest, the most honest with herself. The most alone, perhaps. While we stayed in that room, she never showed one sign of weakness. She sat down in the middle of the mess, just long enough to come to a decision. Then, in a burst of energy, she stuffed our skimpy belongings into the big canvas bag where Joséphine tucked away our dirty laundry. I realized that we were going to leave. Quite far away from Joséphine, who slept on in the bed where she could finally stretch out at her ease, without having to huddle up real small, hugging the wall to leave more space for Corazón's huge body. The trouble is, Joséphine has never been willing to sleep alone. As long as I've known her, she has always needed a man in her bed. A husband or a son. Her favorite is Corazón. Was. He's dead. And I won't be around anymore to replace him, now that the future belongs to the authorities. She truly loved him, Corazón. When he came home later than usual, she'd wait for him before she drew the curtain and went to bed. When he was out all night, she sat up in the chair, her mouth full of prayers. Whenever he stayed away for some time, I was his replacement. Joséphine would call me to come get into the bed. She'd hug me close for a while and fall into an uneasy sleep toward dawn, still murmuring complaints and prayers. If you begin at the end, then we are the chief culprits. No one has the right to take life away. But while we never meant to kill it, that life was turning out badly every single day. Whether he really did ever climb into the ring or whether he was just lying to us, Corazón hit everything that moved, except for Mariéla. So he might have expected that someday someone would hit back. And Joséphine, although you couldn't ever accuse her of loving hatred or violence, is not completely innocent. You might think she lives on nothing because she never asks for anything. The truth is, she rarely uses words to say things. Her expectations take a sideways approach. She has hardly any voice and never shouts "I want," or "I mean," or "I demand." She never raises her voice, but in her eyes there's a whole vocabulary. To get something, her face freezes and grows pitiful. Her face is a lament that weeps over its hopes in a roundabout way. She also invents stories that often have a hidden meaning. For example, she tells how when I was little I used to run away from the clatter of rainstorms on the sheet-metal roofs. How I'd hide in the latrines shared by the small houses of the neighborhood. She believes that story cross-her-heart and tells it to anyone who'll listen. At that time, Corazón wasn't sleeping in the house. He wouldn't accept the idea of this second child. Joséphine, according to her, used to pry me from my hidey-hole, rub my limbs briskly, and keep me in her bed for the night. I don't remember escaping to the latrines, and I've always loved the sound of rain. Especially after Mariéla taught me how to change the water into music by cupping my palms over my ears. During every downpour, I'd compose songs for myself, merry little melodies. That's what I remember. Me being so scared, Joséphine invented that to express a wish: that I would fill in for Corazón in her bed whenever he spent the night drinking in one of those crummy dives where the rum's too cheap to match the label on its bottle. Joséphine, my mother, has always lived in fear that someone else would swipe her spot in her men's hearts. She wanted me to remain her frail child my whole life long. Joséphine, she's unhappy, she has no guarantee that she'll always be needed. That no other woman will ever come along to replace her. She has always been jealous of Mariéla, who asks nothing of anyone. Joséphine's failing was to worry, to believe that one day Corazón and I would both take off and leave her flat. Corazón liked to frighten her and would run away every now and then. He'd come back after each fake departure, though, and Joséphine, reassured, would give thanks for that godsend. And yet that blessing may perhaps have worked more like a curse. Each time he returned, he hated her a bit more, and beat her a bit more to make up for lost time. Me, I never thought about going away. Except for just long enough to come back, my arms full of little pink glasses decorated with hearts and my pockets stuffed with gourdes and sourballs, since Joséphine never allowed herself any whims or treats save for the tons of sticky candies she gorged on every Sunday afternoon. During the week she lived on prayers and watching others eat. It was only on Sunday that she turned greedy. I would never have left, except to go get her candies. And drinking glasses just like the ones she bought from a hardware stall at the Salomon market. I'm sure she likes them better than all the lovely luxury items in the whole wide world. Joséphine, she's had a hard life, she's just suffering itself. I didn't want to abandon her. Still, she shouldn't have invented that story about the latrines. It made me feel smaller every time she trotted out that tale for Mam Yvonne or the neighbor ladies. Especially since, really, I never needed any excuse to love her. She comes right after Mariéla. And in life as in school, second place isn't so bad. Mariéla, she's in first place: I see her from inside, as if we were walking in step. To the point that sometimes I forget that we're two people, after all. Whereas Joséphine I've always loved from a certain distance. Now that I'll never see her again, because after what we've done we can't live together anymore, the distance will grow bigger without changing my feelings. You can love someone from very far away. The way it is in history lessons, which teach about the destiny of navigators who look back on their countries from afar, still feeling affection for that tiny image. Distance, that's something we didn't know how to talk about, Mariéla and I, the day Corazón died. What's far away exists without any outlines. You can't imagine its shape. All you know is, the space isn't defined. It floats a little, like a boat. It's a territory like the night, it needs time to become natural. At the moment we left, when the mailman's footsteps were approaching, Mariéla couldn't manage to explain it to me. The words weren't coming to her. Although she usually didn't have any trouble finding the right words. She has a gift for saying things, but "far away," where we had to go, she just couldn't describe it precisely. The only image that came to me was that we'd be abandoning the slum to live the rest of our lives in a kind of wasteland. I was careful not to walk on the broken glass and crockery or bump into Corazón's long legs, which divided the room almost perfectly in half. His body was still big, too big for a small one-room house with a woman and two children always getting in his way. Only his face had shrunk.

He'd fallen on his side and was showing his bad profile. He had chosen, for his death mask, that fake look of a sad child he always wore after some creditor had been by. Before she took the plane to the United States, Mam Yvonne, who knew religion without being devout like Joséphine, often used to tell us that the power of the Evil One lies in guile. And that God's weapon is compassion. Corazón must have taken after both of them. I realized this on the day he died. Joséphine experienced both those sides of him every day. Why else would she protect her face whenever he approached her with a bottle in his hand? And why did she speak to him at other times as if in supplication? Begging for his presence like a blessing! He was both her demon and her Good Lord. Even in death, he hadn't changed: Corazón was many men, all of them quite different. He could have written the book on schemes to get drunk whenever he liked and never pay his debts. He could also waver like a reluctant convalescent hesitating between the cure and a relapse. He took the worst of life and talked only about the best. That was my father: a brute who could be as gentle as a sheep. Before leaving for the United States, Mam Yvonne often used to visit us to speak heart-to-heart with Joséphine and shower her with advice. As soon as people start living better than you do, that sort of makes them an authority. Mariéla didn't much appreciate Mam Yvonne's way of lecturing us. Mariéla doesn't like wisdom. Mam Yvonne really needed to say those words to us. She felt a touch guilty about Corazón's behavior and meant to pass on to her daughter-in-law her expertise as a capable woman. Men, they're all pigs. A smart woman uses men and doesn't let them push her around. All of them, without exception: pigs, and nothing more. My son's just like the rest of them. And Joséphine, who had a loving heart right out of the movies, would start defending Corazón.

Mam Yvonne admitted that he wasn't bad through and through. But watch out. When he was little, I caught him several times putting burning cigarette butts in the ear of the milkman's donkey or ripping the pages from a schoolbook to avoid doing his homework. He fought frantically to escape the spankings he'd earned. He would put on the face of an angel and soon you'd forgive him. Mam Yvonne warned Joséphine: even as a child, he was always capable of doing terrible things. And now Corazón would lose his temper, start choking, sucking up all the air in the room, and we'd all feel the tension mount. Before the impassive Mam Yvonne, Corazón would be fuming, almost shouting, but he never dared challenge her openly. Yes, you used to do that, she would insist. Then you'd go bragging to your friends, whose mothers would tell me about it. Mam Yvonne would search her memory for years, dates, witnesses, while Corazón gave way, reduced to telling us that his mother had made up that business about the cigarette butts in the donkey's ears just to make us think badly of him and to cause trouble in his own home. Joséphine already doesn't respect me, so if you start sticking your nose in . . . I have to admit that I agreed with him. Mothers, they always come up with stuff that doesn't exactly reflect reality, it's more like the idea they have of their sons. Take Joséphine and those latrines. A mother, she's fine. Except when she sets about telling the story of your life. The more the son grows up, committing his own fresh follies, the more the mother clings to the follies of the past. When there aren't enough, she invents them. On that point, Joséphine was like Mam Yvonne, constantly claiming the right to meddle by deciding what my favorite meal was, or putting her seal on my childhood memories. With a mother, things get complicated if she decides to know you better than you know yourself. Mam Yvonne was describing her son the way she'd wanted him to be, while he put on his lost-child face and seemed about to burst the seams of his overalls, his muscles swelling with vexation. And knowing that soon Mam Yvonne would no longer be there to protect us from the storm she had a talent for stirring up, Joséphine would ask Mariéla and me to go get some Barbancourt rum on credit at old man Eliphète's variety store. Softly she'd remind us to make sure Eliphète put it on her tab, since Corazón had long since exhausted his credit in every business in the neighborhood. We'd bring back the rum. At the sight of the bottle, Corazón would simmer down, relax his muscles, and trot out his favorite saying: Life holds only bad surprises, and the last one will be death. When it comes, I won't put up a fuss. Well, death came. Despite what people say, we didn't go out looking for it. It wasn't cooked up in advance. Violence attracts more violence, and Mariéla lifted up that wrench as if she had become a kind of robot handpicked by horror, or Providence. The teacher had explained to us that despite what historians say (they only ever know the outside of events), it wasn't the lunatic Défilée who gathered up the remains of Emperor Dessalines the evening of his assassination, but a brave spirit passing across the bridge who took over the old madwoman's body. History, she told us, hides a wealth of mysteries and as many surprises. No one knows beforehand who among us will become a hero or a monster. As for Corazón, although there was nothing historic about his death, he was definitely and forever fresh out of surprises. He still lay there, and Mariéla didn't spare him even a single glance. Me, I would have liked to speak with him one last time. To talk. Present our case. Argue with his corpse. Find words that would be halfway between a "Sorry" and "Goodbye." Explain to him. Lecture him. But Mariéla would not have tolerated such a compromise. The mailman's footsteps were drawing closer, leaving us little time. It must have been noon. I could hear the little kids shouting over at the elementary school. Their shrill tumult drowned out the ringing of the bell announcing the end of classes. I recognized the voices of my friends in the uproar: Roland, Ambroise, and all the others. Marcel. And especially Stammering Jhonny, but his voice you can't hear because he needs at least an hour to say the slightest thing. So he prefers to keep quiet. Jhonny is my best friend. If Corazón hadn't drunk up Mam Yvonne's last check, I would have been out yelling with them, yanking the back hem of the proctor's jacket, and maybe Mariéla wouldn't have done what she did. Or she would have done it all by herself. In a way, you might say that it was a blessing in disguise, that habit Corazón had fallen into, of spending my school fee money in the bar. Spending that money, that's one thing I've forgiven him. School I never liked. And I was always a slow learner. Unlike Mariéla. She understands everything right away. My essays, she used to write them for me in no time, while it took me forever to compose the first line. The teacher used to emphasize the importance of an outline, the sequence of ideas, the structure of paragraphs. "You went on a picnic with your parents: tell us about it. Describe a sunset. Draw up the portrait of your favorite animal." I'd try to plan an outline. But I couldn't decide on the right trees and animals to invent. Should I begin the description with the roots or the fur or the tail, the moral or the physical portrait, the frame or the color? Mariéla would take the pencil from my hand. In the time it took me to jump a hedge, or pull on a rope, or lob some dumb I-dare-you at Marcel or Stammering Jhonny, or stroll around the neighborhood spying on the pretty girls who went to the Baptist church without obeying the commandments, she'd whipped me up a landscape all my own, a sea just right for a voyage, a dog, a cat, a big house with real windows and a door set straight on its hinges. She'd even written me some wonderful parents: a father who didn't beat me and a mother with a gift for smiles. At first the teacher had ranked me among the poorest pupils. As Mariéla kept writing for me, my compositions improved along with my grades until I was even held up as an example. Until the day the teacher told Joséphine that I was a born writer. And Joséphine, while she wasn't a blabbermouth, once she'd drawn the curtain and shut herself in with Corazón at the back of the room, after begging us to go play outside so we wouldn't hear her sighs, well, she couldn't keep anything secret from him. Corazón, he soon figured out that Mariéla was the author. He said it was a father's place to keep an eye on his son's work and that he would go to the school to talk with the teacher. Joséphine gave him the money. When I was sent home because my fees were late, she didn't dare ask Corazón about it for fear he'd fly into a rage and beat the hell out of us both. About school, though, it's not so serious. It's really something I never regretted. Mariéla stopped going after she got her certificate. And I mean, school is no party. Fortunately, it's not because of this that Mariéla did what she did. That we did what we did. Together. Corazón's death, I can't say that I'm proud of it. It wasn't worked out ahead of time. You shouldn't claim credit for actions unless you planned them. And it wasn't a success, either, like a discovery you make or when you create something new. We fell into it, Corazón's death. It's a trap life had set for us a long time before. An event that will live on in the annals of the city. Given that neither time nor other people will allow us to forget it. Don't ever think I'm proud of it. Ever since that day, though, Mariéla and I, we're like a community. Even if they separate us, we'll always be together. A team. I'm the one who held Corazón's feet to make him slip. Before that, Mariéla had had to do her best for the both of us. When I was really little, she used to take care of me when Joséphine was lost in her prayers. When I was sick with malaria, it was Mariéla who gave me my medicine, checking the instructions to figure out the dosage. If I had the power, there are times when I'd like to bring him back to life, Corazón. Especially at night. He isn't mean when he's asleep. No, I'm not proud of what we did. But, on the other hand, it's good that she didn't have to do it alone. Mariéla is too all alone. This time, at least she'll be able to say: My little brother helped me.

Hearing the mailman's footsteps, Mariéla grabbed the bag she'd filled with our clothes and pushed me toward the door. Outside, the first thing that struck me was the heat of the sun. Mariéla and I, we prefer the moon. On moonlit nights, shadows are softer than modeling clay, and we used to draw shapes with them. The noonday sun casts a shadow so hard that it follows close on your heels, as if everyone had a personal policeman to drag along underfoot. We always took shelter when the sun beat down too harshly. At school, there was the great oak in the middle of the recreation yard. Mariéla had also shown me other shady places for escaping the sunshine. Sometimes we hid behind the long curtains of sheets hung up by washerwomen. Or we sought out the dampness of the unfinished little houses at the far end of the slum. Out where stubborn folks had begun to build despite warnings from the city inspectors and then reluctantly had to stop work after all, because you cannot lay foundations in a swamp. The two of us had always had our haunts, spots where we could outwit the sun. For the first time, we had to brave the glare without the promise of relief, trying courageously to outrun it, racing for a long time toward the night. After Corazón's death, the first thing I saw was the sun. The second thing, that was the mailman's belly. I ran right into it. He let the whole neighborhood's mail tumble into the stagnant water between our place and the Jean-Baptiste family's house next door. The letters began to spread out into the muddy water and float like sailboats. The neighbors might have forgiven us for just Corazón. Basically, aside from us, no one liked him. He'd wheedled money from even the poorest of the poor, and since the women liked his looks, all the men loathed him without daring to tell him so, because of his biceps. Our real crime was to have knocked the mail into the muck. No one in the world likes having their hopes flung into a puddle. People were going to shred us. There was surely a letter from Mam Yvonne swimming somewhere in there. Corazón could sense them coming and would get the little table ready to welcome the mailman, who loved to chat with him about boxing. One bottle, two glasses. Corazón had a mongrel's flair for sniffing out the arrival of Mam Yvonne's letters and arranged to intercept them so he could spend the money himself. On those days, Corazón, who no longer allowed Joséphine to leave the house, encouraged her instead to go out, reminding her of this or that promise to visit an old friend. He'd set the glasses on the table, roll up his sleeves to admire his biceps, and wait for the mailman. He was rarely off in his calculations, and then only by a day or two. Except for those six months when we went without any news, which was how long it took Mam Yvonne to get the backlog of her Social Security checks from the state of Florida. Floating among the letters was one from Mam Yvonne with a number to be presented at the window of the foreign exchange office and precise instructions as to the usage of the sum in question. But now Corazón would not be there to intercept it.

And anyway, the mail for the whole slum was soaking in the puddle between our house and the Jean-Baptiste place. The mailman had gotten to his feet and was shouting at us to come back. We were long gone when he decided to enter our house to get help from someone with authority. We had already run down half the main alley, passed the entrance to the elementary school, and were climbing over the dilapidated little wall around the property of the pastor of the Baptist church to take the shortcut that came out in front of the furniture factory. Grown-ups avoid that path, especially those with jobs, because they risk stepping on broken glass or cow-pats: the smell of dung is unmistakable, and grown-ups don't always like people to know where they've been. For us, though, it's so simple to jump over the low wall. And since no boss preaches to us on payday about the need for cleanliness, we prefer the shortcut to the adults' long ways around. At the end of the path, only a hop, skip, and a jump from the asphalt where the big city began, Fat Mayard tried to stop us, just for fun. Actually, I didn't interest him. I don't interest many people. To them—aside from Stammering Jhonny, Marcel, and a few others—I'm Mariéla's brother. Fat Mayard felt honor bound to feel up girls' breasts, and he often lay in wait for Mariéla. She had let him do it once, probably because it was a new experience. Mariéla likes trying new things. And he, foolishly convinced he'd acquired some rights, had gone all around the slum crowing victory to make guys jealous. On the day of Corazón's death, he tried to grab her and hold her close. At first it was only a game. When he heard the uproar of the neighborhood shouting our names, he realized something serious had happened. Like everyone who dreams of being in the spotlight, he tried to join in, by grabbing Mariéla for real. And she dodged him. Exactly like Corazón when he worked out at daybreak while the neighborhood still slept, except for the women on their way home from the bakery with bread to sell. That threw Fat Mayard for a loop, but he wouldn't give up. An unarmed girl was supposed to be easy prey. He pounced again. And Mariéla treated him to the shock of his life. She popped him one right in the breadbasket. Just the way Corazón shadowboxed with the morning breeze to keep in shape. In a last reflex of pride, Fat Mayard took the precaution of glancing around. No one was watching. Relieved to have no witnesses, he dropped to his knees, eyes glazed, breathless, gagging as if giving up the ghost. We didn't have time to scold him, to tell him he was going to live and get himself clobbered plenty more times. Flesh isn't as weak as people think. Mariéla and I know that death doesn't kill with a single punch, it's the accumulation of damage that wears the body down from inside, till only the skin is left. Those last weeks, Corazón hit Joséphine almost every day. She didn't even bleed anymore, didn't cry, didn't react in any way. But her battered skin kept breathing. Death hadn't yet risen to the surface. Blows take a long time to kill. Fat Mayard could wait. Mariéla burst out laughing at his look of despair. Some people come into this world with the gift of tears. Mariéla's natural-born talent is laughter. She'd found that out all by herself, no help needed. I don't know if there are places where laughing is taught, but around here you just pick it up on your own. And sometimes life goes by so fast or stays in one spot so long that somehow you run out of time or energy and never get around to learning. Me, for example, I don't like to laugh. In elementary school they teach you the ABCs. The different churches of God teach the fear of the Lord. For wisdom and rules to live by, we take inspiration from proverbs. In our neighborhood, when things go wrong, life leans on proverbs. Everyone has a supply of them. Even the poorest souls. And they're the only possession we share without waiting to be asked. Those times when we have nothing to say to one another, we toss out a proverb at random, and that can start up who knows what conversation. We've got tons of proverbs to fill empty spaces and provide commentary for any occasion. Even those unexpected once-in-a-lifetime events. When the rainy season lasted so long that the water topped the highest roofs of the houses clinging down in the ravines, people were racking their brains to come up with a saying that would explain the deluge. The oldsters invent a proverb every time misfortune trips life up. And children collect them to grow in wisdom. Mariéla's laughter isn't some local custom, it's a personal conquest. Mariéla is her very own creation. Her tears, her ideas, her peals of laughter. And now her destiny. If you can call the trackless life ahead of us a destiny. She was still laughing when we reached a real street. With a name. And cars. A different territory under different rules. In our neighborhood, aside from those who work and always slog home exhausted, we have lots of spare time. So people are available. Our pursuers weren't about to give up the chase, but it would be hard for them to find us in the crowd. We'd become a girl and boy among others. Anonymous in the real city. The one on the map. Once we'd reached the outskirts of the city, we slowed down. I was coughing. Pedestrians were turning around and seemed to study me with a suspicious eye. I can't help coughing after the slightest effort. In the slum, my cough is no big deal. Everybody knows it's part of my nature, a constitutional defect, and no one pays any attention. But strangers always seem a little startled by it. Our headlong run had worn me out, so Mariéla suggested we go on to the Champ de Mars, to rest there on a bench. We walked slowly and my cough calmed down. I had no idea what would happen next, but I felt fine. The anxiety came later, on the bench. And again that evening, when we had to improvise to find a place to sleep. And yet again the next day, when we went to meet Stammering Jhonny and found out the press had gotten involved. Black thoughts, they're like trees. They can take time to grow, budding in your head, and wind up taking root there. During those first hours after Corazón had died for real, after our race to escape the slum, we walked quietly around the Champ de Mars, where the statues of heroes look down indifferently from on high. Mariéla was carrying the sack and thinking for the two of us. We walked side by side, and I advanced calmly, as if I were hidden behind her. She has always been kind to me. She's done heaps of favors for me, a thousand little things you don't think about at the time. Big things too. Like doing my homework or taking care of my health. Plus, since she was Corazón's favorite child, whenever I misbehaved she'd say *we*, to soften him up. If it isn't against the law, I hope we'll be able to write to each other. She and I, we were a real pair. Mariéla is more than a sister. Brother and sister, they're not words we use. In the slum we call everyone by name and we more or less love whomever we like. We can't afford to love from obligation. I had chosen Mariéla. It was already like that before. And for as long as our escape lasted—three days, two moons, and a few hours—until they spotted us on the third day on that same Champ de Mars, watched over by those same statues, me sitting at the bandstand, dreaming about music, and she returning from her bike ride, the two of us formed a real pair.

When we reached the Champ de Mars, we slowed down and looked for an empty bench. To take a rest. Every seat was taken. The only free space was the corner of a marble bench already occupied by a gentleman dressed the old way. In a three-piece suit and tie. And although he didn't say a word, we understood that he spoke a different language from ours. A library language with difficult words. He did not answer our hello. At any other time, Mariéla would have insisted, pressuring the man into politeness. The man did not see us, refusing the accidental company of such offspring from another world. Hands lying flat upon his thighs, he looked into the distance, indifferent to everything, not just our presence. But still. You're supposed to reply when spoken to. Although Mariéla was the sort to make him eat his own tie, we weren't in a position to stand up for good manners. We were rather like him, staring solitarily at our horizon line. Except that ours was behind us. Or maybe off to the side. The man was one of those lucky people who know where to look. A scholar or a man of faith. He was at peace in his world. Still keeping an eye on our strange neighbor, Mariéla asked me to dig the money out of my pocket so we could count up our fortune. Then she wanted to know if I was hungry, and I answered no. I'd been thinking too. After what we'd done, I'd lost the right to be frail. I'd decided to be grown-up. To summon some strength. So I'd promised myself to control my cough. And not to be hungry or thirsty. Ever again. To live without anything. Without daring to feel the slightest need. Not in front of Mariéla, in any case. You're sure you're not hungry? I said no, and besides, it was true. The first day, I didn't want anything. To make things equal between us, I asked her if she wanted me to take charge of the bag. In the future. No, it's not very heavy. Mariéla never speaks with the voice of a victim. There were bloodstains on her dress. More real than the gentleman with the well-cut clothes who continued to stare straight ahead of him without moving his head or his hands, seeing only the portent of that imaginary line he had chosen to target. So I copied him. I gazed at an empty point to avoid seeing the bloodstains on the dress, and all that had happened. Sitting on that bench made me vulnerable. (Before Corazón's death, I lived on silence and would stay motionless for long periods. Now I need movement. And floods of words. Silence awakens the dead.) Corazón was already taking advantage of our stay on the bench to become a kind of ghost. He was there, before my eyes. I looked at Mariéla. Even in the heart of death, Mariéla is like life. But he was coming between us. Enormous. Bleeding from open wounds. Working hard at dying. If you don't want to think about anything, you must take life like an athlete, run all the time, hide behind speed. Once the body is at rest, misery swarms into your head. I stared straight ahead. I looked up at the statues, and I still saw the blood. I closed my eyes to concentrate better. But it's inside your head that you see. The images come from within. That's where everything happens and then happens all over again, real fast. Corazón was dead, and he was alive. Ready to die anew. And now here in the afternoon it's morning once more. It's like a play or a movie. I close my eyes to stay in the afternoon. But the morning is stubborn. Eternal. Unstoppable. Despite all my efforts to stay where we are, Mariéla and I are walking past the garage again. We're returning from the market. A long walk for not much: a pepper and some laundry detergent. The pepper is for Corazón. So's the detergent, for his overalls. The garage isn't too far from the slum. We usually avoid that street. Corazón doesn't like to be bothered at work. And to see him is to bother him. Or not to see him: same thing. Because he doesn't go there every day. The toolbox, the tools, the overalls, all that, it's for show. He doesn't really work at the garage. He's used more like an automobile jack there. He has no claims on the machinery. Or dignity. Or words. Corazón, he's a pair of arms. But we don't know that. Mariéla, who wanted to take that street, she doesn't know that. There's an unbelievable scene going on at the garage. An end-of-the-world. One voice is raised, dominating the others. It isn't Corazón's. On the contrary: the louder that voice grows, the weaker Corazón's gets. We watch what's going on. Mariéla is very upset. On her face I can see astonishment, then disappointment. The scene is hard to describe because what we see is way more humiliating than a kid driven by fear into the shit of the public latrines. This job? The only reason you've got it is because of a promise to your father! Corazón is dying. And don't you dare have any more opinions or touch one single thing without being asked! It's as if one of the grand statues on the Place des Héros had fallen from its pedestal. Physically he's still very much alive and is lifting a section of an engine, those are the boss's orders. But he's a man without an image. And Mariéla, who has always respected him even when she disapproved of him, now realizes she's an orphan. She takes my hand and we leave. We drop the detergent we were to bring back to Joséphine. And the pepper. Mariéla stomps on the pepper and picks up the detergent. She doesn't want to go home right away. We walk. We're looking for an image, a reason to tell ourselves that it's not serious. But the walk doesn't erase the scene. We've already seen everything that's in the street. It's all ugly, all the same: the beggars, the dust, the shop signs, the drunks. And us. There's nothing that could protect us from Corazón's fall. I hear the boss's voice. Lousy good-for-nothing! And lots of adjectives for Corazón run through our minds. None of them positive. He's a man without quality who has no rights or privileges. And Mariéla says to me, He'll never hit you again. She

thought of me, and I of Joséphine. Between Mariéla and Joséphine, there's no love lost. Joséphine adores being pitied and
Mariéla despises weaklings. The sun's broiling our skin and we
decide to go home. But we still dawdle. We need time to accept Corazón in his new version. We're hoping not to see him
again right away. It's like when Jhonny's older brother had his
crazy fit. I saw him. On all fours, like a dog. Wagging, like a
dog, his imaginary tail. Lapping dirty water from a ditch, like a
dog. When Jhonny told me that the fit had passed and that his
brother thought he was human again, I waited weeks before
seeing him. So as not to see the dog. It takes time to get used
to the new reality of a father who gets himself told off and
walked all over like a rag. Unfortunately, when we get home
he's already there. He has set up the table, with the bottle and
the glasses. The dead hero acts as though he were alive. He's
waiting for the mailman. He can't forgive Joséphine for bustling
around the house. For being there. For wearing such a sad
look that you can't miss it. She's busy. And always sad. When
she's not cooking, she cleans house or mends old clothing.
Housework is her passion. It's kind of amazing. If you look
around, you won't find that many objects to put away. We
don't live in a big house, and when she insists on straightening
up the place, moving things around and dusting the glasses,
everyone feels uncomfortable. Especially Corazón, who has no
more room to stretch out his legs. He usually chases her out
when he's expecting the mailman. They're alone in the house,
and he's starting to get cross. That part, I don't see that, it's
something I imagine. He can't bear Joséphine looking at him
even though she's as meek as can be. But he knows perfectly
well that he's a worthless man, and he believes she knows that
too. Even though she has always found reasons to admire him.
She's the only one who can forgive him. Even Mam Yvonne

has lost all hope. She went away to wait until he can't make decisions for us anymore. So that she can salvage us. Mam Yvonne is figuring that we'll find a way to replace him. She gives us presents and is secretly preparing our departure for abroad. Even his mother has abandoned Corazón. His only absolution is Joséphine. Mariéla loved him when she thought he was her equal. They communicated over our heads. Now Mariéla is all alone. Only she has the strength to face up, to decide. She's ready to pay the price. While he lays low like a lizard in front of his boss, to save a lie. You do what I tell you, or you get out. And don't come sniveling back around here. Corazón, he gave in, so he could keep his overalls. And now he wants to play the big guy. Joséphine's presence enrages him. When we walk in, he's hitting her. With each blow he lands, he's trying to hide the truth. He doesn't care that we're there. He has no idea that we saw him die not an hour before. He hits her. To recreate the image he lost. But he's not our champion anymore. Nothing but some poor jerk and our father. We arrive just when his huge fist lands in Joséphine's face and destroys it, propelling her to the back of the room, toward the bed. And he's not finished. He goes after her, defending his imaginary titles. He keeps his guard up, he's Joe Louis again: Joe hoists up Joséphine, who's already knocked out from the first blows. Joe is boxing. And the old skin bag is taking a beating. For Mam Yvonne, whom he never dared to challenge. For the garage owner, who treats him like less than zero. For El Negro, the Dominican boxer against whom he lasted only a single round that one time he ever stepped into a real ring. For the referee, who stopped the fight too early, before I got my second wind. That ref, he fucked up my whole life. And suddenly, he's punching her for Mariéla, who's ordering him to stop. Up yours! Here, I'm the boss! He pummels his punching bag exultantly. But he's been dead ever since the incident at the garage. He's been dead ever since we heard him stammer helplessly. That's why Mariéla goes rummaging through the box where he keeps his tools. She hefts the wrenches, selects the heaviest one. Corazón, basking in his glory, still thinks he holds his audience in the palm of his hand. Mariéla goes up to him, then up on tiptoe to take better aim at his skull, and sweeps her arms in an arc to bring that wrench down in both hands as hard as she can. He's astonished to be attacked by an adversary he hasn't picked out himself. He thinks it's not fair, given that she's the one he loves the most. He moves toward her, perhaps to demand an explanation. He wants to understand. But Mariéla doesn't feel like having a conversation. She strikes him a second time. Head on. Right on the forehead. I hear the sound the bone makes. Now he's furious. He advances in spite of the blows, fist raised, to defend himself. That's when I intervene. I don't want him to touch Mariéla. Joséphine, she's a consenting adult. The only thing you can do for her is help her suffer, and that's all she asks. If anyone told her to leave she'd simply say mind your own business. But Mariéla, she was born to have wings. I crawl toward Corazón. I'm not afraid of him anymore. I'm only afraid of Joséphine, who will accuse Mariéla. I'm afraid because I love Joséphine and hope she will forgive us. Anyway, I crawl toward Corazón. I cling to his feet. The only thing I want is to hold him back. I forbid him to touch her. I try to bite him. My teeth aren't strong enough to get through his mechanic's overalls. He drags me along as he closes in on Mariéla. What's happening is between them; what I'm doing doesn't count. He stopped taking me seriously the day he realized that I had no talent for boxing. He moves forward as if I didn't exist. But because he's already staggering and I tighten my grip, he ends up falling. Mariéla has stopped hitting him. It's the first time I watch someone die, but I know that he's dead. I can't tell if it's the blow or the fall that killed him. Joséphine is sleeping, curled up on the bed. Her husband is lying on the floor, and the blood pools like the rain that sometimes leaks through the roof. At the time, I don't pay attention to a whole bunch of details. I didn't see the blood spurt onto Mariéla's dress. It's only on this bench in the Champ de Mars, next to this apathetic gentleman, that I notice the blood on the dress and realize the permanent nature of what has happened. Violence, that's something we've always lived with: in our neighborhood, the strongest beat up the weakest, and life goes on. This act went beyond anything that came before. Everything we'd ever been or said simply didn't matter anymore. Corazón's death would begin us: Joséphine, Mariéla, and me. I understood that when I saw the blood on the dress. I told myself that it was important for Joséphine not to grow old with the idea that it was a real crime. Mariéla and I, in all our predictions, had never had anything but happy endings. No child in the neighborhood is rich enough to believe in Father Christmas, but sometimes I let myself think that I could stand in for him. Then I would buy a garage for Corazón, and hundreds of glasses and loads of hard candies for Joséphine. Clothes, too, because the mother of Father Christmas deserves a wardrobe, after all. I thought about that on our bench. I saw that Mariéla was shaking, that doubts or worries had made her fragile, and I looked away, toward the gentleman. I felt tears on my cheeks and said, It's nothing, it's my cough. Mariéla pretended not to notice that I was crying.

PART II

SEDUCED

REMEMBER ONE DAY

BY EMMELIE PROPHÈTE

Boulevard Jean-Jacques Dessalines

(Originally published in 1999)

Translated by George Lang

> One day remember
> this dismembered city
> Between noise stupidity and pain
> They created infidelity, the blue sidewalks
> of another continent
> Madness has become useful
> We work at drawing up exits
> From your eyes
> Emptiness is to be reinvented

*

My only point of reference is your face in a spectral light. The desire for you came like a distant murmur. A vague memory of children's books. A lesson learned long ago. I pace the sidewalks of Port-au-Prince. I am late for heart-break. The path I ought to take to know your name. The city where you were born. All is closed for the holidays. My work goes on. I think of you. They told me how my disease began. To this day I do not believe it.

*

I shuffle
Against the stream of your passions
Against the gusts of prison wounds
I shuffle
Turned infinitely
Toward your irrationality

With me night never stops
We left our warmth on a bench
Sand comes up to our eyes

We all dream of sidewalks
The cries of our nakedness
Go without solution
Like your silence

RÊVE HAITIEN

BY BEN FOUNTAIN

Pacot

(Originally published in 2000)

I n the evenings, after he finished his rounds, Mason would often carry his chessboard down to the Champ de Mars and wait for a match on one of the concrete benches. As a gesture of solidarity he lived in Pacot, the scruffy middle-class neighborhood in the heart of Port-au-Prince, while most of his fellow O.A.S. observers had taken houses in the fashionable suburb of Pétionville. Out of sympathy for the people Mason insisted on Pacot, but as it turned out he grew to like the place, the jungly yards and wild creep of urban undergrowth, the crumbling gingerbread houses and cobbled streets. And it had strategic position as well, which was important to Mason, who took his job as an observer seriously. From his house he could track the nightly gunfire, its volume and heft, the level of intent—whether it was a drizzle meant mainly for suggestive effect or something heavier, a message of a more direct nature. In the mornings he always knew where to look for bodies. And when war had erupted between two army gangs he'd been the first observer to know, lying in bed while what sounded like the long-rumored invasion raged nearby. Most of his colleagues had been clueless until the morning after, when they met the roadblocks on their way to work.

On Thursdays he went to the Oloffson to hear the band, and on weekends he toured the hotel bars and casinos in

Pétionville. Otherwise, unless it had been such a grim day that he could only stare at his kitchen wall and drink beer, he would get his chess set and walk down to the park, past the weary peddler women chanting house-to-house, past the packs of rachitic, turd-colored dogs, past the crazy man who squatted by the Church of the Sacred Heart sweeping handfuls of dirt across his chest. There in the park, which resembled a bombed-out inner-city lot, he would pick out a bench with a view of the palace and arrange his pieces, and within minutes a crowd of mouthy street kids would be watching him play that day's challengers. Mason rarely won; that was the whole point. With the overthrow and exile of their cherished president, the methodical hell of the army regime, and now the embargo that threatened to crush them all, he believed that the popular ego needed a boost. It did them good to see a Haitian whip a *blan* at chess; it was a reason to laugh, to be proud at his expense, and there were evenings when he looked on these thrown games as the most constructive thing he'd done all day.

As his Creole improved he came to understand that the street kids' jibes weren't all that friendly. Yet he persisted; Haitians needed something to keep them going, and these games allowed him to keep a covert eye on the palace, the evening routine of the military thugs who were running the country—the de facto government, as the diplomats and news reports insisted on saying, the de factos basically meaning anybody with a gun. Word got around about his evening games and the *zazous* started bringing chess sets for him to buy, the handcrafted pieces often worked in Haitian themes: the Vodou gods, say, or LeClerc versus Toussaint, or Baby Doc as the king and Michèle the queen and notorious Macoutes in supporting roles. Sometimes during these games the crowd grew so raucous that he feared drawing fire from the palace guards. And, regardless of the game, he always left in time to get home by dark. Not even a *blan* was safe on the streets after dark.

Late one afternoon he'd barely set up his board when a scrap of skin and bones came running toward him. *Blan!* the boy shouted, grinning wickedly. *Vini, gen yon match pou ou!* Mason packed up his set and followed the boy to a secluded corner of the park, a patch of trees and scrub screening it from the palace. There on the bench sat a mulatto, a young Haitian with bronze skin, an impressive hawk nose, and a black mass of hair that grazed his shoulders. His T-shirt and jeans were basic street, but the cracked white loafers seemed to hint at old affluence, also an attitude, a sexually purposed life that had been abandoned some time ago. He simply pointed to the spot where Mason should sit, and they started playing.

The mulatto took the first game in seven moves. Mason realized that with this one he was allowed to try; the next game lasted eleven moves. "You're very good," Mason said in French, but the mulatto merely gave a paranoiac twitch and reset his pieces. In the next game Mason focused all his mental powers, but the mulatto had a way of pinning you down with pawns and bishops, then wheeling his knights through the mush of your defense. This game went to thirteen moves before Mason admitted he was beaten.

The mulatto sat back, eyed him a withering moment, then said in English: "All of these nights you have been trying to lose."

Mason shrugged, and began resetting the pieces.

"I didn't think it was possible for anyone to be so stupid, even a *blan*," said the mulatto. "You are mocking us."

"No, that's not it at all. I just felt . . ." Mason struggled for a polite way to say it.

"You feel pity for us."

"Something like that."

"You want to help the Haitian people."

"That's true. I do."

"Are you a good man? A brave man? A man of conviction?"

Mason, who had never been spoken to in such solemn terms, needed a second to process the question. "Well, sure," he replied, and really meant it.

"Then come with me," said the mulatto.

He led Mason around the palace and into the hard neighborhood known as Salomon, a dense, scumbled antheap of cinder-block houses and packing-crate sheds, wobbly storefronts, markets, mewling beggars underfoot. Through the woodsmoke and dust and swirl of car exhaust the late sun took on an ocherous radiance, the red light washing over the grunged and pitted streets. Dunes of garbage filled out the open spaces, eruptions so rich in colorful filth that they achieved a kind of abstraction. With Mason half-trotting to keep up, the mulatto cut along side streets and tight alleyways where Haitians tumbled at them from every side. A simmering roar came off the closepacked houses, a vibration like a drumroll in his ears that blended with the slur of cars and bleating horns, the scraps of Latin music shredding the air. There was something powerful here, even exalted; Mason felt it whenever he was on the streets, a kind of spasm, a queasy, slightly strung-out thrill feeding off the sheer muscle of the place.

It was down an alley near the cemetery, a small sea-green house flaking chunks of itself, half-hidden by shrubs and a draggled row of saplings. The mulatto passed through the gate and into the house without speaking to the group gathered on the steps, a middle-aged couple and five or six staring kids.

Mason followed the mulatto through the murk of the front room, vaguely aware of beds and mismatched plastic furniture, a cheesy New York–skyline souvenir clock. The next room was cramped and musty, the single window shuttered and locked. The mulatto switched on the bare light overhead and walked to an armoire that filled half the room. That too was locked, and he jabbed a key at it with the wrath of a man who finds such details an insult.

"Is this your house?" asked Mason, eyeing the bed in the corner, the soiled clothes and books scattered around.

"Sometimes."

"Who are those people out there?"

"Haitians," snapped the frustrated mulatto. Mason finally had to turn the key himself, which went with an easy click. The mulatto sighed, then pulled two plastic garbage bags out of the armoire.

"This," he announced, stepping past Mason to the bed, "is the treasure of the Haitian people."

Mason stood back as the mulatto began pulling rolls of canvas from the bags, stripping off the rag strings, and laying the canvases on the bed. "Hyppolite," he said crisply, as a serpentine creature with the head of a man unfurled across the mattress. "Castera Bazile," he said next, "the crucifixion," and a blunt-angled painting of the nailed and bleeding Christ was laid over Hyppolite's mutant snake. "Philomé Obin. Bigaud. André Pierre. All of the Haitian masters are represented." At first glance the paintings had a wooden quality, and yet Mason, whose life trajectory had mostly skimmed him past art, felt confronted by something vital and real.

"Préfète Duffaut." The mulatto kept unrolling canvases. "Lafortune Felix. Saint-Fleurant. Hyppolite, his famous painting of Erzulie. There is a million dollars' worth of art in this room."

This was a lot, even allowing for the Haitian gift for puff. "How did you get it?" Mason felt obliged to ask.

"We stole it." The mulatto gave him an imperious look.

"You stole it?"

"Shortly after the coup. Most of the paintings we took in a single night. It wasn't difficult, I know the houses where they have the art. A few pictures came later, but most of the items we took in the time of the coup."

"Okay." Mason felt the soft approach was best. "You're an artist?"

"I am a doctor," said the mulatto, and his arrogance seemed to bear this out.

"But you like art."

The mulatto paused, then went on as if Mason hadn't spoken. "Art is the only thing of value in my country—the national treasure, what Haiti has to offer to the world. We are going to use her treasure to free her."

Mason had met his share of delusional Haitians, but here were the pictures, and here was a man with the bearing of a king. A man who'd gutted his best chess game in thirteen moves.

"How are you going to do that?"

"There is a receiver in Paris who makes a market in Haitian art. He is offering cash, eighty thousand American dollars if I can get the paintings to Miami. A shameful price when you consider this is our treasure . . ." The mulatto looked toward the bed and seemed lost for a moment. "But that is the choice. The only choices we have in Haiti are bad choices."

"I guess you want the money for guns," said Mason, who'd been in-country long enough to guess. There were fantasts and rebels on every street corner.

"Certainly guns will have a role in this plan."

"You really think that's the solution?"

The mulatto laughed in his face. "Please, have you been drinking today?"

"Well." Like all the observers, Mason was touchy about appearing naive. "It took the army a couple of million to get Aristide out, and they already had the guns. You think you can beat the army with eighty thousand dollars?"

"You are American, so of course everything for you is a question of money. Honor and courage count for nothing, justice, *fear*—those people in the palace are cowards, okay? When the real fighting starts I assure you they will run. They will pack their blood money in their valises and run."

"Well, first you have to get the guns."

"First the paintings must be carried to Miami. You are an observer, this is the same as diplomatic immunity. If you take them no one will search your bags."

Mason laughed when he realized what was being asked, though the mulatto was right: the couple of times he'd flown out, customs had waved him through as soon as he flashed his credentials.

"What makes you think you can trust me?"

"Because you lost at chess."

"Maybe I'm just bad."

"Yes, it's true, you are very bad. But no one is that bad."

Mason began to see the backward logic of it, how in a weird way the chess games were the best guarantee. This was Haitian logic, logic from the mirror's other side, also proof of how desperate the mulatto had to be.

"You must," the mulatto said in a peremptory voice, and yet his eyes were as pleading as the sorriest beggar's. "For decency's sake, you must."

Mason turned as if to study the canvases, but he was

thinking about the worst thing that had happened to him today. He'd been driving his truck through La Saline, the festering salt-marsh slum that stretched along the bay like a mile-wide lesion splitting the earth. At his approach, a thin woman with blank eyes had risen from her squat and held her baby toward him—begging, he thought at first, playing on his pity to shake loose some change, and then he saw the strange way the baby's head lolled back, the gray underpallor of its ropy skin. The knowledge came on like a slow electric shock: *dead*, that baby was dead, but the woman said nothing as he eased past. She simply held out her baby in silent witness, and Mason couldn't look at her, he'd had to turn away. With the embargo all the babies were dying now.

"Okay," he said, surprised at the steadiness of his voice. "I'll do it."

It turned out that the mulatto wasn't really a doctor. He'd had two years of medical school at the University of Haiti before being expelled for leading an anti-Duvalier protest, "a stupid little thing," as he described it, he'd done much worse and never been caught. As far as Mason could tell, he eked out a living as a *doktè fèy*, a kind of roving leaf doctor and cut-rate *ougan* who happened to have a grounding in Western medical science.

He'd cached stolen paintings all over town. Mason never knew when he'd turn up with the next batch, a bundle of wry Zephirins or ethereal Magloires to be added to the contraband in Mason's closet. But it was always after dark, almost always on the nights when the shooting was worst. He'd hear a single knock and crack open the door to find the mulatto standing there with a green trash bag, his hair zapping in all directions, eyes pinwheeling like a junkie's. Mason would give him a beer and they'd look at the paintings, the mulatto tutoring him on Haitian art and history.

"Something incredible is happening here," he might say as they sat in Mason's kitchen drinking beer, studying pictures of demons and zombies and saints. "Something vital, a rebirth of our true nature, which is shown so clearly in the miracle of Haitian art. *'Ici la renaissance,'* how strange that this was the name of the bar where Hyppolite was discovered. *Ici la renaissance*—it is true, a rebirth is coming in the world, a realization that the material is not enough, that we must bring equal discipline to the spiritual as well. And Haiti will be the center of this renaissance—this is the reason for my country, the only slave revolt to triumph in the history of the world. God wanted us free because He has a plan."

He could spiel in this elevated way for hours, forging text in his precision English like a professor delivering a formal lecture. If Mason kept popping beers, they'd eventually reach the point where paintings were scattered all over the house; then the mulatto would pace from room to room explaining tricks of perspective and coloration, giving historical reference to certain details. "But the dream is dying," he told Mason one night. "Those criminals in the palace are killing us. As long as they have the power, there will be no renaissance."

"They're tough," Mason agreed. "They've got all that drug money backing them up. The CIA too, probably."

"But they're cowards. Fate demands that we win."

He wouldn't tell Mason his name; he seemed to operate out of an inflated sense of the threat he posed to the regime. Some nights Mason was sure he'd fallen in with a lunatic, but then he'd think about the chess, or the reams of Baudelaire and Goethe the man could quote, or the cure he'd prescribed for Mason's touchy lower bowel—"You must drink a glass of rum with a whole clove of garlic." Mason did, and the next day found himself healed. If at times the mulatto seemed a little erratic, that might have something to do with being a genius, or the stress of a childhood spent in Duvalier's Haiti. One night Mason suggested a game of chess, but the mulatto refused.

"I don't play chess since I was a boy. The match with you, that was the first time in fifteen years."

"But you're brilliant!"

The mulatto shrugged. "I was third in the national championship the year I was twelve, and when my father found out he threw away my chess set and all my chess books. He said there is no place in the world for a Haitian chess player."

"But if you were good enough—"

"He said I would never be. And he was probably right, my father was a very smart man."

Mason hesitated; the past tense was always loaded in Haiti. "What was he?"

"Doctor. *Ophtalmologiste.*"

Again Mason hesitated. "Under Duvalier most of the doctors left."

"My father stayed. He was an eminence. The last Haitian to deliver a paper to the International Congress of Opthalmology." He fell silent for a moment, seemed to gather himself. "If you were noted in your field, that could protect you, but this also meant that Duvalier perceived you as a threat. You could be famous but you could never slip, show that you were vulnerable in any way. One slip, and they'd take you." The mulatto paused again. "My father never slipped, but I think it made him a little crazy. He kept a gun in the house— we lived on the Champ de Mars, and at night we could hear the screams of people being tortured in the palace. One night he took this gun, my father, he held the bullets in his hand and he said to me: 'This bullet is for you. This one is for your brother. This one for your mama. And this one, for me. Because if they come they are not going to take us alive.'"

What could Mason say? Any sympathy or comfort he might try to offer would be false, because he'd lived such a stupid life. So he kept his mouth shut and listened, though on nights when the mulatto seemed especially bleak Mason insisted that he sleep on the couch. Sometimes he did; by morning he was always gone. Mason would straighten up the couch, eat his toast and mango jelly, then drive over to the office and get his detail for the day. Some days he drove around in his white 4Runner with the powder-blue O.A.S. flag rippling in the breeze: "showing the blue" this was called, letting the de factos know that they were being watched, though after a time Mason realized this was a strategy that assumed some capacity for shame on their part. Other days he was assigned to the storefront office that took complaints of human-rights abuses. Not much happened on those days; it was common knowledge that the building was watched, and walk-in complaints were depressingly rare.

Once a week he'd drive over to Tintanyen and make a count of the bodies dumped out there, and often these were horrible days. Tintanyen was a wide plain of shitlike muck held together by a furze of rank, spraddling weeds. You entered through a pair of crumbling stone portals—the gates to hell, Mason couldn't help thinking—and stepped from your car into a pressure cooker, a blast of moist, dense, unwholesome heat, silent except for the whine of flies and mosquitoes. The mosquitoes at Tintanyen were like no others, an evillooking, black-and-gray-jacketed strain that seemed to relish the smell of insect repellent. Mason and his colleagues would tramp through the muck, sweating, swatting at the murder-ous bugs, hacking away the weeds until they came on a body, whatever mudcaked, hogtied, maggoty wretch the de factos had seen fit to drag out here. From the shade of the trees bor-dering the field a pack of feral dogs was always watching them, alert, anticipating a fresh meal. Those dogs, the Haitian driver once confided in a whisper, were de factos.

"The dogs?" Mason asked, wondering if his Creole had failed him again.

Sure, the driver explained. They were *zobop*, men who could change into animal form. Those dogs over there were de facto spies.

Mason nodded, squinting at the distant dogs. M *tande*, he said. I hear you.

Each week Mason photographed the bodies, drafted his report, and turned it over to his boss, the increasingly demor-alized Argentine lawyer. They were all lawyers, all schooled in the authority of words, though as their words turned to dust a pall of impotence and futility settled over the mission. The weakest on the team gave themselves up to pleasure, taking advantage of their six thousand tax-free dollars a month to buy all the best art, eat at the best restaurants, and screw strings of beautiful, impoverished Haitian girls. The best lapsed into a simmering, low-grade depression: you had to watch, that was your job, to *observe* this disaster, a laughable, tragically self-defeating mission.

"What does it mean?" Mason asked the mulatto one night. They were sitting in Mason's kitchen during a blackout, studying Hyppolite's *Rêve Haitien* by candlelight. The picture was taped to the back of a kitchen chair, facing them like a mute third party to the conversation.

"It is a dream," said the mulatto, who was slumped in his

chair with his legs thrown out. The first beer always went in a couple of gulps, and then he'd sag into himself like a heap of wet towels.

"Well, sure," said Mason, "*Haitian Dream*, you told me that." And the colors did have the blear look of a dream, the dull plasma blush of the alternating pinks, the toneless mattes of the blues and grays, a few muddy clots of sluggish brown. In the background a nude woman was sleeping on a wrought-iron bed. Closer in stood an impassive bourgeois couple, the man holding a book for the woman to read. The room was a homely, somewhat stilted jumble of curtains, tables and chairs, framed pictures and potted plants, while in the foreground two rats darted past a crouched cat. As in a dream the dissonance seemed pregnant, significant; the sum effect was vaguely menacing.

"I can't make heads or tails of it," said Mason. "And that thing there, by the bed," he continued, pointing out what looked like a small window casement between the bed and the rest of the room. "What's that?"

"That's part of the dream," said the mulatto, almost smiling.

"It looks like a window."

"Yes, I think you are right. Hyppolite puts this very strange object in the middle of his picture, I think he's trying to tell you something. He's telling you a way of looking at things."

On these nights the gunfire seemed diminished, a faint popping in their ears like a pressure change, though if the rounds were nearby the mulatto's eye would start twitching like a cornered mouse. Here is a man, Mason thought, who's living on air and inspiration, holding himself together by force of will. He was passionate about the art, equally passionate in his loathing for the people who'd ruined Haiti. You don't belong here, Mason wanted to tell him. You deserve a better place. But that was true of almost every Haitian he'd met.

"You know, my father thought Duvalier was retarded," the mulatto said one night. They were looking at a deadpan Obin portrait of the iconic first family, circa 1964; Papa Doc's eyes behind his glasses had the severe, hieratic stare of a Byzantine mosaic. "It's true," he continued, "they worked together treating yaws during the 1950s, every week they would ride out to Cayes to see patients. Duvalier would sit in the car wearing his suit and his hat and he would never say a word for six hours. He never drank, never ate, never relieved himself, he never said a word to anyone. Finally, one day my father asked him, 'Doctor, is something the matter? You are always so quiet—have we displeased you? Are you angry?' And Duvalier turned to him very slowly and said, 'I am thinking about the country.' And of course, you know, he really was. Politically, the man was a genius."

Mason shook his head. "He was just ruthless, that's all."

"But that's a form of genius too, ruthlessness. Very few of us are capable of anything so pure, but this was his forte, his true métier, all of the forms and applications of cruelty. The force of good always refers to something beyond ourselves—we negate ourselves to serve this higher thing. But evil is pure, evil serves only the self of ego, you are limited only by your own imagination. And this thing Duvalier conceived, this apparatus of evil, it's beautiful in the way of an elegant machine. An elegant machine that may never stop."

"I can see you've thought about it."

"Of course. In Haiti we are forced to think about it."

Which was true, Mason reflected as he made his rounds, Haiti shoved it in your face sure enough. During the day he'd drive through the livid streets and look for ways to make the crisis cohere. At night he'd lock his doors, pull down all the shades, spread twenty or thirty canvases around his house, and wander through the rooms, silently looking. After a while he'd go to the kitchen and fix a bowl of rice or noodles, and then he'd wander around some more, looking as he ate. It was like sliding a movie into the VCR, but this was better, he decided. This was real. With time the colors began to bleed into his head, and he'd find himself thinking about them during the day, projecting the artists' iridescent greens and blues onto the streets outside his car, a way of seeing that seemed to charge the place with meaning. The style that seemed so primitive and childish at first came to take on a subversive quality, like a sly commentary on how the world had gone the last five hundred years. In the flattened, skewed perspectives, the faces' confrontational starkness, he began to get the sense of a way of being that had survived behind the prevailing myths. The direct vision, the thing itself without the softening filter of technical tricks—the vision gradually became so real to him that he felt himself clenching as he looked at the paintings, uneasy in his skin, defensive. An obscure sophistication began to creep into the art; they were painting things he only dimly sensed, but with time he was starting to see a richness, a luxuriance of meaning there that merged with the photos, never far from his mind, in the mission's files of the Haitian dead.

Life here had the cracked logic of a dream, its own internal rules. You looked at a picture and it wasn't like looking at a picture of a dream, it was passage into the current of the dream. And for him the dream had its own peculiar twist, the dream of doing something real, something worthy. A *blan's* dream, perhaps all the more fragile for that.

He packed sixty-three canvases in a soft duffel bag and nobody laid a hand on him. He had to face the ordeal all by himself, with not a soul to turn to for comfort or advice. There hadn't even been the consolation of seeing the mulatto before he left, the last sack of paintings delivered by a kid with a scrawled one-word message: *Go*. But Mason was white, and he had a good face; the whole thing was so absurdly easy that he could have wept, though what he did do on getting to his hotel room was switch on the cable to MTV and bounce on the bed for a couple of minutes.

He'd gone from Haiti to the heart of chic South Beach. His hotel rose off the sea in slabs of smooth concrete like a pastel-colored birthday cake, but for a day Mason had to content himself with watching the water from his balcony. When the call finally came, he gathered up the duffel bag and walked three blocks to The Magritte, an even sleeker hotel where the men were older, the women younger, the air of corruption palpable. Well, he thought, here's a nice place to be arrested, but in the room there was only the Frenchman and a silent, vaguely Asian type whose eyes never left Mason's face. There were no personal items about; they might have taken the room for an hour. Mason had to sit and watch while the Frenchman laid the paintings across the bed like so many bolts of industrial cloth. He was brisk, cordial, condescending, a younger man than Mason expected, with a broad, coarse face only slightly refined by a prissy mustache and goatee.

They wore dark, elegant suits. Their hair was smooth. They looked fit in the way of people who obsess over workouts and what they eat. New wave gangsters—Mason sensed a sucking emptiness in them, the void that comes of total self-absorption. It made him sick to hand the paintings over to these people.

"And the Bigaud?" the Frenchman asked in English. "*The Bathers?*"

"He couldn't get it."

A quick grimace, then a fond, forgiving smile; he was gracious in the way of a pro stuck with amateurs. He acted like a gentleman, but he wasn't—it was only since he'd lived in Haiti that Mason found himself thinking this way. Only since he'd met the first true gentleman of his life.

They gave him the money in a blue nylon bag, and he made them wait while he counted it. Later, perversely, he would think of this as the bravest thing he'd ever done, how he endured their stares and bemused sarcasm while he counted out the money.

When it was finished and he'd zipped up the nylon bag, the Frenchman asked: "What will you do now?"

Mason was puzzled, then adamant. "I'm going back, of course. I have to give him the money."

The Frenchman's cool failed him for the briefest moment. He seemed surprised, and in the silence Mason wondered, Is my honor so strange? And then the smile reengaged, with real warmth, it seemed, but Mason saw that he was being mocked.

"Yes, absolutely. They're all waiting on you."

At the house in Pacot he stuffed the cash up a ten-dollar Vodou drum he'd bought months earlier at the Iron Market. Then he settled in and went about his business, staying up late at night to listen for the door, going down to the park in the afternoons to take his daily drubbing at chess. He realized he was good at this kind of life, the lie of carrying on his normal routine while he kept himself primed for the tap on the back, the look from the stranger that said: *Come. Meet me*. Late at night he could hear machine guns chewing up the slums, a faint ghost-sound, the fear a kind of haunting. During the day he would look at the mountains above like huge green waves towering over the city, and he'd think, Let it come. Let it all crash down.

He missed the paintings with the same kind of visceral ache as he'd missed certain women who'd meant something to him. He missed the mulatto in a way that went beyond words, the man whose aura of purpose burned hot enough to fire even a cautious *blan*. My friend, Mason thought a hundred times a day, the phrase so constant that it might have been a prayer. My very good friend whose name I don't even know. The air felt heavy, thick with delay and anticipation, though the slow sway and bob of palm fronds seemed to counsel patience. Finally, one evening, he'd waited long enough. He carried his chess set past the park into the Salomon quarter, an awful risk that the mulatto would surely scold him for, but he couldn't help himself. He had trouble finding the street and had almost given up when it appeared in the ashy half-light of dusk. He turned and walked along it with a casual air. Just a glance at the house was all he needed: the green walls streaked with soot, the charred stumps of the trees, the blackened, empty windows like hollow eye sockets. Just a glance, and he never broke the swing of his stride, never lost the easy rhythm of his breathing.

The next day he went back with his truck and driver, poking around under the guise of official business. He knocked on doors and explained himself; the neighbors shuffled their feet, picked at their hands, glanced up and down the block as they talked. Lots of shooting one night, they said, people shooting in the street. Bombs, and then the fire, though no one actually saw it—they'd rolled under their beds at the first shot. The next morning they'd edged outside to find the house this way, and no one had gone near it since.

When did it happen? Mason asked, but now the elastic Haitian sense of time came into play. Three days ago, one man said. Another said a month. Back at the office Mason went through the daily logs and found an incident dated ten days earlier, the day he'd left for Miami. The text of the report filled a quarter of a page. They had the street name wrong but otherwise it fit, the shooting and explosions and ensuing fire, then the de factos' response to the O.A.S. inquiry. Seven charred bodies had been recovered from the house, none identified, all interred by the government. The incident was characterized as gang activity, "probably drug-related." Mason winced at the words. The line had grown to be a bad joke around the mission, the explanation they almost always got whenever a group of *inconnus* turned up dead.

Still, Mason hoped. He made his rounds each day through the stinking streets, past old barricades and army patrols and starving street kids with their furied stares, and every afternoon he wrote his report and watched storms roll down the mountains like the hand of God. Finally, he felt it one day as he was driving home, he just knew: his glorious friend was dead. It caught him after weeks of silence, a moment when the cumulative weight of days reached in and pushed all the air from his chest, and when he breathed in again, there was just no hope. False, small, shabby, that's how it seemed now, the truth washing through him like sickness—he'd been a fool to think they'd had any kind of chance. Inside the house he got as far as the den, where he took the Vodou drum from its place on the shelf and sat on the floor. Wearily, slowly, he rocked the drum over and reached inside. The money was there, all that latent power stuffed inside the shaft—

something waiting to be born, something sleeping. He cradled the unformed dream in his hands and wondered who to give it to.

HEADING SOUTH

BY DANY LAFERRIÈRE

Kaliko Beach

(Originally published in 2006)

Translated by Wayne Grady

Brenda

My husband and I both come from the same small town north of Savannah. The middle of nowhere. I won't even bother telling you its name. I've never met anyone who's even seen it on a map. I've known my husband since we were little children. We don't come from the same religious backgrounds. He's a Methodist and I'm a Baptist. The way I see it, it doesn't make any difference what you call yourself as long as you believe in God. That's what my husband told me after we got married, and now we're both Methodists. I talk about it, anyway, but I haven't been confirmed yet. If my husband were here, he'd say, "That's Brenda all over!" His name is William, but he likes to be called Bill. Actually, Big Bill. Oh, I almost forgot: you don't have to know what to call him, because he didn't come with me on this trip. That was my idea. I didn't think I could ever do it, leave him alone up there like that. This isn't the first time I've been to Port-au-Prince. It's the second. The first time, Bill came with me. I've been wanting to come back for two years. Pamela, I call her Pam, she's my best friend, she says that I've been like a drug addict in withdrawal for two years. I tell her that no drug addict ever went through what I went through. My whole body suffered, my head, my chest, my blood, every possible pain you could ever imagine, I suffered. For two years. Every day. Every night. Every hour. Can you imagine such a thing? I don't think anyone who isn't called Brenda Lee, and who didn't come from a tiny little town north of Savannah, and who hasn't lived for twenty-five years with a man named Bill who hasn't touched her more than a grand total of eight times in all those years, could ever understand what I went through.

Ellen
I've always been attracted by the South, but I never thought of coming to Port-au-Prince. As far as I was concerned, Port-au-Prince was for nymphos. Not for me. One big sex park. Anyway, I've been coming here now for five years. I come down every year and spend the whole summer. My courses end the last week of June, and generally a week later I fly to Port-au-Prince. I always stay at this hotel. It's quiet, it's clean, and it's on the beach. This is how you know you're getting old: you want everything close at hand. Port-au-Prince. Who would have guessed that this is where I would spend my holidays? I went to a private school, and for the past twenty-five years I've been teaching at Vassar. I teach stuck-up little bitches to keep their knees together so they can trap husbands. And if you think things have changed in that regard you've got one very long finger stuck like this in your eye. [She makes the gesture.] Actually, I'm supposed to be teaching contemporary literature, but all they want to know is how to go about making the best of what the good Lord gave them to work with. A tidy little mouth, two little tits that they check for signs of growth every day, blond hair, and a pretty little ass. Scrumptious little packages. And who can blame them? The boys are worse. Complete ninnies who don't deserve any better. I hate

that country, even if it is my own. You can't imagine how much I loathe those little sluts and their asshole boyfriends. All they think about is getting laid and producing litters of more brats and, when they've bought as much junk as they can at their supermarkets, washing up on a beach somewhere in the Caribbean like so many overstuffed sperm whales. Always with their hair in curlers, always wearing sunglasses, always shoving their shopping carts into your legs at the checkouts. So will someone please tell me what the hell I'm doing here, where that's exactly the type of person who forms the majority? [She motions with her chin to the line of her compatriots covered in sunscreen trying to get a tan on the beach.]

Sue

I've tried every diet known to science and I still look like a blues singer from Harlem. And I've never set foot in Harlem. I never go anywhere where there's more than ten blacks. It's not that I'm afraid of blacks, it's just that black men aren't my thing. Now you're going to say that I'm not making any sense, because I'm really crazy about Neptune, and Neptune is as black as the ace of spades. But Neptune is Haitian. To me, when I say black, I mean American black. All American blacks think about is cutting white throats, and we do everything we can to help them do it. You're shocked, hearing me say that, aren't you? Well, that's what I think. Who built all those schools American blacks go to? Not them! Well, I say that, but I've also got to say that I can't stand white American males, either. They never look at a woman like me. If you want to get an American white male to notice you, you have to weigh less than a hundred and twenty pounds, and I weigh twice that. I'm still light on my feet. I work in a factory and there isn't a man there who works harder than me. I can carry a heavy box a long way. I'm strong as an elephant and light as a butterfly. If he knew how to handle me, a man could do anything he wants with me. He could make me his slave. But those idiots, all they want is some anorexic bimbo. They have no idea that under all this fat I'm as thin as a razor. Neptune is the first man who ever paid me a compliment about my weight. To him, being big isn't a fault. It's a quality. He's a fisherman. He has a little sailboat. He fishes not far from here, near the Île de la Gonâve. His philosophy is very simple: fish, eat, drink, sleep like a baby, and fuck like a lion. Not a bad life, eh?

Brenda

I'm going to tell you what happened the first time we came here, my husband and me. I wanted to wait a bit before opening up to you like this. If my husband were here, he'd say: "Brenda, you've never kept a secret longer than a day." But that's not true. There are many things about me that he doesn't know, and that he'll never know. That no one will ever know. Well, you, but it's not the same with you. I don't know you. It's good to talk like this to someone you don't know. I get the feeling you're very young to be doing this; this kind of thing requires a certain amount of experience. I'm not finding fault or anything, but back home, inspectors are usually older men. And I also don't see what use all this information will be to you. I must admit that I'm still a bit surprised, even though, as you reminded me, each country has its own ways. It's also true that people who come from rich countries tend to want to impose their ways of doing things. I apologize again for getting mixed up in things that don't concern me. I usually avoid politics like the plague . . . Well, to get back to my story, it all started when my husband took pity on this young man who hadn't had anything to eat for two days. A young man from Ouanaminthe, a small village in the north. You must know him, surely. His name is Legba. His mother called him that because it seems he was the first of her children to survive after six miscarriages. The name suited him. In any case, my husband asked him to join us at our table. Albert—that's the maître d' at the hotel—he wasn't all that pleased. My husband told him that if we're paying for a room we can invite anyone we want to our table. And my husband added in a lower voice, so only Albert could hear him, that he wasn't going to let any nigger stop him from doing what he wanted. That's the way he talks, my husband, but he isn't racist or anything. In our town that's how everyone talks about black people. Anyway, Legba came over and ate with us at our table. He didn't look like he was more than fifteen years old. Right off I noticed his gleaming white teeth and his radiant smile. My husband told him he could order anything he liked. I've never seen a human being eat so much in my life. When he went to the toilet, my husband said, "He's a nice young man." Albert was still making signs to us to get rid of the boy, but my husband pretended not to notice. From the first, Legba made me think of a lost dog. Anyway, he wasn't bothering anyone, because that day we were the only guests in the dining room. But even if there had been others it wouldn't have made any difference to my husband. Methodists are like that, they'll walk all over anyone who tries to stop them from doing what they think is right. Not me, I was born Baptist. I only became a Methodist because of my husband. But in some ways I'm still a Baptist. I would have found a way to get food to Legba without offending Albert. But my husband isn't like that. Like I said, he's a Methodist. Sometimes I think people shouldn't marry outside their religion.

Ellen
If I had my way I'd rid the earth of everything that's dirty, and there's more of what's dirty here in this town than anywhere else I've ever been. So why, dear God, did you plant, in this dungheap, a flower as radiant as Legba? I turned fifty-five last month. I can tell you there are worse things in life. And this young man is as beautiful as a god. Do you think I could find anyone like him in Boston? Don't tell me I could because I've been in every bar in that snobbish whore of a town a hundred times, and believe me, there is nothing in the North for women over forty. Nothing, nothing, nothing, you bunch of bastards!

Sue
People bring their illusions with them when they come to Port-au-Prince. Even Fat Sue. There is sun here. Fresh fruit, grilled fish, the sea.

And I have a lover.

Brenda
My husband and I got into the habit of having every dinner with Legba. He seemed shy at first. Every night we'd spend hours talking to him about his life, his family, his future. It's like we adopted him, and he seemed to have accepted us too. One day we suggested he join us for an afternoon on the beach. My husband knew an isolated spot. The three of us were stretched out in our bathing suits on this enormous rock, facing the sun. Legba's body fascinated me: long, supple, delicately muscled. His skin glowed. I could hardly take my eyes off him. I drank him in, trying not to be too obvious about it. It didn't take long for my husband to notice the state I was in,

though, and when Legba got up to walk lankily down toward the water, my husband gave me a wink that I took as a kind of permission. When I pretended not to understand what he was on about, he told me straight out that he didn't have any objections to me giving in to my obvious inclinations. I tried to look offended, but just then Legba came back and my husband only had time to whisper, "I want you to." I was totally taken aback by his behavior; it was the first time he'd ever acted like that. I completely lost my head. Legba was lying beside me on his back, with his eyes closed. I didn't dare look his way. My husband elbowed me and made me look at Legba's young, almost naked body. So I let my eyes travel over his flat, sleek stomach, his long legs, his bathing suit with its enticing mound. From then on I was in a kind of trance, hypnotized by Legba's firm yet trembling skin. I was irresistibly drawn to this body that seemed like it was being offered to me on a platter. My husband took my hand and guided it toward Legba's torso. When he let go, my hand fell on his chest and I kept it there. Legba briefly opened his eyes and then shut them again. Encouraged, I moved my hand down to his stomach. I felt an incredible thrill of pleasure traveling up from the young man's soft skin through my fingertips. My hand was trembling. I tried to stay calm but couldn't. Legba didn't move a muscle. It was as though he was making me a gift of his body. I slid two fingers under his bathing suit and took hold of his penis, which quickly began to harden in the palm of my hand so that it poked out under the string of his bathing suit. Seeing his black cock, so long, so tender, made me completely lose control of myself. My lungs were on fire. I felt waves of heat flooding between my legs. I feel awkward telling you about such an intimate experience, but believe me, it's been two years and I haven't been able to tell a soul, and yet I've relived each moment a thousand times in my head. I remember each second as though it happened yesterday. I'm not ashamed of it anymore. I am a very sensual woman. I hadn't known that about myself, but now I totally accept who I am. I'm a good Christian, but why else had the Good Lord put me in this degrading situation? I had absolutely no control over my desire. It was as if someone had thrown gasoline over my whole body and then lit a match. I tried, oh yes, I tried, but I couldn't stop myself. I turned into a sexual animal. Look at me—even telling you about it I'm breaking out into a sweat. [There is a long pause.] Do you want me to go on with my story? All right, but I still don't understand how it's going to help you find the man who did this. Yes, you're right, man or woman. I'm a bit lost, I'm afraid . . . Oh yes, with his arms lying by his sides, Legba was barely breathing, but regularly. I looked around quickly to see if anyone was coming our way, then I gently spread Legba's legs apart and knelt between them with my face above his penis. I took it in my mouth. I breathed up and down its length, covering it with my saliva. Then I took it into my throat as far as it would possibly go. When I couldn't stand it any longer I sat up, took off my bathing suit, and impaled myself on his rod. It tore so deep into me I couldn't hold back a howl. It felt like it was piercing me all the way up to the middle of my chest. I hadn't even recovered from the shock of it, the pain and pleasure all mixed together, before I started going up and down on him. He was breathing harder now, almost panting. But still he didn't move. My husband was lying right next to us, taking it all in. His eyes were riveted on the long black sword that was splitting me in half. I was going faster and faster, knocking my forehead against his chest, making his cock go in farther, deeper. I think I was crying out constantly. The sight of his young body drove me even crazier.

Finally, I felt powerful jets of hot sperm deep inside me. They went on and on. I came too, almost at the same time as him, completely out of my mind. I clutched at his fresh and fragile chest like a woman possessed, and jammed myself one last time on his cock, as deep as I could get it in, and held it there for a long time. He opened his eyes. He was as exhausted as I was. His eyes were red and timid and a bit frightened. Moved by a wave of gratitude, I threw myself on him, kissed him everywhere, and cried like a baby. It was my first orgasm. I was fifty-five years old . . . I feel so tired now. Would you mind if I went and lay down for a bit . . . ? Thank you . . .

Albert

I was born in Cap-Haïtien, in the northern part of Haiti. My grandfather was also born there. You may already know this, but my whole family fought against the Americans during the occupation of 1915. I come from a long line of patriots. My father died never having shaken a white man's hand. For him, whites were lower than monkeys. Whenever he saw a white man, he used to say, he always wanted to turn him around to see if he had a tail. My grandfather didn't even go to that much trouble. As far as he was concerned, a white man was an animal, pure and simple. He'd say "the whites," but he was talking mainly about Americans. Those who dared invade Haitian soil. The supreme insult. A slap in the face to a whole generation. I came to work in Port-au-Prince when I was twenty-two, after my father died, and got a job in this hotel right away. If my grandfather knew that his grandson was serving Americans he would die of shame. This new army of occupation isn't armed, but it has packed its suitcase with a scourge much worse than cannons: drugs. The Queen of Crimes, and she always comes with her two sidekicks: easy money and sex. There's nothing here, sir, that hasn't been touched by one or the other of these plagues. There was a time when we had morals. Now I look around me and I see that everything has come crashing down. I look at our customers, respectable women who twenty years ago, when I first started working here, would have been with their husbands. And what do I see? Lost women, animals lusting after blood and sperm. And whose fault is it? His, the master of desire. He's seventeen years old, he has eyes like glowing embers, a perfect profile. Legba: the Prince of Storms.

Ellen

When the police found his body on the beach one morning, they immediately assumed that a drug deal had gone wrong. They didn't give a shit about the delinquents. Legba was what they call well-known to the police. He sold drugs to everyone on the beach. You don't think for one minute that the Port-au-Prince police, one of the most corrupt forces in the Caribbean, would waste time investigating the death of a young prostitute, do you? You'll have to excuse me, I'm used to saying what I think. That's why I don't really understand what you're doing. You say you work for a self-regulating department? Criminal Investigation Services, is that what you called it? I don't know what good that can do now that Legba is dead. And I also wonder why you are so interested in such intimate details. I know it's probably none of my business, but you're going about this inquiry in a very strange way, sir. What else do you want to know? . . . Yes, he was a hoodlum, but Lord, was he good looking! What's more, he knew how to make love to a woman. It's true, he could have got what he wanted just looking like a young god, and as far as I'm concerned that would have been enough to make me happy.

I could have spent hours just looking at him. He could do whatever he wanted with me. And in that he was indefatigable. I mean, think about it: I spent eighteen years in the best universities in the States learning the best ways of improving my quality of life on this planet, and that whole time all I really needed was an adolescent here in Port-au-Prince. He played my body like a guitar, and believe me, he knew how to handle his instrument. There were times when I thought I was going to die, I kid you not. My body felt completely drained, as though he'd pumped everything out of it. He could bring me to orgasm almost without touching me. Me, who had always intimidated American men, who are supposed to be the most powerful men in the world, at least in terms of economic and political power, and here I was completely in thrall to a boy in Port-au-Prince. With him I was no longer Ellen the Cynic, I was a little twit who wanted nothing more than to be touched in the right places. And he knew them all, by instinct. The first time I laid eyes on him, down by the hotel, I was afraid of making a fool of myself; after all, I was in my fifties. And I wet myself. I had to go up to my room to change. I stood in front of my mirror and masturbated, thinking about him. He had such an insolent mouth, and my God did I want that mouth. I dreamed about him caressing me with his hands so often that when he finally did touch me it was like we'd always been lovers. But what I wanted most, what gave me the highest orgasms, was to have his long, fine penis in my mouth. I would wake up in a sweat in the middle of the night. By day it was different, I could be Ellen the Cynic, able to thumb my nose at the rest of the world. My punching bag at the time was that fatty, Sue. I didn't care at all that she was fat, but I could never understand why she would choose Neptune when Legba was available. I didn't understand it then, and I don't understand it now. How could she not get down on her knees before such a black sun? To me, anyone who feels nothing in the presence of such beauty is dangerous. Of course, if she had once dared to look at Legba I would have scratched her eyes out.

Albert
One day I came upon them by the stairs. She was hanging on his neck and complaining that he was driving her crazy. You know who I'm talking about? That intellectual from Boston, the one with her nose always up in the air. Legba wasn't saying a word, as usual. His face was blank. He knew how to drive that kind of woman around the bend. She was crying like a teenager who'd just lost her first love. Yes sir, as I've always said, it's the cynics who are the hardest hit.

Brenda
I always try to speak well of people, but since you asked me what I truly think, I have to admit that Ellen isn't a woman, she's a bitch in heat playing at being an intellectual. She was lost the moment she first laid eyes on Legba. Really, it was disgusting to watch. People like her don't know the difference between sex and love.

Sue
It's true, Brenda is very discreet. She's not one of those women who shows her emotions. Her face is always calm. I would never have known what she was going through if she hadn't confided in me. That day she seemed totally lost. I'd never seen her like that. She came into my room, which she'd never done before, and said: "I can't do it anymore, Sue. I think I'm going to kill him, and then kill myself." Coming from Brenda, I didn't know what to think. I didn't even know who she was

talking about. I vaguely thought she was talking about her husband, because I knew they weren't getting along very well. I thought that this was why she'd come down here on her own this time. That's what I thought, anyway. Until she admitted to me that she was in love with Legba. How a woman like Brenda, who is so serious, such a devout Christian, could fall in love with a little gigolo like him was beyond me. He acted like a prince because this German woman had given him a gold chain that he wore around his neck like a leash. A pitiful little drug dealer. Surely you know he sold cocaine on the beach? Since his death the other young prostitutes have vanished into the woodwork. I haven't seen one of them on the beach. Gogo, Chico, not even the handsome one, Mario. All gone off somewhere, like a cloud of flies attracted by the smell of a fresh corpse. Anyway, when Brenda came out and told me point blank that she was in love with the little rat, I had the surprise of my life. But there's no point going on about it. People's feelings are part of life's impenetrable mysteries, I must have read that somewhere. Oh, I stopped wondering about life a long time ago. I take things as they come. Brenda told me that Legba had stopped coming to their rendezvous, and she couldn't stand the pain of it any longer. She couldn't sleep, she couldn't eat. All she could think of was him. And he couldn't care less about her. The only thing he was interested in was money. She spent the whole day in her room, she said, bawling her eyes out under a pillow. She couldn't go on living like that. She was talking quietly, sometimes so low I couldn't understand half of what she was saying. Just saying his name, over and over. *Such pain*, I thought. There's nothing I can do for her. She's the only one who can control her destiny. That's just the way it is. I suggested she take some tranquilizers, and she just looked at me in alarm, and I knew she'd already tried that. That's when I realized that if Brenda was confiding in me it could only mean one thing: she wanted me to stop her from committing a crime. Of that I am certain.

Ellen

I love love so much—love or sex, I don't know which anymore—that I've always told myself that when I'm old I'll pay to get it. I just didn't think it would happen so soon. That boy was Satan personified. The Prince of Light. But the kind of light that can kill you. He showed me what hell was like. I'd never been afraid of suffering, but this was too much. I'd given him everything. In return, he'd humiliated me in ways I'd never imagined possible. He dragged me through the mud. I took it all. It makes me laugh, now, the way Brenda goes around acting like the weeping widow. I'm the widow. Brenda couldn't have known a hundredth part of what I had to put up with just to be near him. The flames of hell. Imagine a young, arrogant kid like he could be, with a woman of my age. Can you even imagine what it would be like with him and his friends? There's Ellen Graham, the hag. But time heals all wounds. Brenda spends her days in her room, crying. Me, I don't cry.

Sue

It's a terrible thing to say, but I'm sure it was either Ellen or Brenda who killed him. He drove them to it, them and others too, and what was bound to happen one day happened. All because of the contempt that Northern men have for women of their own race.

Albert

That morning I went to see a friend who works at a small hotel not far from here. When I came back, I walked along the beach. It was dawn. The beach was empty except for some-one who looked as though he'd spent the night there. As I got closer I could see it was Legba. He looked like a sleeping angel, curled up on the sand like that. His face in complete repose. When I reached him it seemed to me that the night had been pretty rough on him. But even then all I saw was a frail young man. He even looked like he was smiling. I don't know why, but I sat down beside him. There was no one else on the beach. There was that strange dawn light. The feeling of being nowhere. I began to stroke his hair. He shivered as though he was cold. I lay down beside him and took him in my arms. I can't tell you how bizarre it all seems to me now. It was like I was watching my double. I remember that light in my eyes. That music in my head. That young body on the beach, almost naked. And no one else about. *Careful*, I told myself, *beware of the sweetness of this skin*. And I . . . kissed him. I kissed Legba. It was the first time I'd ever kissed a man. I kissed him. Everywhere. He responded to my caresses in his sleep, I think it was probably out of habit. I should have got-ten up and run away, but it was too late. I was already caught up in the fiery ring of desire. I hadn't known that such physical happiness could exist. That morning I ate of the fruit of the tree of good and evil. Strange, isn't it, that without even ask-ing me any questions you've made me bring up all the secrets that I kept hidden in the deepest recesses of my being.

Ellen

Well, he certainly hid his light, didn't he, the hypocrite! Every time I went out looking for Legba I'd get this mean look from him . . . Because he was a rival. I wanted to go up to him and slap him in the face. I can tolerate anything but bigotry. Al-ways with his nose stuck in the Bible, the little shit-ass! Now that he's got a taste for it, as he says, he's not going to switch to another road. I don't believe a word of what he told you: the dawn, the light, the music of the spheres, the forbidden fruit—it's all just shit in a silk stocking. Oh sure, once it was over he had to rush off and do his penance. I'd like to have seen him whipping himself. He's the worst kind of sadist. And let me tell you something: that's the kind that can kill.

Brenda
Of course I can't go home. I don't have a home anymore, or a husband. I don't want to have anything more to do with Northern men. I'd like to spend time on other Caribbean islands. Cuba, Guadeloupe, Barbados, Martinique, Dominica, Jamaica, Trinidad, the Bahamas . . . They all have such pretty names. I want to get to know them all.

THREE LETTERS YOU WILL NEVER READ

BY GEORGES ANGLADE

Quina

(Originally published in 2006)

Translated by Anne Pease McConnell

In the collective memory of Quina there had only been two judicial executions in all the history of the town court. And since both of them took place during the same month of August in 1956, they became as unforgettable as a cyclone. I am not, of course, referring to the frequent extra-judicial executions, dating back to the mists of time, in the abject jails of the provincial police. No! I mean a sentence of death on paper, in due form, pronounced by a judge on the recommendation of a jury. Such extreme sentences were not rare in Quina, but from appeals to commutations of sentences, everyone knew that these games among the local members of the bar guaranteed that no one would ever have to face a legal firing squad. To get to that point, not only did bad luck have to have been involved, what's more this had to happen to Little Innocent who in his grandstanding threw himself into the thing so energetically that the impossible occurred.

He was really named Little Innocent, this the first man to be executed that August. The son of Madame Innocent of Porte-Saint-Louis, not to be confused with Madame Innocent of Porte-Gaille, the mother of Yvette and Fernande. Little Innocent was fairly badly named, given that he was neither little nor innocent, but no one could do anything for this younger brother whose older brother had been named Big Innocent before him. It was if he had been branded by fate from birth always to end up in the wrong place at the wrong time. Quina was the only province that invented names that brought about hilarious associations in the midst of tragedy. And so let us imagine a Little Innocent inextricably compromised in an affair of double adultery followed by murder, rapid-fire executions, sordid revenge, all against the political background of a year when a presidential campaign was being prepared. The summer of 1956 will not be outdone by any other summer in Quina!

The affair, which was neither commonplace nor ordinary, grew nevertheless out of events which were conceivable in any province. A new and quite young junior officer fresh from the military academy would be stationed somewhere and would find himself delighted, with the help of his uniform, to be a little village Casanova, pursued by promising winks from ladies whose marital passions had grown cold. Some of these officers would succumb to a provincial melancholy against a background of boredom, especially the ones who came from the capital. The most recent to arrive in Quina had everything required to let himself be tempted by the calls of its Sirens: he came from Port-au-Prince, wore his khakis with a haughty air, and his *kepi* at a jaunty angle, while an attractive, perpetual smile indicated how highly he thought of himself. A future colonel, undoubtedly, or even a general, who knew? But for Quina he was just another stud, with all the risks implied by the term. The observers from the galleries did not give this latest arrival much of a chance as he passed by them morning and evening on the plaza, strutting to beat the band. The competing women would swallow him whole. And it was the very beautiful Madame Little Innocent who won this obstacle course among the chosen finalists.

It must be said, as a balm to the disappointment of the losers, that Madame Innocent was a woman from Fond-des-Blancs, blue-eyed, with a lovely mane of hair and black aquiline features. The ingredients of this beauty could be traced back to the Polish brigades of the War of Independence, who had deserted Leclerc's French army to join the ranks of the indigenous army in the south. The racial mixture that was to result from this became a sort of Ethiopian type, the *marabout* that the local language had transformed into the diminutive *boubout*, a title for a woman who might elsewhere be called a lady friend, a girlfriend, a lover. My *boubout*. This lady was a *boubout* worth looking at twice. The little junior officer hadn't a chance.

He took the shotgun blast from the front, point blank, while trying to jump over a fence at two o'clock in the morning on Tuesday, August 3, his trousers still at half-mast. Caught in the act, he had tried to flee. But it was buckshot meant for large quadrupeds which had wandered into other people's fields. In Quina, a sort of common law said that any animal that had wandered out of its master's enclosure to feed on forbidden fruits was considered wild game, and because of this was subject to being legitimately shot. The court-appointed defense attorney would later point out this analogy. The young officer had been found bloodless and bent in two over the barbed wire he was straddling, his crime perpetuated, as the defense will insist, and no form of help would be of any use to him with his chest wide open from the impact of the unforgiving buckshot.

Naturally, Little Innocent was not home that evening, and he was not arrested until around four o'clock in the morning, with dawn approaching, when he was quite simply returning to the conjugal home as if nothing was wrong. The crowd in front of his house and the swiftness of the police who took him into custody really seemed to surprise him. When his rights were read and he was shown the reason for his arrest (that was still done then, really; I was in the crowd of on-lookers), he indignantly proclaimed his innocence as a town bourgeois, but refused categorically to say where he was at the time of the murder—*of the execution*, according to the defense lawyer, who will later plead justifiable homicide. The most he would say was that as a gentleman, it would be impossible for him to compromise a lady with whom he had spent the night. And so Little Innocent had no alibi; and what is more, he had all the motives. The case had the earmarks of revenge: the husband keeps watch, forces the lover to flee, and brings him down. What is more, Little Innocent was a good hunter and he knew (as did everyone else) that no ballistic tests could identify the twelve-gauge shotgun that had fired buckshot at the imprudent boy. He also knew that every family in Quina had at least one twelve-gauge and a few buckshot cartridges on hand. The investigation was turning out to be difficult, but everyone in Quina also knew that it was completely unlike Little Innocent to kill anyone, least of all his wife's lover. He had lived with her for a long time under a nonaggression pact formed by old lovers whose fire has died out.

The case was handled quickly, under orders from above telephoned to the prefect by the general-president in person. This hinted at the approaching elections. The victim was a military officer and the leader, who had his eye on a reelection prohibited by the constitution, could not let the death of a young first lieutenant—guilty of adultery or not—go unpunished six months before the coup which he believed would bring about a second term. And so an extraordinary court session was decreed from Monday, August 9, to Friday, August 13, by the town authorities; and Little Innocent was immediately dragged before the judge who was assisted by a mixed civil and military jury composed of three soldiers and three civilians. It was unusual, but Quina had always made broad interpretations of the civil and military codes in effect in Port-au-Prince.

For five days, Little Innocent would take advantage of this unhoped-for platform to deliver a performance which those who were there fifty years ago still talk about. First, he made sure he would represent himself, in order to take the fullest advantage possible of his opportunities to speak. He claimed to have no knowledge of the facts before the time of his arrest, and that besides, his wife, his *femme-chance* (woman-through-luck), had no reason for self-reproach and nothing to justify, since she was assured of the honor of his highest esteem. That did not prevent him from having a mistress, like everyone else, his *femme-douce* (sweet-woman), whom he would not compromise for any reason, even to gain an alibi which would save him from death. He concluded each of his flights of oratory with *C'est ainsi que les hommes vivent*—That's the way men live—addressing himself to the numerous youths present who would applaud and take up the refrain, singing it with him and imitating the voice of the great singer Léo Ferré, in spite of the judge's threats of removal from the courtroom and the hammering of his gavel. *That's the way men live . . . and their sins follow them from afar.* All that smacked of the end of a regime.

Toward the middle of the week, the matter of the letters arose in response to a question from the judge: if he could not provide a direct alibi through the testimony of the person he was with at two o'clock in the morning on Tuesday, August 3, was there some indirect alibi that would prove the existence of this liaison which was the only thing that could demonstrate his innocence? Yes, there were three letters, three marvelous letters written some ten years ago by his lover in such a sensuous style that he had reread them every day that God had granted him since receiving them. For ten years! In the face of his refusal to submit them as evidence, even if it might mean escaping a firing squad, the judge was reduced to asking him to outline their contents in order that their existence could be decided upon. That was the turning point of the trial. The testimony of Little Innocent was to reach a level of eroticism rarely heard in a courtroom. He knew by heart the three letters and their amorous laments, which he recited while acting them out, like the dubbing of a love scene in a porno film. At times, naughty sighs arose from the spectators' section, which irritated the judge intensely, his eyes going from one row to another searching for the culprits. But when Little Innocent came to the salutation at the end of each letter, *I kiss you everywhere you like to be kissed*, daring to bring up that great feminine art, things had gone too far. The judge ordered that everyone under the age of twelve leave the courtroom so that the testimony could continue, rated "triple X," he ordered the court reporter, who did not miss a word.

The next morning, Thursday, the judge imposed a court-appointed attorney and a gag on the defendant so that he would remain silent and the trial would not be drawn out interminably. On the insistence of the powers-that-be, it was necessary to bring in a verdict by Friday the thirteenth at the latest; which was a bad omen for everyone. That day, Little Innocent was found guilty of first-degree murder and condemned to death, not without a final scene created by the defendant, railing this time against his lawyer who, wishing to save him, requested the court's leniency since this was a crime of honor committed by a cuckold. Hearing that word, Little Innocent had thrown himself on the lawyer, pouring out abuse on him for insulting his wife. Nothing remained but the task of setting the conditions of the execution in a ruling that would be given on the following Monday, August 16.

A crowd formed even before the trial reconvened, for if they expected the normal delays that would finally make the sentence null and void, there was also the fact that they were dealing with the army in a case of the murder of an officer. You see, it is well known in this country that laws are made of paper but bayonets are made of iron. The judge had obviously worked hard during the weekend, for he gave his ruling in a severe tone that brooked no protest. He ruled that Little Innocent had abused the court to such an extent that before he could be executed he was required to reimburse the State for the cost of the bullets in the Springfield rifles to be used by the firing squad; and what was more, he must pay off, through forced labor, the rental of his prison cell and the court costs incurred. All this was at the usual exorbitant interest rate of 1.5 percent per month commonly used by banks with embarrassing aplomb. Since Little Innocent was a pauper who ended up living from hand to mouth by the end of each month, he was insolvent and had no means of raising the round sum of six thousand three hundred and twelve gourdes and thirty-five centimes, which he was to pay by the end of August before the interest began to accrue, making the debt he was required to pay before he could be executed heavier each month. This ingenious idea on the part of the judge was commented on at length and with admiration—he must have dug deeply to come up with the Chinese tradition of making the condemned man pay for the bullets used to kill him, and with the Australian practice, used against illegal immigration, which required that stowaways refusing to leave of their own accord must reimburse the costs of their imprisonment through a life of forced labor. The judge must have kept late hours to come up with these penal curiosities, and all Quina showed him discreetly, with a more pleasant smile or a more marked doffing of a hat, the esteem in which they held him for his skillfulness. Little Innocent would not face the firing squad.

But two days later, in the sickly pale dawn of Wednesday, August 18 (for all such dawns are sickly pale), the second detonation of the month rang out. It was rumored that Little Innocent had been executed by the captain who had been assigned temporarily to the post during the crisis. He had carried out his orders immediately upon receiving an anonymous envelope containing exactly the sum the condemned man was required to pay before he could be executed. His task done, the officer went to the judge to give him the six thousand three hundred and twelve gourdes and thirty-five centimes in their original envelope. The town was in shock. All the ingredients for a riot were in place, and the authorities reported immediately to Port-au-Prince that something was brewing and the situation had to be defused. Who could have paid the ransom that wasn't meant to be paid? The army, immediately suspect, swore that they had not done it, and you-know-who, at around eleven o'clock in the morning, telephoned the prefect for the second time to vindicate that institution and to promise an immediate investigation to find the anonymous donor. This was not necessary.

At noon precisely, a woman dressed all in black and heavily veiled in black crepe falling from an equally black wide-brimmed hat, crossed the plaza in front of the church where she had just gone to confession, and went to the courthouse where she brought proof that her jealous husband, the awful man from whom she had been separated for a long time, had arranged the whole thing—from the buckshot to the fine—to bring down her lover.

The third detonation of the month took place at the Angelus on Saturday, August 28, market day, against the wall of the cemetery adjoining the landing strip. No one jumped this time—all Quina, speechless with astonishment at the month's events, was present.

THE PORT-AU-PRINCE MARRIAGE SPECIAL

BY EDWIDGE DANTICAT

Delmas

(Originally published in 2008)

T hey told me, Madame, that I'm going to die."

I don't know if it was a dreadful gut feeling that had sent Mélisande to that particular clinic, rather than other healing places, but she'd gone down near the bicentennial park downtown and had gotten her arms pricked and her blood drawn, only to receive a death sentence. She'd been coughing for some time, soft and discreet at first, then more and more thunderously, which had led to my removing my young son from her care. But only this morning when she got a fever and developed a level of sluggishness, which I instantly recognized, from my late father's battles with various types of respiratory illnesses, possibly as pneumonia; only then did she finally decide to seek medical care.

She was sobbing now as she stood in the doorway of my bedroom, her body as flat as one of the doorframe beams. Leaning against the somber wood, she hiked up a flowered silk skirt to wipe the tears from her face. I immediately recognized that skirt as one I'd formerly owned. I had paid about seventy dollars for it at a sale at a fancy boutique in Miami—back when I was in college, before I married a classmate, a fellow Haitian, whose family owned a hotel in Port-au-Prince.

"Have you told your mother?" I asked her.

She was a child really, a girl, fifteen or sixteen at most. Her mother worked as a cook at our hotel. They had lied about her age so that Mélisande could get the job as one of our son's nannies, but given the fact that the mother had six younger children in the provinces, in Léogâne, I figured that Mélisande had plenty of experience for the job. I don't know why I trusted Mélisande. Perhaps it was because she was from my parents' hometown. Some of her relatives might have known some of mine. I didn't trust that many people with my son, but it was obvious as soon as I placed him in Mélisande's arms and she probed out of him the loudest laugh he'd ever tried, that he loved her. Perhaps what drew him to her were the same things I found appealing about her: her elfin face, her reedy voice, her slightly hesitant walk, as though she was never really sure it was safe to touch the ground.

Roland, my husband, had thought that Mélisande should be in school, but we hadn't forced it or insisted, as we could have, that she go. Or at least that she attend some type of vocational class in cooking or sewing when she wasn't looking after our son. Sometimes, during her free time, we saw her helping her mother cook or I saw her joke with the hotel maids as she cleaned the guests' rooms with them. The agreement she had with the maids was that whenever she helped them out, whatever was left behind in the rooms would be split with her.

Sometimes, aside from the tips, they'd find small pieces of gold or silver jewelry—mostly earrings and bracelets—that my husband would hold on to for a while and then, after no one had called or come back to claim them, would allow the maids to sell them to the jeweler down the street who'd pay a few dollars just so he'd melt them again into other pieces to sell back to other hotel guests. This was a bit of extra money that she might not be making if she were in school, I sometimes told myself. But school might have helped with the future. And now she might not even have a future.

Shame on me, I think now. I'd kept hoping that she'd find a good night-school or an adult literacy class on her own, but I never did more than hope. I never even talked to her about it, never offered her the evenings off to do it. I was prepared, however, to let her go if she asked, but she never did. Now I would right this wrong. Somewhere between when she came to work for us (or maybe it was before) and now, she had contracted this disease. Perhaps if she had been in class, and had had homework and exams and yearly promotions, it wouldn't have happened.

"Come in and sit down," I told her.

I got up from my bed and walked over to the doorway. I was still in my pajamas, pink silk pajamas that she'd probably inherit from me one day, assuming she wasn't in fact dying. My son was downstairs with my husband in his office. As I guided Mélisande toward a rocking chair by my bed, she felt extremely light to my touch, almost like paper, cloth, or air. Even though her feet were gliding across the wooden floor, I still felt as though I was carrying her. Her body slid down into the chair where I immediately piled up a few cushions around her. I pulled an ottoman from a corner and pushed it under her feet. Resting my arms on her shoulders, I felt some of the warmth of her lingering fever through her plain white T-shirt.

"What did the doctor say exactly?" I asked.

"He said," she replied, with her face buried in her hands, "that I have SIDA. AIDS."

I had been expecting anything but that. Perhaps pneumonia or some bronchial infection, but not that. When she came home from the doctor, I was prepared to lecture her about not waiting so long the next time to get herself checked out. There were things that could kill people in the countryside that could easily be treated here in Port-au-Prince. This is what I had prepared myself to tell her. I thought at most she would need antibiotics.

"Even with the SIDA," I was telling her now, "they have all these drugs. People live for years on them."

This provoked a new flurry of sobs from her. Her shoulders were bobbing up and down and I began to panic. My son. My boy. She had touched every part of his body, had washed, had wiped, had kissed and cuddled him. Had they accidentally exchanged saliva, blood? I suddenly wanted to leave her there and run through the hotel and find my son. As usual he had woken up earlier than all of us and my husband had taken him to his office. He was probably even now crawling under his father's desk, giggling, singing with delight.

Mélisande was still sobbing, her face soaking in the pool of tears gathering in her hands. We'd have to get Gabriel tested. And how would we deal with it? How would I live with yet another loss? How would I live with myself—how would I live—if he had been infected?

I decided that I would simply let Mélisande cry. Let her get it all of it out of her system before we tried to come up with some type of solution. There were just a few clinics which offered retroviral treatments. Some offered them for free. Others expected you to be a guinea pig in some questionable experiments. The clinic where Mélisande had been tested offered some counseling but no treatment.

Why hadn't I suspected all this sooner? I stepped away from her and staggered to the edge of the bed. I should have urged her to go to the doctor when she first began to lose weight. I should have stopped her not-so-secret flirtations with many of the hotel's male guests. The concierge, a former brothel manager, had told Roland that Mélisande liked to seek out some particular guests—the fat white ones—who she thought, because they seemed to have never missed a meal in their lives, were rich. It didn't seem to matter to her that most of the time she had no idea, until they lewdly grabbed some part of her body, what they were saying. The exchanges of "What?" and "Who?" were a delightful game to her. By repeating the sometimes obscene things they said to her, she thought she was learning English or Spanish or whatever language they spoke. She would disappear for a few minutes with them into their rooms, but it never seemed to me long enough for her to have had sex with them, only to make a rendezvous perhaps for a later encounter, during her free time. Again, I didn't want to cause trouble for her. There were six young children counting on her and her mother for food, clothes, and school fees back in Léogâne. I thought she was protecting herself, *aux moins*.

She stopped crying for a few minutes because she seemed to run out of tears. And now she had the hiccups, which forced her head to jerk back and forth.

"We have to find you a place where you can get a second test performed," I told her.

She raised her head and glared at me, then she opened her eyes really wide as though a beehive or a bird's nest had suddenly appeared on top of my head. Her eyes were extremely red, the bulging capillaries having taken over her eyeballs.

"They told me there was no cure," she said.

"Let me talk to Roland. We'll find you some care."

I had no idea where to find the best treatment in town, but I knew Roland would. He knew something about nearly everything, especially things that involved worst-case-scenario types of problems. This was a hotelier's job, he sometimes reminded me. If someone shows up hungry, you feed them. If they want a drink, you ply them. If they want to be left alone, you make yourself scarce. If they want company, you entertain. If they are lovelorn, you find them love. And if someone shows up sick, you find treatment quickly, before that person expires on your watch.

My sigh of relief was as loud as a hundred-mile wind. My son was negative. The same Canadian doctor who performed his HIV test was the one who'd help us get the retroviral drugs that Mélisande needed. The best thing, he told us, was a new one-pill treatment that many of his patients were opting for because it made compliance easier. Someone like Mélisande, he could already tell, was not going to be compliant. First of all, she was claiming that she'd never had sex with anyone, and since she'd never injected herself with a dirty needle and had never had a blood transfusion, all he could conclude was that she was in terrible denial.

"If you won't even own up to the possible ways that the disease might have entered your body," he'd told Mélisande in French-accented Creole, as she sat across a desk from him, her eyelids fluttering between open and closed, staring, when they were open, at a back wall full of framed diplomas, "how can you hope to treat this disease aggressively?"

Once the doctor provided us with a month's worth of pills from his own private stash—at ten American dollars each—Mélisande was a lot more compliant than any of us expected. I had told her to come and find me every morning so I could watch her take the pill as we ate breakfast together, and she had done it for over two weeks now. Most of the time we ate something quickly on the patio outside my room. Other times we ate in the hotel dining room, with my son at our side. Mélisande was gaining weight, my old clothes fitting her a little better now. She cried less and less too at breakfast, in part, I think, because she knew the staff was watching us. But what she never did again was touch my son, who reached his tubby little arms out to her, contorting his face into a grimace that would turn into wails, then tears, when she simply ignored him or turned away.

I stopped bringing my son to breakfast with her after a while. It was too much for both of them. By the time Mélisande had to return to the doctor for another month's supply, I cancelled the breakfasts altogether and passed on the job of monitoring her compliance to her mother, who from the day she learned that Mélisande was sick never stopped calling her a *bouzen*, a whore, even as she took a break from whatever she was doing every morning to make sure that her oldest child swallowed the pill and chased it down with at least a piece of bread. Some mornings I'd watch this exchange between them from the bungalow in the hibiscus garden where I sometimes sat with my son. The mother was no taller than Mélisande herself, but was a strapping, muscular woman. I could almost see a line of veins popping out under the rolls on her flabby neck as she continuously berated Mélisande, who'd try to put an end to their transaction by swallowing the pill quickly and rushing off.

"What are you going to do when Monsieur and Madame stop paying for your 400-gourdes pills?" the mother would occasionally shout, like a drill sergeant hazing a recruit. Her fear was palpable. Her daughter's survival now completely depended on Roland and me. If we decided to sell the hotel and move elsewhere, her child could die. What if the drug companies, who provided the doctor with the free supply that he unethically resold to us, stopped making the drug or no longer sent it to Haiti? What if that doctor took off as well? If any part of the chain that ran from the creation of the drug to our ability to get our hands on it broke down, she could lose her daughter.

One morning, I heard her asking Mélisande as she was taking the pill, "What if the white man starts keeping all of the pills for himself? What if Monsieur and Madame are killed in a terrible car accident?"

"You will never have a healthy child," she told her another day. "You will never have a husband."

"You should talk to her," Roland said to me after overhearing this too. "All illness involves state of mind as well as state of body. It can't be helpful for the poor girl to be treated that way."

I felt like a coward for not intervening sooner.

"Where do you want to be buried?" the mother said soon after. "You better start saving now if you want a fancy coffin."

In the Haiti of my time and place, death was always looming around some corner. In car accidents. Illness. Kidnappings. Suicides. Unlike the rest of us, Mélisande's mother could not afford the conditional optimism this tiny little pill allowed. I could easily imagine myself in the mother's place. I'd probably have many of the same concerns and fears.

That morning, after Mélisande had gone off to breakfast, I asked to have a word with her mother, who as soon as I closed my husband's office door behind us, began to cry.

"Mèsi, mèsi," she sobbed, grabbing my hand. "Thank you for not throwing her out. Thank you for not letting her die."

"There are people all over the world being kept alive in this way," I said, gently tugging my hands out of her grasp.

"Besides, you're wasting precious time with your daughter. You can help her the most by not cursing, but loving her."

"Love her?" She frowned and her eyebrows nearly became one.

"Yes, love her." It must have sounded like an order. "You must love her."

I knew what she was thinking. These silly half-assed outsiders, these *dyasporas* with their mushy thinking, why does it all come back to love with them? Love the world. Love life. Love yourself. Love your children. Don't yell at them. Don't hit them. Don't give them away. Don't these *dyasporas* know that there are many other ways to show love than to be constantly talking about it?

"Of course I love her" she replied, spreading both her arms wide as if to prove it. "That's why I am so rough with her."

Sitting on a cushioned bench near the office door, she looked unconvinced, but also ashamed that I, on top of everything, now had reason to scold her, ashamed that she had no choice but to sit there and take it. I too felt ashamed for having made her feel that way. Pressing both her hands down as if she'd suddenly realized how much they protruded from her body, she then responded to what I had *not* said.

"You loved your mother too, didn't you?" she said. "I saw you. I saw you the day she drowned herself."

I moved from behind the desk and closer to her. Both our faces were now soaked the way Mélisande's had been the day she'd made her announcement to me. Sitting across from her, our protruding knees nearly touching, I said, "You did?"

"*Wi.* I was in the kitchen cooking when I heard your scream. I rushed out and saw her floating facedown in the pool. It was unkind of her to come all the way from Miami to kill herself in your new husband's pool."

I didn't know whether she was being unkind, but I wanted to tell her that this is what had happened. My mother had never been a good swimmer, neither in Miami nor in Léogâne. She had only gone near streams and oceans and pools when my father was with her. When he died, she had no one to protect her from water.

"I saw you with her body in your arms," she continued, her eyes fixed on her worn-out sandals, on her feet, on the floor. "When I heard you scream, I thought the sky would open up and it would start to rain because I thought even God would have no choice but to cry with you."

It did rain that night, I reminded her ("*Ou sonje?*"), a torrential rain that caused mudslides that pulled dozens of houses from the hillside shantytowns into trash-strewn ravines all over the capital. God had shown, I now said, that his tears only brought further losses. Still, I hadn't been able to feel sad for the others. I felt no solidarity with the mudslide victims, the mothers and fathers and babies whose bodies were engorged by the red earth like my mother's had been by the meticulously maintained pool water. Why should I be the only one grieving? I had thought. Why should my mother be the only one to die? I had not felt truly bad for even one person's loss since, I realized. Until I'd learned about this woman's daughter. I didn't want Mélisande to die, I told her. I didn't want her to cry to the heavens for her daughter the way I had for my mother. I didn't want another type of sky to open again and carry others away.

"Okay," she replied, somberly, giving in to my tirade.

I knew that even after our talk there would be no reconciliatory embrace between her and Mélisande. There would be no apologies.

* * *

The next morning, I watched from my patio where my son was jumping up and down in a playpen next to me as she silently handed Mélisande a glass of water.

"What did you tell her?" Roland asked as we ate breakfast at the same table that Mélisande and I had occupied for a few weeks.

"You know . . ." I said, which he knew meant that I didn't want to talk about it.

At the end of the month, just when Mélisande needed another refill of the drugs, the doctor mysteriously left Haiti and moved back to Montreal. As Mélisande's supply dwindled to nearly nothing, Roland called everyone he knew but couldn't track the man down. Mélisande had no choice but to start seeing another doctor, a Haitian woman this time, who ordered a new series of tests, dredging up the distressing diagnosis, the counting of T cells, which I could tell, when Mélisande came back with now several bottles of pills, had taken away whatever illusion she might have harbored that she was getting well.

The new regimen did not agree with her. She had stomachaches, diarrhea, and nausea, and spent her days in bed. It would take time for her body to get used to the new drugs, the doctor said. Roland made a few more calls and we found Mélisande yet another doctor to confirm that she was indeed getting the right treatment.

She wanted the one-pill treatment back, Mélisande told the third doctor as he examined her on the small cot in the bedroom of one of the hotel's workers' bungalows, a small wallpapered room that she shared with her mother. Fishing out an old prescription bottle from one of my old purses, she handed it to the doctor, a tall Cuban man who spoke Creole with only a slight Spanish accent.

"Ay!" the man exclaimed when he saw the Canadian doctor's name.

"What's wrong?" I asked from where I was standing by the door.

It turned out, the Cuban explained, that what Mélisande had first gotten from the Canadian doctor was a placebo. It was more or less aspirin. It had not been doing anything for her at all. The doctor who had prescribed and sold them to us had suddenly fled Haiti because he'd been discovered selling useless pills to unsuspecting patients all over town.

"Your long-term treatment begins now," the Cuban told Mélisande as her tiny body sank deeper under the thin cotton sheets on the bed. "You must be vigilant about it."

I saw Mélisande's eyes sink along with her body. She had lost precious time, he was telling her. The disease had probably advanced further.

"He was playing with her life," the doctor told me as we walked out of Mélisande's room. She turned her face away from us, burying it in her pillow while I pulled the door shut behind me.

What would it have cost me to have trusted less? This is what I would have done for my son. I would have questioned, made deals, insisted, yelled.

"We've gone way beyond the call of duty," Roland said when I met him for lunch under a sun umbrella by the pool.

"How? By getting her a quack?"

"We tried to give her a chance," he said. "We tried to do everything we could have done for our own child."

Our own child, whose second test by another doctor was also negative, could have left the country. If a quack had intentionally fed our child a placebo instead of treating him, Roland himself would have hired the hit man.

* * *

That afternoon, Mélisande's mother served us a late lunch on one of the terraces while our son napped. She was sweating in her tight gray cotton uniform and dirty white cooking apron. Her head was wrapped in a black scarf, and though this was something she wore every day, it suddenly looked like mourning garb.

"We're sorry," Roland told her, "but she was probably sick before she came to work with us. Maybe someone was with her when she was young."

She lay the food down quickly, turned her back to us without saying anything, and walked away. In her mind, we were possibly just as bad as the quack, and now we were insulting her child too. Had we not fed Mélisande the hope of that pill, perhaps she might have taken her home to a bòkò or a leaf doctor or someone else who might have really tried to help her. If intention counted, her people might have better intentions than ours. They might have tried harder than we did to help her.

Perhaps I should apologize to her too, I told Roland, reassure her that we really tried, were doing the best we could. We had been duped, just as she had been, as her daughter had been. But our child's life was not in danger.

I got up from my seat and started to follow her, but Roland grabbed my hand and pulled me down.

"Leave it alone," he said, sounding now truly angry, not at me or at Mélisande's mother, but rather for us, for her.

After lunch, I went back to the bungalow to see Mélisande. She was lying in bed in a deep sleep and did not even stir when I walked in the room. Her body, stripped except for a matching set of polka-dotted bra and panties, would eventually adjust to the new cocktail, the Cuban doctor had told us. And slowly she could once again rejoin our lives at the hotel.

Watching her sleep so quietly, without even a hint of a snore, I thought about the strength of her will. Her symptoms had completely disappeared while she was taking that useless pill. It had seemed to help her once she believed it could.

Yet there was something different about her face now. She no longer seemed so young. Perhaps it was because of her sudden weight gains and losses, but she appeared to have wrinkles, some between her eyebrows, some around her mouth, a few under her eyes.

A week later, her body did begin to finally adjust to the cocktail and Mélisande got out of bed again. I noticed her one morning sitting by the pool staring in the water, then up at the sky, while my son and I ate breakfast on my patio. She reached into her pocket and pulled out something that she traced against the lifelines in her palm, then made a fist around it before placing it in her pocket again. She did this a couple of times—pulled the thing out of her pocket, then looked down at it and put it back. At some point, I noticed it was shiny, a little ring with some kind of stone that, though minute, was catching the light.

I took my son's hand and walked down to the pool. She was startled to see us. Her eyes had been closed and I had to call out her name to let her know we were there.

"How are you?" I asked while Gabriel and I slid onto on the lounge chair next to hers.

Sitting there, I couldn't help but think of my mother, so lost after my father had died. They had married when she was nineteen and, aside from me, he had been, whatever that meant now, her whole life. When I finished school and retraced my steps back to our beginning, to Haiti, she had dutifully followed, then at the first opportunity had leaped into a pool and drowned herself. Her death had been the most recent in a series of goodbyes. In many ways, my mother and I had been like Mélisande and her mother, without the friction, without the harsh words, without any words at all. For so long, before my mother had died, we had already been separated by water.

My son reached out for the shiny object and Mélisande's hands, but she pulled them away and shoved them into her pocket.

"What's that?" I asked.

She must have been wondering how long I had been looking at her, watching her pull this thing in and out of her pocket. Slowly she reached in deeper and out came the tiny ring once more. The gold was as thin as a strand of angel hair pasta, with a small glass stone that was once again capturing the light.

Drawn by the glint of the stone, my son reached for the ring again, but Mélisande yanked it away.

"Did one of the guests leave that behind?" I asked her.

She shook her head no.

"Did someone give it to you?"

She nodded.

"A man?"

Another nod.

"Did he give it to you before you were sick?"

"Maybe," she answered softly, two lines of tears suddenly running down her face.

"Did he say he loved you?"

"*Wi*," she replied with her head bowed, her eyes on her feet.

"He said he was going to marry you?"

He did, then he left and never came back.

It was worthless, of course, one of the fake gold *krizokal* rings made by the corner jeweler down the street. I had seen a bunch of them on the hands of young girls who came to the hotel for drinks and sexual exploits with both foreign and local guests. That type of ring even had a name. It was called the Port-au-Prince Marriage Special.

"Mélisande . . ." I began, trying to think of the best way to tell her. That ring was like the pills she'd been taking at first. There was no hope or healing in it.

"*M konnen*," she said, "I know," signaling with a wave of one bony hand that she no longer wanted to talk about it.

TRUE LIFE

BY MICHÈLE VOLTAIRE MARCELIN

Rue des Miracles

(Originally published in 2008)

Translated by Nicole Ball

My mother weeps. And the continuous murmur of her tears is so intense that it's impossible not to hear it all over the world. If she were a fountain, barefoot girls—ragged graces—would rush to her to gather the water from her eyes in enamel vessels, plastic goblets, and banged-up aluminum basins. But she's neither a drinking or luminous fountain, she's only a woman with swollen eyes, pregnant with a tiny tadpole splashing around in her amniotic fluid. The cause of the present tragedy: my father doesn't seem to care. Indifferent to the flood, he hitches up the legs of his trousers so as not to get them wet in the puddles. Goes right through my mother's arms, removing those clinging hands, those fingernails—bird's claws sinking into his flesh—and gets out of bed.

Maurice, don't leave! The threats become moans. *Maurice, come back!* My father doesn't turn around.

Men, they say—and they may be right—don't like unhappy women. Especially if the men are the ones who cause their grief.

My father, like so many others, takes refuge between the thighs of some Didine, Rosita, Alina, who demand so little and laugh so much. Ah, *amor de mis amores, vamos a gozar*, she probably says in a singsong voice, while dragging him toward the bed. My mother's jealousy was such that she could burn down churches, skin children alive, or tear stones with bare hands from the walls of her house. But she remained defeated by those very young girls whose only ambition was to make my father happy. I met one of the Alinas one day, and despite her smile, I hated her right away. Because she was beautiful and because it was her fault that my mother's eyes were perpetually red.

I don't know what had provoked this last scene. The smallest thing could ignite the anxious spark in my mother's eyes, firing up a swarm of Spanish wasps in her heart. A note studded with spelling mistakes, carelessly left on the dresser. *And she doesn't even know how to write "Maurice." She's a fool, an utter fool, Maurice.* The moaning of another woman's name in a moment of sexual abandon. *Who's that Didine? Rosita? Alina? Another whore. A damned slut!* And this time? What was the proverbial straw that broke the camel's back? The smell of another woman, her sweat or her perfume on my father's body, on his cock? But I'm wandering off, I'm dreaming, I'm hypothesizing. What is certain and the real truth is that in her anger she shouted that the child she was carrying, that child in her womb—me—was not his.

My father laughs and finally turns back around to face her. *I don't believe you, Marie Thérèse, you're crazy!*

My mother doesn't blink.

Think carefully about what you're saying, Thérèse.

Then, in a low voice, details drop from her mouth, one after the other.

In my father's eyes, a storm rises. And in a silence that fades into another silence, he gets dressed, puts on his shoes, and walks out the door.

* * *

After my father left, and as far back as I can remember, there were only women's voices in that ancient house. The cries and whispers that remained inside the walls of our home had the high, deep, or severe tones that I can match with the photographs of dead women pasted to my mirror. There they are, these women who gave color to the days of my life, that line of women from which I come. My great-grandmother Sélitane, baptized Julia, had eaten African earth before drinking the ocean she crossed with the court of King Béhanzin. When she was very old she went blind, and for a long time her monotonous chant, a litany repeated from continent to continent, floated through the house. She was as greedy as a magpie, grabbing everything that wasn't nailed down. Shoving her pitiful treasures into a cardboard box she jealously kept under her bed, to inspect her riches at her own leisure before sleep claimed her.

After the death of that simple, illiterate woman, virtuoso of the bullwhip, they found among her worthless papers a heart in chiseled silver tarnished by the years, with the word *Happiness* inscribed on one side and the intertwined initials G.S. on the other. During a stay in the French Antilles, she had met a certain Gaston Sarogance, an innkeeper whose pleasure she had submitted to in the storeroom every God-given evening until she got pregnant. He disposed of her with a promise to support her and her child, and sent her by boat to the other end of our island.

From this little guinea hen of a woman, all black and gray, my grandmother Félicité was born. Tall, beautiful; so beautiful. Majestically displacing her weight in air when she walked, flowing like a breeze that picked up dust and withered leaves everywhere she went. At sixteen, she had men drooling over her. Their pants would swell with surges of sudden desire that would tear the fabric and bring migraines so strong that they would rush to the nearest pharmacy to buy painkillers.

Even Alcantère Debramme, a seemingly rich old gentleman the color of a corpse, lost his head over her. One day he came to ask for her hand. Félicité, however, born and named for happiness, had preferred the love of Anselme. Anselme, with shoes held together by string, with a notebook always under his arm and a pen behind his ear, had stolen her heart with poems he passed to her over the fence. Little pieces of paper rolled into a ball where *lover* rhymed with *forever*, and *mine* with *thine*. *Verba volant, scripta manent*: words fly away, writings remain. Madame Julia had said, *No, no, and no*, as she had higher ambitions for her daughter. Faced with this refusal, Félicité's heart had become a garden of brambles. Dry thorns. For two years she carried a lover's mourning for that thwarted love, up to the day when she saw Anselme squatting next to a wall, relieving himself after a sudden bout of diarrhea brought on by an abundance of stolen figs. The fruit seller had pointed an accusatory finger at Anselme, and Félicité could not forgive her poet's gluttony. Had she looked again toward Alcantère Debramme, she would not have found him—the old gentleman, dropped like an old hat, had consoled himself with a neighborhood Primrose and had never walked past their fence again.

Félicité's free heart blossomed again with the arrival of Estime Placide, who owned the house in which my mother was born. She fell madly in love with my father, Maître Derville—*maître*, the title one gives to lawyers—Maurice to his friends. They were happy at first, but after a few years, things changed. Isn't love always a wonder at the beginning? My mother, my poor sweet mother, was too fragile to resist the charm of this man, whose smile alone always lured young turtledoves.

My father liked to laugh and sing, drink and dance. He had a table reserved for him in all the best cafés of the city and every barman had a bottle marked with the name *Monsieur Maurice* within arm's reach. One evening, while out with a group of friends, he let himself be tempted by a little outing near the city. *To each man his woman*, and they woke up in a brothel at noon. At that time, he still had scruples and would have offered my mother sweet talk as consolation. Then one of his friends, a colonel, suggested that he lock him up in the town jail. The best way to get him out of this tricky situation. That very evening, a rumor circulated that Maître Derville had been arrested. There was talk of a denunciation, of subversive acts. My tearful mother was informed that she would have to approach the colonel to free her husband. She was so terrified that she fainted and fell on a stove. The flaming coals burned holes in the thin cotton fabric of her dress. Screams. Lamentations. Ice to cool the wounds. He would laugh as he told the story later. My mother never learned the truth.

So in that terrible year of 1955, assisted by her mother and a midwife and without fanfare, Marie-Thérèse gave birth to me. For a long time afterward, she stayed in bed praying for my father's return. So here I am. She called me Lola, a whore's name.

My mother had lied. I really am my father's daughter. I inherited his selfishness. The lust and passion that carries me toward many different men is my father's. We share the same taste for adventure. The brutality of our stubbornness is such that a pack of wild horses couldn't turn us away from any pleasure we have promised ourselves. And when I talk to you about my father's love affairs and lies, I'm also talking about my own.

Among my love affairs, some were scandalous, others secret, and one was particularly cruel. Some were only trifles. There were also some that were uninspired and without grace; one ending as another was beginning. And all of them existed to forget just one love, Jean.

In my life, there had been suicides, divorces, and an infestation of bedbugs—they'd had to air out all the mattresses in the sun to get rid of them. There had been the birth of a three-eyed older sister Rose, whose fetus was kept in a jar in our house. There were illnesses that dragged despair in their wake: Grandmother Félicité drowning her suffering in liquor, refusing to show the doctor the crab gnawing at her anus, but howling her pain like a dog wailing at the moon. Yet if you happened to ask me, I would tell you that none of those things affected me nearly as much as my love affair with Jean.

It was a magnificent and extravagant love. Old as the world. Fluid as time. He himself would claim with a smirk that we had been in love for centuries. For me, there only existed the time before him and the time after. The first part all childhood memories. The second part filled with days and nights of intertwined cruelty and tenderness.

As is almost always the case with love affairs, this one was born by chance. December, which others found fun, had always been a dark month for me, marking another year of loneliness. It was on a Friday, the thirteenth day of the month, during the longest year on earth. At a dance at a private house, I was distractedly counting flies while my girlfriends were dancing to an old bolero, a sentimental tune.

You have not changed
You're still that young man, so strange . . .

The air smelled of sweat and perfume. The colored paper

lanterns punched holes in the darkness. Romantic conversations were blooming in every corner while the Bengal lights whirled around in the garden. Suddenly—I didn't see him coming—there he was in front of me.

Mademoiselle?

I was changed forever.

His breath on my neck, the warmth of his hand, that pointed star burning the middle of my back—these sensations communicated a secret to me, something that I felt in my blood, that this man's hands all over my body would bring me peace.

His long past of conquests had accustomed him to the passions he aroused in the eyes and hearts of young girls. Accepting their feelings with indifference, watching them after making love like so many useless things, and chasing them away with a frown, like silly birds. What he liked most about me—what he hadn't found with the others—was my deep and uncompromising devotion. I loved him furiously and shamelessly, and he in turn was skilled at hurting me. He rejected my love and then cajoled me like a child. Who can explain how far love can go? Sometimes, passion only ends at the brink of madness; at the point of no return. It seems that you have to let time pass. You only die the first time. The other times, you cry. And the only way to get rid of the taste and smell of the man who left you is to replace him with another man. How many bodies must one love to forget just one? Is it possible for a man's smell to haunt you through time?

I remember that body. I loved that skin, the smell of tobacco on it. And the scent of absence is so strong that I never had to smoke tobacco or dab my wrists with his cologne to make him relive in me. But everything fades, everything in the end is exorcised. It's a matter of covering painful memories with others, with less important, more ordinary ones. The way you cover filth with dried leaves.

Happy lovers have no stories to tell. The moment before you fall in love is the most mundane, innocent moment of your life. There are no omens, no portents, no premonitions. Yet in that timeless, motionless universe, I could have foretold the day, the hour, the minute, and the second when I met him. And in my memory, it all begins on that day when Jean, with his sculpted, chiseled face, got married, and was thus made inaccessible. I was absolutely smitten. And I created an entire story that only I remember. I'm fifteen and I'm at a dance. Jean is merely an unknown man smiling sweetly. His eyes meet those of a slightly frail teenager in siren-blue sandals and dress, sitting on the sidelines. Ceremoniously, he asks me to dance. Out of pity? On a bet? I, who only know the arms of boys my own age, I am stirred, intoxicated, bewildered in the arms of this thirty-year-old man. And when the music stops, I don't want to be free. I want him to keep me in his arms. He smiles and says, *Thank you, mademoiselle.* But I am still hanging on to him. Impossible to tear myself away. In the short silence between two songs, a new land is discovered. And I read a desire in his eyes: he must have said words whose color differed from those I was used to hearing. *Mademoiselle, my name is Jean. You have a beautiful mouth. I'm going to kiss it.* Words said practically without breathing. Words that you never hear when you're fifteen, words that shake up my sleepy fatherless life. And then he draws near and in a moment everything else disappears, because I had become blind and deaf, a moment so brief I'm not sure I dreamt it. All he had done was lick my mouth. In the time it took for me to smother a cry, he was already gone. The sad voice on the record is singing:

If I hurt you when I left you that evening
Without a word, without a look
To soothe your feelings . . .

A sleepless night, filled with dreams. Filled with Jean. The next day, I looked for him across the city. All day long and on every face I search for Jean, and I write these lines in my notebook:

I will no longer go to dances in a blue dress
For I lost my heart by chance, to the rhythm of a dance

The great madness of love is blowing through me. I am fifteen and finally life mirrors literature. I am not one of those girls men lose their heads over. I've become one who loves men to death. And I have loved them all. Without demanding or expecting that they love me back, and sometimes despite their obvious indifference. I have made myself completely available to them. Transforming their lukewarm feelings into love has been my challenge, my persistent desire. Today I see how obviously selfish and flighty those men have been. But at that time, I wanted the pride of having lived exceptional adventures. Jean had become the longed-for tormentor this consenting victim was awaiting. He taught me the skill of smiling while suffering.

I believe everything he tells me. A paragon of sensitivity and truth, he only lies to his wife. I reserve my lies for my mother. I've developed a love of music and have resolved to learn the piano. Jean gives me private lessons. Every Saturday when Madame is away, the yellow cover of the Hanon exercise book leaning on the black varnish of the instrument,

Jean runs his hands over me while I play the wrong notes. The maids might be listening and silence would be suspicious. Sometimes he's the one who sits at the piano and I between his legs. When it's my turn to sit on the stool again, the staccato of the "Indian Waltz" is the only rhythm that resists his assaults and the only one I'm able to control. Even today, it's the only piece I can play from memory. I played that waltz to the point of exhaustion, while his hands and mouth were playing other games.

I don't know what kind of relationship he had with the woman I always called Madame. She seemed to me very old, as old as Jean, and I had no interest in her. Did she suspect what was happening in her house? It was certainly not Jean's first affair. I wasn't his only pupil, and I did not have a monopoly on his affections. But it was probably the most reckless of his adventures. Like all lovers, we were exhibitionists and gave ourselves away without realizing it, by the trembling of our hands, our looks of complicity, our furtive smiles, light caresses that we thought imperceptible but must have been obvious to everybody else. Revelations as precise and terrible as a vibrant *Te amo* aria sung on stage by a soprano. *È finita la commedia.*

The next year, without having learned the sonatas other students played in recitals at school, I got into the habit of visiting him in his friend's apartment. I would cut my classes and meet him in the afternoon. The heat of our naked bodies would mingle on the bare mattress in that bachelor pad. He would turn on the radio. The first time, the song might have been "Náufrago" or "María Bonita," but later I learned he liked to do it with Mozart in the background.

He kisses me. No one has ever kissed me like that. He

devours me. He eats my mouth. He eats me up whole, my flesh, my body. Not a part of me escapes his mouth, his lips, his teeth, his tongue. A cannibal feast. He nibbles, sucks, licks, rips, brands me with his teeth. He touches everything, plunders and devours. Voracious, greedy.

But no matter how much I wanted to melt into Jean's body, my own body—still so frail—refused to let him enter. What happened next, and what was repeated many times throughout that year of torment, I would rather not recall—but he ordered me, at age fifteen, to make love with someone else before coming back to him. Which abandoned sweetheart could I go to for this favor? Who might turn me down? Who would take Jean's place?

I kept returning again and again with my head hanging low. I would keep going back to that bed where Jean had deflowered other girls while we were apart. But this was of no importance. I would have accepted anything from him.

PART III

LOSING MY WAY

I JUST LOST MY WAY

BY ÈZILI DANTÒ

Anba Dlo, Lan Ginen

(Originally published in 1997)

i just lost my way.
i had it once, when i didn't know any better.
My earliest memories, if i go way back to infant times, are blank.
A wall of black.
Like when i'm in a dreamless sleep.
There's no light, no noise, no color, no smell, no movement,
only a still, airless black.

i'm there in that silent airless black.
But without thoughts, without flesh.
Joined one energy to another, no air between,
i cannot be sundered down through all the millenniums.

i've no links here. No involvement, no kinky hair, no caramel skin,
no sexual urge, no community, no foreparents, no hunger to take or
give shape or to resist the shapes the Universe, its powers and
polarities impose on me.

Here, in this airless, senseless emptiness,
there's no torment about harvest and things,
no dialectic, no contrasts, no time, no reference points, no
contradictory inclinations, no everyday-rhythmic-organic-urge to
expand, no impatient temperament getting in the way, no

interminably long roads, forests and thickets.
And,
most liberating of all,
no impossible dreams—that everyday struggle to overcome social
injustice and inequality of opportunity.

When the i who stands before you here withdraws.
Sleep without dreams. There's just black and the i that i am, is lost.
No witnesses to find me and define me narrow.
The narrow that's daylight black.
The narrow that's flat.
One-dimensional.
A shadow.

Where i come from, All is one.
And that oneness is as black as the center of the sun.
As dynamic as the silence of celestial inspiration,
compassion, love, peace, death.

When everything drains off me, All is empty,
wide and deep as my crown chakra
and as black as the known cosmos.

i'm learning to accept i've been lost for longer than i can know.

THE MISSION

BY MARIE-HÉLÈNE LAFOREST

Bonair

(Originally published in 2002)

Rusted wheels, half-buried copper caldrons, and a windmill's sails still lay about Bonair, remnants of the distillery which had once been the center of life in the village. Six huts crowded in the clearing while several more stood along the trail made by horses, donkeys, and the barefoot people of Bonair.

"A white man's coming, a white man's coming!" A boy ran, firmly gripping his oversized shorts at the waist, jumping like a kid goat over the rocks on the trail, whizzing past the huts. "A white man's coming!" he yelled, reaching his mother pounding corn in a tall wooden mortar. The corn chaff rose above her head like golden dust and the deep, low thumping stopped.

"Alone?" she asked.

"No, with a priest," the boy answered.

"A priest?" Lumène's eyes opened wide. There hadn't been any foreigners in Bonair since Pè Milcent was shipped out of the country four years ago. Chef Section came with the order one morning: all foreigners must leave Haitian soil within forty-eight hours. The converts assembled outside Pè Milcent's shingle house. When he stepped out in civilian clothes, carrying a small bag, two women flung themselves at his feet. "Don't forget us, Pé." "Pé, it's goodbye then." Pé Milcent, too

192 // Haiti Noir 2

moved to speak, shook hands, patted heads, and left. Lisette, his housekeeper, got the sheets and towels he didn't have time to take to the Sisters of Mercy in town. He must have arrived home safely; otherwise, they would have heard that he was dead or in jail.

Lumène resumed her pounding, rhythmically marking time until the priests reached the bend in the trail. Two men in their late twenties, in gray suits with clergyman collars, approached. The light-skinned one had square shoulders and a thick mustache; the darker one was smaller, with a smiling face.

"Chef Section's not here," Lumène said without looking up.

"Do you know where he is?" The clergymen stopped.

"He'll be here soon, at three o'clock."

The clergymen went back on their steps to wait for the rural guard in the shade of a tamarind tree.

"She knew where we were headed," the lighter man smiled.

"Where else could we be going?" the darker one said.

"Chef Section wasn't there, was he?" a man called out from the porch of his hut.

"He'll be back at three," the clergymen answered.

"Yes, he's usually back at three. Yes . . . you can come sit over here." John set two chairs against the wattled walls of his hut. Blotches of white glared in his hair as if he had just whitewashed a house. He stretched his long legs before him, ready to make conversation.

"You're priests from Port-au-Prince?"

"We're from the Pentecostal Church."

"Oh, Baptists, Protestants. There was a Baptist church here once, before Pè Milcent came. They were here when I was this tall, still in short pants. No one here is old enough to remember. That's why my name is John, after Pastor John. My mother was baptized in the river behind Chef Section's house. Pastor John, afraid of the water spirits, stood on a big rock to dip my mother's head in the water. He began to build a church down the road over there. He made some nice songs. *God is everywhere . . .*" John intoned, tapping his foot.

A breeze blew and stirred the leaves of a silk cotton tree. The clergymen looked up. Calabashes with offerings swung from the branches. John stopped talking, turned left and right, scrutinizing the sky.

"Then we had a Catholic priest called Pè Milcent . . ." he continued.

"When did Pastor John go away?"

"Oooh . . . a long time ago. I tell you, all the people you see around here weren't even born back then. He left one Easter Sunday. The rara bands were out every night, *dum-tum, dum-tum*, bamboo sticks, drums, *dum-tum, dum-tum*. On Holy Saturday everyone was out dancing. No one was under the arbor to pray. After that, he left. You can't serve God and Satan . . ." John pointed to the path with his cane, interrupting his talk. "I think he's coming." He sucked his teeth, like everyone in Bonair did every time they saw Chef Section. They had found out he was trying to get a pistol from the Macoutes in town. But what for, they asked themselves, to shoot one of us?

Through the heat, the clergymen saw the thin guard in a blue denim suit with large silvery buttons waddling toward them, feeling his whip. He cracked it in the air, the sound sharp like a single gunshot. They rose to meet him, followed him, watching his uneasy steps in the shoes he'd worn to town.

"Want to build a church, eh?" Chef Section asked.

"Apparently there is an old house . . ."

"The priest's."

"If we could rent it . . ."

The priest's house, with a slanted roof and a porch, was built like those of the better-off country folks' on the main road. The rains had washed away the paint, but the jalousies, which opened in long painful creaks, had kept the water out. Small rodents had left their black trails in the two rooms. The men agreed on a price.

The next morning the two pastors arrived on foot carrying two duffel bags, a broom, and a pail.

"What good will these poor pastors on foot be to us?" the people of Bonair whispered, remembering missionaries in Land Rovers, who carried their trousseaus in trunks like young brides. They grew perplexed as they watched Pastor Ben: a white clergyman drawing water from the well in the garden, scrubbing the porch on his knees.

Pastor Ben sat under the tamarind tree to wait for the wooden floors to dry. He smiled to himself as the branches swung their lacy leaves above him. He drew out a penknife with a shiny blade to shave a few sticks; green flakes curled around him. He threw the sticks in the air, stood up, and stretched his arms. He strolled in the garden, pulling a blade of grass, stooping over, feeling the coppery soil through his fingers. The sun, setting for the night, found him reading out of a small book, the breeze blowing through his hair on the front porch. When it was too dark to see, he went inside. On the bare floor that night, he lay, head resting on his folded arms, as if he were on a sandy beach, the rustle of geckos and lizards through the tall grass keeping him awake. He savored the smell of cut green wood and loosened soil. He had planned so long for this day.

Ever since the massacre at Caserne Dessalines five years

ago, he had thought of nothing else. At the time, he was a medical student in Paris. A group of men assaulted the barracks next to the presidential palace. They were caught. Duvalier displayed their mutilated bodies to the public. By decree, all schoolchildren were taken to the square to see the fly-ridden, foul-smelling corpses.

The trip back to Port-au-Prince was the longest he had ever embarked on. To elude Duvalier's spies, he went through Madrid, Mexico City, Pointe-à-Pitre, waited there three days before flying to Port-au-Prince. When he stepped out of the plane, a wave of emotion swelled inside him. He didn't expect the dry heat to smell of his childhood, of his summers in a mountain house, of geranium bushes and fig trees. He clutched the small Bible with one hand and fingered the silver cross on his chest with the other. The first local member of the secret Committee for Freedom, Pastor Paul, met him. The Church of Hope was about to begin its activity.

He had three sermons written on the theological virtues to ease the rural population into his teachings. He would have to deliver them like someone who has recently learned to speak Creole. He was determined to be patient; after all, Fidel Castro had lived two years in the Sierra Maestra. The Church of Hope would gather enough followers from within the country to fight the dictator. He had a mission. He had returned to free the country and its peasants, the most oppressed of the oppressed. The sun rose so early that it was already day and he had not fallen asleep.

The rattle of a vehicle stopped all activities in Bonair the next morning. Springs, mattresses, chairs, and boxes in its bed, the pickup truck, Pastor Paul at the wheel, jostled about. When it became clear that they were bringing Pastor Ben's furniture, the hoeing and weeding resumed. From a distance the people saw the pastors extend the beams of the porch, hammering and clobbering. They laid straw mats for the shade and hung a kerosene lamp from the porch ceiling. At dusk Pastor Paul drove away, leaving Pastor Ben alone.

On Sunday he lined up the foldable chairs for his first service. John limped to the porch-turned-church leaning on his cane. Following John's lead, the people of Bonair hesitantly approached. To the few curious present, Pastor Ben spoke of his plans for a practical school, without slate tablets or books. He would teach them about growing and selling crops. The church garden would become the community's, everyone sharing in the work and dividing the yield equally. The people were surprised that Pastor Ben brought seeds to sow, instead of used clothing and powdered milk.

In the coming weeks, Pastor Ben spoke of hope and charity, finding it difficult after that to write any more sermons. For fear of being searched at the airport he had taken no books and it was risky for Pastor Paul to travel with printed material. Every night he closed his doors early and wrote furiously. He was working on the theme of awakening.

Wake up, wake up to a new life, he wrote, *the Kingdom of God is of this world*. He said the words aloud and crossed out the last line.

Each morning he tended the garden, John in his trail, following him all the way to the riverbank where root vegetables grew.

"You like yam, Pastor Ben? Pè Milcent only ate potatoes," John said.

"Everything that grows on this soil is blessed."

"Pastor Ben, you're not married?"

"Marriage would interfere with my mission."

"Some pastors have wives. You're not ready to start building the church? Chef Section asked me when you're going to build the church. Pè Milcent used to go to town to buy bricks, planks, a little at a time."

Pastor Ben suspected John was trying to tell him he found his behavior eccentric. He began to plan construction of the church. The news pleased his nine followers.

On Wednesday Pastor Paul came for him. They drove to Mombi to order cement, sand, and bricks. The following Monday, when they returned to town for trowels and plumb lines, it was market day. From the surrounding villages, people had flocked to Mombi to trade. Pastor Ben stood on the side of the road looking at the market shacks and at the masses of women squatting before their baskets. Unknowingly, his eyes became misty. He breathed in the smell of cod and herring, of pig's feet and hot peppers. Gusts of pine wood fire and whiffs of fried pork filled his avid nostrils. He stood there, his thoughts going back to memories from his youth, his parents and their mansion, to scenes he had forgotten, hierarchies he'd felt vaguely uneasy about. He remembered the analyses of oppression and repression in a Paris university room with the men of his Communist cell. It was in Paris that he fully understood the society in which he had lived all his life and the mechanisms enacted to perpetuate economic and social injustice.

Seeing Pastor Paul struggling with a sack of rice, Pastor Ben stepped down into the market area to help him. Bending forward to grab the other side of the sack, his face neared that of a small woman selling rice who locked his gaze.

"Monsieur Michel," she breathed.

He heaved the bag and hurried to the Church of Hope's truck. His heart was beating fast, sweat ran down his face, his hand stroked his thick mustache, his mind in turmoil. The woman's eyes had seen behind his mustache.

As planned, the two men met a Pastor Henri along the road. He was to bring them news from abroad. Pastor Ben could hear in Pastor Henri's shrill voice that there was news, which he would later whisper inside the truck. The coded message was clear, the day had come.

Matilde knotted her rice in a burlap cloth and left the market. She had seen Monsieur Michel, but what was he doing there, dressed like a clergyman with a big brown mustache? She'd taught him to walk, taught him his first words, fed, washed, dressed him. She was his Mati. She couldn't be fooled by his get-up. Madame Saint-Armand should be told.

With her market clothes on, her worn sandals flapping, and a pack of rice balanced on her head, she set off for the city. She waited on the road for a vehicle going to Port-au-Prince.

The dog began to bark when she arrived at the Saint-Armands' gate. The yardman let her in and opened the front door, recognizing the woman who had raised five of the six Saint-Armand children. He led Matilde into a room where she sat under a photograph taken the day Michel left for France. She remembered how the Saint-Armands had talked about sailing to France to visit him. But when the time came, ships had stopped coming, curfews were set, properties seized, and she'd gone back to Mombi to watch over her plot of land.

"Matilde, what happened?" Madame Saint-Armand's arms, which Matilde remembered being fuller, reached out to her.

"I didn't have time to change," Matilde replied, thinking of her clothes, but staring at Madame Saint-Armand's gray suit, the color of mourning.

"Business bad?" Madame Saint-Armand asked.

"When they don't take money from us every time we sell something, we manage."

The two women drew long sighs. Madame Saint-Armand picked up her handbag. She was opening her purse to give Matilde money, out of habit.

"Madame," Matilde waved a hand at her, "sit down, I have something to tell you . . . I saw Monsieur Michel. I called him, but he didn't answer, but it was him."

"Michel?" Madame Saint-Armand whispered. "Michel . . ." Sadness glazed over her eyes. "You saw Michel?"

"Madame, it was him," Matilde repeated, lowering her eyes so as not to stare at Madame Saint-Armand's distress.

There was silence.

"It couldn't have been him," Madame Saint-Armand struggled with the words.

"I, Matilde," she hit her chest, "I wouldn't recognize Monsieur Michel?"

Madame Saint-Armand nodded.

"Maybe . . . you'd better speak to Monsieur Saint-Armand." She rose slightly from the chair and turned toward the wide staircase. "Frantz, Frantz!"

Matilde told Monsieur Saint-Armand that her eyes had crossed Michel's. She went on describing his clothes, the clergyman collar, and the bushy mustache as often as the Saint-Armands asked her.

"Matilde," Madame Saint-Armand hesitated, "we have no news of Michel . . . He left medical school six months ago." She stopped and Matilde watched her shoulders sink. "No one has heard from him since," she choked on the last word.

Matilde was in tears. She had not known. She had seen Michel and had not held on to him. There was nothing they could do at this late hour. The Saint-Armands would wait until tomorrow morning to drive to Mombi where Matilde had seen him.

The people of Bonair woke up hearing a rustling at daybreak. A bad air is coming from the earth, John thought. It is a bad sign when the night breeze grazes the grass and does not reach the trees. A hiss cut through the dark. John groped for his cane. Flares lit up the dawn, a volley of shots, grenades exploded. Chef Section stormed out of his house to try out his new pistol.

The people of Bonair remained shut inside their huts and waited for the tremors to subside. When they glanced out, machine-gunned soldiers surrounded the area where the pastors' house had been. The people gathered on the opposite side of the trail, slapping their cheeks in despair. They saw John walking through the rubble, trembling, stammering, while heading in the direction of the soldiers. A woman rushed over, clenched his hand, and drew him to where the population of Bonair crowded. The villagers remained silent, immobile, staring at the soldiers until the sun rose high in the sky.

Matilde and the Saint-Armands woke up at daybreak with a heavy heart. Unaware that Duvalier's *léopards* had pounced, they set off for Mombi.

Fifteen years after Duvalier's death, on February 7, 1986, his son, Baby Doc, fled the country. That day the people of Bonair renamed their village Pastorbenville.

BARBANCOURT BLUES (EXCERPT)

BY NICK STONE

Pétionville Square

(Originally published in 2007)

Max left La Coupole at around two a.m. The Barbancourt rum was making his head reel, but not in an unpleasant way. Booze had always promised to take him up someplace good only to fuck with his controls and leave him stranded midway, tasting the inevitable crash. This was a different kind of drunk, closer to an opiate float. He had a smile on his face and that good feeling in his heart that everything would be all right and the world wasn't such a bad place really. The booze was *that* good.

Dark telegraph poles leaned out of the concrete, tilting slightly forward, toward Pétionville's brightly lit center. The wires were slung so low and loose Max could have touched them if he'd wanted to. He was walking in the street, barely feeling his footsteps, bracing his body against the downward pull of gravity, which threatened to send him sprawling flat on his face. Behind him, people were coming out of the bar, spilling conversation and laughter, which faded to murmurs and splutters in the deep silence that confronted them. Some Americans tested the rigidity of the stillness with a one-off scream or shout or a bark or a meow, but the quietness sucked the noise into more silence.

Max didn't know exactly which street he had to turn down. He couldn't remember how many he'd passed on his way up before he'd noticed the bar. He was close to the center of town, but not that close, somewhere in the middle. He passed one road, looked down it, but it wasn't the right one. There was a supermarket on the left and a graffitied wall to the right. Maybe the next road. Or the next. Or the one before. He'd meant to ask Huxley for directions, in between one of the four or five other drinks they'd had together. He'd forgotten. Then he'd stopped caring sometime after he'd lost count of the drinks he'd had. The Barbancourt had told him he'd find his way home *no problem*. He carried on walking.

His shoes were starting to pinch the sides of his feet and scrape off the flesh on his heels. He hated them, those nice, new, shiny, leather slip-ons he'd bought at Saks Fifth Avenue at Dadeland Mall. He should have broken them in before he'd put them on. He didn't like the *clack-clack* the heels were making in the road. He sounded like a young horse in *its* first shoes.

And then there were the drums—not any closer than when he'd first heard them, but clearer, the sound raining down from the mountains like rusty cutlery; a full battery of snares, tom-toms, bass drums, and cymbals. The rhythms had a jagged edge. They'd gone straight for the drunk part of his brain, the part he'd hit when he'd fallen off the wagon, the part that would hurt like a motherfucker in the morning.

Someone tugged at his left sleeve.

"*Blan, blan.*"

It was a child's voice, hoarse, almost broken, a boy's.

Max glanced from side to side and saw no one. He turned around and looked back up the road. He saw the bar's lights and people in the distance, but nothing else.

"*Blan, blan.*"

Behind him, the other way, downhill. Max turned around, slowly.

His brain was on the graveyard shift, everything taking its time to fall into place, adjust, calculate. His vision had dancing ripples before it, as if he were at the bottom of a deep lake, watching pebbles falling through the surface.

He barely made the boy out in the darkness, just a hint of silhouette against the orange neon.

"Yes?" Max said.

"*Ban mwen dola!*" the boy shouted.

"What?"

"*Kòb, ban mwen ti kòb!*"

"Are you—hurt?" Max inquired, stumbling in and then out of cop mode.

The boy came right up to him. He had his hands out.

"*Dola! Ban mwen dollaaarrrggh!*" he screamed.

Max blocked his ears. The little fucker could scream.

"*Dola?*" Money. He wanted money.

"*No dinero*," Max said, putting his hands up and showing the boy his empty palms. "No money."

"*Ban mwen dola donk*," the boy whined, breathing hotly all over Max's still-open palms.

"No dollar. No peso, no red fucking cent," Max said and carried on walking down.

The boy followed him from behind. Max stepped a little faster. The boy stayed on his heels, calling after him, louder: "*Blan! Blan!*"

Max didn't turn around. He heard the sound of the child's feet scuttling after him, soft footfalls underscoring his cracking heels. The boy wasn't wearing any shoes.

He walked faster. The child stayed right on his tail.

He passed a road he thought looked familiar, and stopped

abruptly. The boy thudded against the back of his legs and pushed him. Max bounced two steps down, losing his balance and his bearings. He took a couple of wild, desperate steps to steady himself but put his foot through a sudden empty space where there should have been road. His leg went down, down, down. And then his foot splashed into a puddle. By then he'd already tilted too far over. He fell straight down, landing hard on his front, bumping and grazing his chin. He heard something scrape away down the road.

He lay still for a few seconds and assessed the damage. His legs were okay. No real pain. His torso and chin didn't hurt much. He was conscious of something nasty, the notion of pain, waving at him behind opaque glass, but it was a crooked shadow in a still-beautiful, silky mist. In the days before general anesthetic, they must have given future amputees Barbancourt communion.

The boy cackled over his head: "*Blan sa a sou! Blan sa a sou!*"

Max didn't know what the fuck he meant. He got up, pulled his leg out of the crater, and turned around, uphill, pissed off as hell, his chest now stinging with pain. The rum's spell was broken and all the nightmares had come rushing back. Half his trouser leg was soaked in a cocktail of piss, dead oil, and matured sewage.

"Fuck off!" he shouted.

But he couldn't see the boy. The boy was gone. In his place, in front of Max, stood about a dozen street urchins, all no taller than ten-year-olds. He pick out the edges of their heads and their teeth, those who had them or were baring them, and the whites of their eyes. He could smell them—stale woodsmoke, boiled vegetables, earth, moonshine, sweat, decay. He could feel them peering at him through the darkness.

There were no lights on this stretch of road, no inbound or outbound cars. The bar lights were now pinpoints in the distance. How far down had he come? He stared quickly to the street on his left. Two rows of boys were standing across it, blocking his way. He wasn't even sure it was the street he wanted. He had to retrace his steps, maybe go back to the bar, start again. Ask for directions this time.

He started forward but stopped. He'd lost his shoe in the crater. He looked down at the road, but he couldn't find the hole he'd gone down. He touched the ground with the ball of his foot but felt solid asphalt.

The drumming had suddenly stopped, as if the players had seen what was happening and come over to look. Max felt like he'd gone deaf.

He took off his other shoe, slipped it in his jacket pocket, and started to walk up the hill. He stopped again. There were more kids than he thought. They were stretched out all the way across the road. He was standing right in front of them, close enough to inhale nothing but their gutter-fresh stench. He was going to say something but he heard small whisperings behind him, words evaporating in the air like raindrops on a hot tin roof.

When he turned around, there was another cordon of boys, roping off the way down. He noticed shapes now moving up from Pétionville town center. More children, heading his way. They were carrying things—sticks, it seemed, big sticks, clubs.

They were coming for him. They were coming to kill him.

He heard a rock fall off a pile to his left and roll down into the street. The whispering around him increased to tones of rebuke, all coming now from the same direction. He followed the sound and traced it to the doorway of an empty building.

He looked closer, pushed into the darkness for the lightest tones, and he saw that they were passing out rocks, to each other down the line. Half of them already had one in their hands, held down by their sides. When everyone was armed, he supposed, they'd rain them down on him. Then the others would beat the life out of him with their clubs.

His mouth went dry. He didn't know what to do. He couldn't think. He couldn't sober up.

The rum came rushing back to him. His body suddenly felt good, his throbbing chin dulled, his head was light again. He was brave and invincible.

It didn't seem so bad. He'd been through worse than this. He could push his way through. Why not give it a try? What the hell?

He took a couple of steps back and squared his shoulders for the bulldozer run. He could hear them behind him. He didn't look. Could they see what he was doing? Probably. These kids lived in the dark. Had they second-guessed him?

When he charged, he'd knock three or four of them down. They'd pelt him with rocks, but if he kept his head covered and ran like a motherfucker, he'd escape the worst of the barrage.

Uphill, drunk, not so young anymore. Where was he going?

They'd chase him and he wouldn't know where to turn. He'd worry about that later.

And how many were there?

A hundred. Easily. He was dead.

The rum rush deserted him. Optimism split on him too.

The drum started again—just the one, the same deep slow beat he'd heard in the courtyard earlier in the evening. This time it sounded like bombs dropping on a distant town or a battering ram striking a city's gates. The beat didn't go into his heart but right behind his ears, every note a grenade exploding in his skull, sending shock waves down his spine, making him wince and shudder.

Think again, he told himself. One more try. If that fails, run.

"You want money?" he pleaded, despite himself. No response. The rocks were passed on in silence, the kill hands filling up, the circle almost closed. It seemed hopeless.

Then he remembered his gun. He was armed, full-clip.

Suddenly a motorbike roared into life at the top of the hill, the engine shocking the night like a chain saw in a chapel. It was the kid in the white suit.

He came down the hill, the bike slowing to a growl and then a purr as it neared the circle around Max.

The kid put his bike down and came over to Max.

"*Sa w ap fè la blan?*" He spoke in a deep, ragged voice that belonged to someone five times his age.

"I don't understand," Max slurred. "You speak English?"

"Inglishhh?"

"Yeah, English. You speak?"

The kid stood his ground and looked at him.

Max heard it before he saw it, something slicing through the air, something heavy, aimed right at his head. He ducked and the kid in the suit swung into space.

Max dug a furious left-right combination into the kid's ribs and solar plexus. The kid gasped and cried out as he folded over like paper, sticking his chin straight out for a right hook, which Max slammed home and sent him sprawling to the floor.

Max grabbed the kid in a choke hold, pulled out his Beretta, and jammed the barrel through his mouth.

"Back the fuck up or he dies!" he yelled, looking all around him. The kid was flailing at him with his hands, kicking at the ground, trying to tip Max over. Max stamped on one of the kid's hands with his bare heel. He heard bones give and a strangled cry boil in the middle of the kid's throat.

No one moved.

What now?

He couldn't exactly drag the kid around with him as he looked for his way home, checking every street until he found it. No way. Maybe he could use him as a shield, push him as far away from the crowd as possible, then cut him loose and go on his way.

No way would they let him.

He could try and shoot his way out.

But no, he wouldn't use it. Not on fucking *children*.

He'd fire in the air and run as they hit the deck or scattered or panicked.

"Put your gun away!"

Max jumped.

The booming voice had come from above, in the black sky, behind him, downhill. Still keeping his hold on the kid, Max shuffled around toward Pétionville. The view ahead was completely blocked by the man's body, which Max couldn't see but sensed, massive and heavy, the thunder in dark, roiling clouds.

"I *won't* ask you again," the man insisted.

Max took his gun out of the kid's mouth and slipped it back in his holster.

"Now let him go."

"He tried to fuckin' kill me!" Max yelled.

"Let him GO!" the man boomed, making some children jump and drop their rocks.

Max freed his assailant.

The man barked something in Creole and blinding-white overhead lights came on. Max looked away, hand up against the glare. He saw the kid on the ground, blood all down the front of his suit.

Suddenly Max could see every millimeter of the immediate street. The children were standing around him three rows deep. They were all skinny, dressed in filthy rags, many only in shorts, turned away from the light, hands shielding their eyes from the glare.

The same voice barked in Creole again.

The kids all dropped their rocks in a collective crash. The rocks rolled down the road, some thudding into Max's bare feet.

Max squinted into the lights. The voice was coming from above the row of floodlights.

The voice boomed again and the children scampered, a stampede of tiny, mostly bare feet ripping down the road, puttering away as fast as they could. Max saw them running through Pétionville's square, over a hundred of them. They would have torn him to pieces.

He heard the sound of a big engine turning over and saw twin sets of exhaust fumes rising up behind the lights, in the shape of upended pine trees. It looked like a military jeep. He hadn't even heard it coming.

The man's accent was straight-up English—not a hint of French or American in it.

Max felt the man looking down on him, at least a good extra foot taller. And he felt his presence—powerful, magnetic, and crushing—enough to fill a palace.

He came closer to Max.

Max looked but couldn't see his face.

The man reached down and grabbed the kid by the middle of his jacket and plucked him clean off the ground, as though picking up something he'd dropped and come back for. Max only saw his bare forearm—thickly veined and heavily muscled, bigger than one of Joe's biceps—and his fist—blunt and heavy and crude as a sledgehammer head. Max swore the man had six fingers. He'd counted five knuckles, not four, when he'd seen the hand bunch up the boy's suit jacket into a handle.

The man was a giant.

The overhead lights went out and the main ones flicked on, dazzling Max all over again. The engine kicked into action.

Max's vision regrouped in time to see the jeep reversing quickly down the hill. It reached the roundabout, turned left, and headed off down the road. Max tried to see the people inside but he couldn't make anyone out. From where he stood, it looked empty, driven by spirits.

DAME MARIE

BY MARILÈNE PHIPPS-KETTLEWELL

Dame Marie

(Originally published in 2007)

O n the morning I was leaving Port-au-Prince for Dame Marie, stopping through Jérémie, a mourning dove paused an instant below my window, and when it flew away, it dropped an underbelly feather that descended to the ground calmly like a large snowflake.

It was hot in the plane, so small that we had to bend down to get in and take our seats. During all of takeoff and a good while afterward, a red rooster in a cage stacked in the back with luggage kept screaming for glory, for the thrill, for the torment. The pilot smiled each time he heard it.

The singing of the rooster, however, made me think of the sounding of the bugle that I imagined Gustave heard so strongly in his heart when, in New York, he made the decision to change the course of his life—perhaps he hoped to change that of his countrymen as well—by joining the rebel groups. He must have heard it also when he said farewell to his family, over the phone with some, or over coffee as he did with Uncle Edward who tried to dissuade him.

The sound of the bugle must have been present still when he disembarked at night with his companions on the white beach at Petite Rivière de Dame Marie; also present when he saw that they had been abandoned by those who had trained them and that the thirteen others who were to join them with a greater stock of munitions ten days later did not appear over the water's surface or at the edge of the white sand where they had been expected; and still again present when the winds blowing strongly over the ocean saw him disappear toward the mountains to hide with his companions—one black man and twelve pale-skin mulattoes in a country of black people.

And at last, he must have recognized the now-familiar sound when he faced death in the mountains of L'Asile with the remainder of his companions, survivors of this retreat that was a two-and-a-half-month fight against government forces—finding himself discovered and finally out of munitions, he cried, "If we must die, let us die like brave men!" And, lacking bullets, he started throwing stones.

It is bullets, then, that killed him, not decapitation.

I have waited numerous years to learn that, years spent uselessly holding up under this weight lodged in the heart of memory, personal memory and family memory.

Years to suffer this image, the emotion, the anxiety over this other death by decapitation that we always thought had been his own because of the gruesome newspaper front-page photograph of his severed head that had publicized his capture.

But he is no less of a martyr, and is a political martyr for sure. But for me, and of greater importance still, he is a martyr of the faith, of *his* faith. I long thought of the day when I would stand on the beach at Dame Marie, holding a candle—humble luminary to celebrate the man with a great heart.

If it is true that one can weep eternally for a life that seems wasted, cut off too young at twenty-three, it is also true that there are hearts whose sensitivity is so great, so vibrant, so intensely impregnated by all of life's experiences, that their life is in fact, in its substance, infinitely richer, denser, more profound, and, in a way, longer because it is fuller.

I think of the internal journey that it must have been for Gustave, this last travel going from New York to L'Asile, stopping through Dame Marie. I see it as a rite of passage going toward what parcel of divinity he carried in him, a rite that would allow his giving birth to the Jesus of his being.

To come to Dame Marie by the road, leaving from Jérémie, means that one arrives from high up, over the hills. The church nests in the village under a vast, clear sky and shines like a pearl, first from afar and minute, then growing more and more at every turn of the road, down to the public square's small green garden on the coastal strip, at the edge of the blue sea.

So, I was finally standing on the white sands of the beach at Dame Marie. Under the midday sun, I held a votive candle for Our Lady of Perpetual Help. It would have burned seven days if winds allowed it—because winds always blow there, the same winds that would have pushed them, these thirteen companions, whipped them, caressed them, drunkened them, even.

I dug a small hole at the foot of a coconut tree so the candle would be stable and protected from the winds. I wedged it with sea rocks. I prayed with both the humility and presumption of prayer that requests and hopes for the well-being of the soul of the one we cherish and miss or for continued strength on its journey. But I mostly thanked Gustave for this great gift that he has made to us, his family.

More than of his life, he has made us the gift of his death. He taught us what death can offer life. Since Gustave, we carry in us this grand gesture he made of his death.

I don't think that either Uncle Edward or anyone else could have convinced him not to embark for his country. A man of great heart is forcibly a man of great dreams. Logic can do nothing against such men. A decision like the one he made does not come from the domain of reason: it comes from the most profound region of who he, Gustave, was; it is born out of a temperament that drags along with him the sensitive image of all that he has lived before he could arrive at that point, at that decision, and that pushed him to make it.

It would not have been possible to tell him, "You can neither avenge your father's death nor bring him back. Think of him who would not have wanted you to take such a risk. Think of your mother, think of yourself. This makes no sense—a handful of men cannot fight, and win, against a state."

To reason with him would not have been possible because what he was about to do was more profound than reason, more vast than vengeance, greater than himself: the call from the father was that of his soul. He found a unique moment in time that allowed him to act to the measure of his soul. Like all of us, he came on earth to surpass himself. Like very few of us, the élan in him was so strong that there was no need for a long life of dull repetitions, of meager satisfactions, vain and selfish, of reductive fears erected in the name of common sense, to finally be able to arrive, crawling and out of breath, at the foot of the Almighty.

It was standing up that Gustave presented himself to the Light.

Because he had a hero's soul.

In his *Imitation of Christ*, Thomas à Kempis wrote:

You are wrong, you are wrong if you seek anything than to suffer trials; for this whole mortal life is full of miseries and is marked on every side with crosses. The further a man advances in Spirit, so much heavier are the crosses he often finds, because the pain of his exile increases with his love . . . Great fruit and benefit will be his by the bearing of his own cross. For while he willingly submits himself to such trial, then all the burden of tribulation is turned into assurance of divine consolation . . . It is not the virtue of man, but the grace of God that enables a frail man to attempt and love that which by nature he abhors and fears.[1]

Hard to say how, in his childhood, Gustave knew where to glean examples and life experience that could fill and give shape to a soul with heroic appetite. Grandfather Jules acted as his father, and ours too in a way. I always had the feeling that my own father spent his life trying to live up to the bravery Grandfather showed during the First World War. For my father, no human qualities equaled the courage, loyalty, and righteousness exemplified in the character and lives of great soldiers. There is no doubt in my mind that, for Gustave the child, his grandfather, decorated with the Iron Cross, his father the colonel, and his uncles, even, were at some point *the* great men, the braves, the example to follow, the way.

One could also say that his grandmother, an ardent Christian, shaped his childhood. It is in his bedroom that she painted the life-size Saint Jude Thaddeus, patron of desperate causes, whose feet and hands I complained were too small while I watched her paint, thus making her laugh without feeling any compulsion to enlarge them. Her laughter cascaded in the air and fell like big water bodies that have unfathomable, unseen repercussions into the rock and deep in the earth; it slid down in waves along her great breasts, softened by age, until it finally went and lost itself in the large cove of her hips and belly, sitting as she was, her small legs opened up, spread

1. Thomas à Kempis, *Imitation of Christ*, bk. 2, ch. 12 (Zwolle, ca. 1418–1427).

out, the flowery blue cloth of her skirt pulled across the chair as is done by legs of old women who have become too fat and indifferent to their physical grace.

Gustave's laughter, on the other hand, as soon as it was carried out of his throat, which appeared to me then an unshakable column singularly marked at the disturbing point of his Adam's apple, seemed to be engulfed back down the same throat, descend all the way down his body to his feet, and die down at the earth wherefrom I would receive it, a small child, him so tall, teasing him about trivial things so he would laugh again—a child's stratagem that reveals the love felt and hides its embarrassment.

Gustave's bedroom was at the end of the hallway, straight down from the top of the stairs that I would sometimes silently crawl up to, like the Indian I imagined myself to be, in order to spy on our grandmother: she seemed large and anchored while she painted this emaciated Saint Jude whose eyes looked like two black embers in a bearded face. But actually, we were the ones who were being observed, by the gaze emanating from Gustave's portrait: a photograph hung over the little bed of all of Gustave's coddled childhood, showing Gustave in a US Army uniform, a man now, standing, his right hand resting on the airplane he flew, but his head and eyes looking toward us.

Grandmother gave away her Saint Jude to the Christ-Roi Church in Bourdon where we grew up. I imagine that someone hurried to put this painting in the oubliette, in a depot, because no one knew of its existence when I inquired about it a few skinny years later.

Now it is the example of Gustave-the-man that stands before us, before me. His gesture changed us and continues to transform and defy us while it lives within us. Without Gustave, we would have been different: we are who we are because Gustave was.

In his essay "Religion and Poetry," Paul Claudel wrote:

> *Religion did not just fill life with drama but it created at the end of it, with Death, the highest form of drama which, for any true disciple of our Divine Master, is found in sacrifice.*[2]

This, Gustave died to teach us. We would not do him justice and we would even be robbing ourselves of a precious gift we were bequeathed if we were not able to recognize this, admire him for it, and if we were afraid to remain as willing witnesses of a life that expressed its greatest dimension.

The town of Jérémie also remembers my cousin and godfather, and it is a face in mourning that it still bears today. Is it possible that it carries in its memory a living remorse that gnaws at and grinds its old walls, and covers them with the gray mood of a coat made from dust and refuse?

However dilapidated it has become, Jérémie still keeps its beautiful cemetery that glows on the hillside like a miniature Rome with its domes, arches, and porticos. The poet Émile Roumer is buried there.

One hears that men from Jérémie have pretensions to a kind of inspired singularity: they often succeed at it. It is one of those who, in the evening, at an Auberge Inn table, told me what he knew of Gustave's death, and this man, himself looking like a great grasshopper of a man wearing full clothes, and seen to fold his long, dry limbs over a din-maker of a motorcycle which he hangs onto like some insects do onto their wings;

---

2. Paul Claudel, "Religion et Poésie," in *Réflexions sur la poésie* (Paris: Folio Essais, Éditions Gallimard, 1963).

his high legs seem to want to make him trip over himself while he comes toward you; his hair is a fleece full of obstinate curls, white hills that start from the top of his forehead and follow one another all the way and out of sight around the curvy horizon of his head; of an eagle, he has the fixed stare: one eye that absorbs you because the man has passion, because he watches, and one eye that is no longer one but that continues to see the last image received, this eye said to have been lost at guerilla warfare of another people than ours.

He also told me about Roland's death, Gustave's father—pushed out of a plane above Jérémie's ocean. I learned about the entire Villedonne family's death—men, women, children, and the elderly, all of them gathered naked on the airport landing strip and machine-gunned. He showed me the Villedonnes' family house and talked about his childhood friends—the Sansonne, the Chavigny, the Drouet, and many more—because Gustave was not the only one whose family came from Jérémie.

In this Haitian country, history is passed orally from one generation to the next, whether it is religious history, familial, or political. At Dame Marie, an eighteen-year-old fisherman showed me the beach where the group of *guerilleros* had landed. He understood, having only overheard me pronouncing Gustave Villedonne's name, to which exact spot he needed to take me.

The sea appears to cover all, drag all to engulf all, and forget all. On a night of a full moon at a Grande Anse beach, winds push the waves until they come and topple over each other on the beach. The same sea that delivered Gustave to the shores of Dame Marie continues to edge this island as it did our lives.

Our lives go up high like waves for only a brief moment,

and then die down on the littoral. But they don't get wasted and lost there as we think—the sea takes them back, ebbs, and contains them. In its water's depth, the sea keeps the world's memory. This immensity where one would like to be dissolved, that attracts and frightens us, also allows us to touch God with the mind. Mystics say that what is below reflects what is above. In Haiti, popular belief has it that the world under the sea reflects all that is on earth. The journey underwater is a mystical voyage wherefrom one returns transformed and powerful. Sky, earth, and sea: maybe all that is but a single great canvas on which color zones touch each other without interrupting the thread. I do not know in which color zone Gustave now happens to live, but I know that he is nevertheless able to reach, and continues to touch my being in the zone where I find myself captive.

SURRENDER (EXCERPT)

BY MYRIAM J.A. CHANCY

Port-au-Prince Central Prison

(Originally published in 2010)

Early Afternoon, March 7, 2004

The moment of awakening reaches Romulus Pierre in the depths of the dank corner of a jail cell, surrounded by the stink of urine, of human and bestial feces ground into the dirt floors, with only a small square of light streaming in from a brick-sized opening up above that allows the prisoners to know when the sun rises and night falls. Some count off the days by etching lines into the pitted walls of the cell; others, without hope of ever being able to wake from the nightmare of their incarceration, let the days run one into another.

For Romulus, awakening comes in the form of muscle tremors, stomach spasms, and hallucinations. The tissues binding his muscle and cartilage hunger for an infusion of narcotics—cocktails of prescribed and illegal drugs—cocaine, heroin, antidepressants, uppers—anything he can get his hands on.

For one hundred and eighty-six days, his hands have had nothing to grasp in the regular schedule he has grown accustomed to—not the comforting smoothness of a small pink pill or the cool plastic cylinder of a needle case.

His hands roam the puckered and uneven walls next to his cot as he tries to grasp the outline of a face floating there, then they cling to his body frame when the convulsions shake him so hard that he feels the bones of his vertebrae lurch back and forth as if ready to leap from his body and leave the flesh behind.

In the span of the first weeks of his incarceration, once it was known who he was and why he was being held, some heady substances did find their way to the cell like the miracle of rain after a long drought. For a few days he was his old self again, bleary-eyed, smiling, stoned, feet on the ground, elbows on his knees, hands cavorting in the air above his thighs as they animated a story he told of his travels to a prisoner listening at his feet, while others turned away from his suffocating self-importance. They would defecate against the walls in silent protest as Romulus spoke. There wasn't much room for movement. There wasn't any room for heroics.

Romulus did not seem to notice the turned backs. He attended only to the face upturned toward his, as he spoke with authority of things he has seen, even as his tongue became thick and unintelligible, even as he lost track of the events in the tale he was telling and grew silent as the drug took over and left him dumb. He seemed only to notice the punctuated indifference of some of the men in the cell when the drugs leached from his system and left him, insomniac, craving more. He would have drunk his urine if there had been any privacy in the cell, in case the drugs were still lurking in the warm liquid. For him, these were desperate times.

When the doors of the cells are broken open, he has been sitting there in doubtful company for one hundred and eighty-six days. He has counted each and every one of these days without pencil and paper, without scratches on the wall. Any drug addict worth his salt needs to keep track of things like an eagle-sharp accountant, to count how many pills, how many possible hits, how many highs, and how many hours between, how many days to the next drop, the next payment, the next OD, the next stomach pumping, the next withdrawal, the next averted death. The minutiae of time becomes a science, a honed sequence of small events toward ecstasy, briefly experienced and furiously repeated over and over again in a frenzied pantomime that provides the necessary illusion of having a worthy goal. It functions like an ill-paid but time-consuming occupation; time, therefore, has to be made an ally. Not other people's time, mind you, but the time related to the ups and downs of addict life. Time is a relative invention and a good pal in the world of hallucinations and deprivation. It is all that will remain after the wives are gone, taking their children with them, gone with the friends bearing that look of disgust and despair on their righteous faces. Romulus can do without the lot of them. He thinks this even while imprisoned, surrounded by men he is sure have committed heinous acts against humanity and nature.

On the last of those one hundred and eighty-six days, even in the haze of his drug-addled mind, as an empty pocket of time forces him to think about those who once peopled his life, the stadium seats he'd filled with fans, the money he made from records that had gone platinum in the Caribbean and in Europe (he'd never tried to conquer the North American market: it was too vast, too fast, even for his adrenaline-driven life), Romulus has an uncommon realization. He lies there on his cot and grasps that beyond the drugs, beyond the hallucinations and the gripping nature of the loss of time, he has had no life whatsoever for at least twenty years.

It is a sad moment, an empty epiphany that someone of his intelligence should have deciphered earlier had he not been thinking of the next hit, the next score, the little bags of dust floating in his suitcases, many of which had mysteriously gone missing from his last transaction, which was why he found himself penned in between steel bars and an impacted floor of red dirt on his own native ground, a land which, some ten years prior, he had been forbidden by law to reenter. He had somehow forgotten about this pithy detail when he had agreed to smuggle the suitcase of cocaine past international borders.

When the doors are finally flung open by men in military garb, he is too sad to stand and walk out with the others who jubilantly jump up and down in the mucky excrement of the stall in which they have all been kept, brothers in criminal excess, many for longer than one hundred and eighty-six days. Romulus has sat there like a prince amongst his people, the only man with a cot to sleep on while the others slept rolled up in rotting blankets stinking of more than a hundred years of servitude. Romulus thinks that he is unlike the other jailed men. He has had money, position, fame. But, he has come to realize, by the time the doors creak open and the cries of *Libere, nou libere* go up, that he has thrown away his freedom for little more than year upon year of escape from reality.

Romulus sighs to himself and watches the men throwing themselves into the sunlight, their bodies floating, emblazoned by the light, the darkness they are leaving behind giving them form: dark angels spilling out into a fallen paradise.

Romulus thinks about the faces that have hovered above him throughout his time in the prison. They have been mostly women's faces. They speak to him, he is sure of this, but he is often unsure of what, exactly, they are saying. They seem to be as lost as he is, lost to time, in fantastic worlds of their own making. He sometimes wonders if they are the product of women hallucinating elsewhere in the world. He wonders if being in an altered state can make a person fall into another's dream. He likes this feeling of ambiguity. That and the floating feeling he experiences when taking the drugs make the trips worth it, like traveling without ever having to board a plane.

At times, the faces seems to prophesy great things that he has yet to do, though he is never sure what those things might be. It is just a feeling they give him, as if there are unexpected heights still to achieve, as if he could undo the train wreck that he has made of the last twenty years of his life. Other times, there are children in these hallucinations, but none look like the children he has fathered. All of them are white, or white-appearing.

He isn't sure that they should be trusted, those faces. After all, they have come to him in the throes of delusion. One apparition has been especially persistent, a woman with a long, pointy face, a white woman who resembles his first love, with skin so translucent beneath her eyes that he can see the filaments of a blue circuitry of veins. She hovers there, right above his head, whispering crazy pronouncements that Romulus does, in fact, understand, much to his surprise, even though she speaks in a language different from his own.

She speaks to him of rivers below the ground and spirit-dwellers who hide in hollowed trees and vales. She speaks of a landscape unfamiliar to his senses but he follows her there to a country so green it makes his Haiti seem like a heap of bones, a cemetery. She wants him to return to this forgotten place, this place of her first beginnings. He wants her to go away from the space above his eyes, a space gouged by many desperate fingers trying to find a way out. *Go there*, she whispers persistently, ignoring him, in the speech he can't quite place. They are almost mystical, these drug-induced delusions. Why would he ever stop? The only thing that *might* make him stop is the fact that he is afraid of this particular apparition. She makes him question his sanity. The more he sees her, the more he feels that he must be nearing his own pivoting point, walking a line he has crossed many times before with the aid of his many hallucinogens, a line between rationality and destruction, between the real and the fantastic.

He usually prefers the fantastic to anything else life might offer, even the first love of his life with her translucent skin and fine bone structure, her body so narrow that it labored to produce a first child, who then died in utero, and then contorted itself to produce a pale-as-roses son who survives still. He would be twenty or twenty-one, that first son. A full-grown man Romulus didn't even know, born in the years when he was still on the cusp of remaining in the real world. He had not quite been an addict then. But by the time the boy was three, he had already lost a sense of up and down. They had called him Christian.

She had taken everything, that first love. Her name was— is—Ellen. She had taken the house and the pool and the rights to the royalties from most of his early recordings. The apparition who looked so much like this first wife, who had been there even before he had a first wife, told him to forget such details in her strange tongue that made him think of the word *brogue*. As other faces receded into the wall, hers became more pronounced, coming and going like the fine breath of air that sometimes wafted in from the brick-sized opening up above.

In the end, Romulus did not have the strength to tell her to disappear. He closed his eyes instead and felt her hovering above him, penetrating the soft matter of his mind. He wished she would disappear when the pink pills found their way into his open palms, held out like a supplicant receiving communion after a long period of retreat and contemplation.

After a few weeks, the pills stopped coming. All he was left with was his slackening body, tired muscles, shortening sinews, sluggish blood, rattling bones and rattling teeth, hair falling out, skin flaking.

Romulus did not think that he could bear the periods of withdrawal, his muscles quivering intensely as if in shock.

To distract himself from his own failing form, he watched all the other bodies around him, defecating, peeing, peeling, brown skins turned to odd shades of dullness out of the sun's reach. Smiles turned to grimaces; folds of skin became grotesque as each of them lost weight. They were thrown dirty aluminum bowls filled with a greenish-brown slop once a day, if they were lucky.

He had never seen such shit.

For the first month, he waited for his sister to bring bowls of white rice with dark beans and a stew of chicken falling from the bone. For a time, he traded those meals for his drugs and then, when the pills ran out, he traded the food for his cot and quiet. His frame became lighter and the apparition resembling Ellen haunted his dreams.

L ap pèdi tèt li, the other men said of him when he would scream at the walls to leave him alone. They laughed at him under the cover of their thin arms and elongated fingers, looking day by day more like the figures of emaciated peasants Romulus had seen captured in the paintings that hung in his Miami houses. He laughed wryly to himself: he had become one of the figures in his own paintings.

She told him to forget about the paintings. He had work to do beyond these prison walls. A land to go to so far away from everything he had known, a history to resurrect. If only he would awaken.

Romulus struggled with her every night. His stomach

clenched at the sight of her. His dreams were polluted with her image, the sounds of her foreign tongue. She took him to her land so green it seemed touched by the hand of God. There, the skies hung low above the hills; the clouds embraced their roundness like the suckling child its mother's breast and threw shadows down like blankets of protection. Yet, in places, there were barren mounds without pasture, small crosses by the side of rocky roads weathering heavy rains to commemorate the dead.

Romulus could not understand it but he vowed to her that if he ever got out of this stinking hole of despair, away from the men whose humanity rotted steadily from within, if they hadn't already lost whatever shred of decency they had been born with—if ever he got out, he would go to this land, if she would only leave him alone after that, if she would only relent and let him regain his right mind.

He did not imagine, as he made this promise, that deliverance was already on its way. He had not imagined that he would ever again walk further than five paces forward and two to the right where he urinated against the wall every day, burning a hole of anger into the limestone, washing away someone else's trace of existence with each impotent outpouring, each erasing the other in a dark dance of expiation.

On the one hundred and eighty-sixth day of Romulus's captivity, deliverance arrived.

On that eighty-sixth day beyond the first hundred, Romulus sits on his pallet and looks out at the sea of legs and arms before him. The stink emanating from the walls and floor is at its worst. He has almost become immune to the shit, the constancy of anxious sweat rising from the serpentine, coiled bodies before him. And then, suddenly, the earth trembles beneath them. The doors are pried open and blinding light streams into the darkness.

Men wearing worn and mismatched army fatigues pull the thronged arms and legs out into the daylight. Romulus has his vision of dark angels in flight. He sits like a rock on the cot while the others precede him. He sees a dark arm hovering in the open space of the door, a space the length of a man, tall and broad, much larger than the brick-sized opening above they have all gotten used to for light. The arm motions in his direction. Romulus does not know if he can move. He closes his eyes and *She* comes to him.

Kanpe. He thinks he hears her tell him to stand up, as if all these days and nights of communication have taught her *his* language.

Kanpe, he hears again, but this time it is a man's voice. The dark arm gestures toward him.

Romulus rises and walks toward the light, knowing it could be the death of him. The prison doors have never been opened in all the time he has been there. No one has left. No one has entered. The cell has been filled to capacity with no hope of exit. It is the kind of thing one gets used to in Haiti.

Romulus realizes he is still alive when the heat of the sun hits his skin and the winds play with his tightly curled hair. The dark arm he has seen in the cell is attached to a burly man dressed in army fatigues. Romulus suppresses laughter: the man's head is topped with a red beret recalling scenes from Ramboesque American films.

It surprises him, the gurgling well of happiness in his chest, the desire to feel mirth rather than his stolid apathy. He looks away from the man in the red beret and the fake general turns from him and begins to exclaim to the company of men that they are all free. All the criminals and innocents, free.

Romulus begins to walk away from the jubilant, stinking men (for they are all men, young and old, well and decrepit, all shades of brown) as they scream their freedom to the blue canopy of sky, as if their deliverers are emissaries from the heavens rather than rogues in borrowed clothing.

Romulus walks away from the group with only one idea pulsing in his mind: to walk all the way through dust and fire, from the hell's edge of the prison walls and into the city's glowing inferno to reach its other side, to reach the roads leading out toward the country of his cursed birth.

March 7, 2004
Streets of Port-au-Prince

Romulus pursues his path with driven intent. *Focus,* he thinks, *focus.* He speaks to himself in a colonial tongue, a language he learned in order to get by in the world. Without it in America, *ou bannann*: no one with nowhere to go. You might as well be left hung out to dry, as the Americans liked to say, like a sheet of banana leaf.

As soon as he is out of the prison walls, and far enough away so that the men he had been jailed with cannot see him, Romulus begins to run, homeward, not thinking about who might be there to greet him, or if he will be welcome. He does not stop to think about his disheveled appearance, his sunken cheeks that make his eyes seem as if they are bulging out, frog-like.

He has lost many pounds in the prison, pounds he cannot afford to lose from an already slight frame. His shirt is torn in places, missing buttons. Still, he runs. How could his sister turn him away? Blood is blood, as his father had always said, despite his own lack of attention to matters of loyalty. Blood comes back to blood, always, like rivers to their beds.

There is an indescribable stench in the air. Romulus is used to the smells of rotting garbage, has gotten used to the putrid odor of disintegrating human waste. But what he smells in the air now is even more overwhelming than what he has endured in prison. His eyes trail the spumes of smoke rising from behind the crowded buildings on both sides of the road. He is startled, as he looks left and right, to see rubber tires piled high burning in the middle of what had been open roads.

In one alleyway, a car sits, torched, stripped of its tires, its windows smashed. Grocery stores that had been off-limits to the poorest of the poor stand looted, usually full shelves empty, products strewn on the floor rendered inedible. He falls into a sea of demonstrators, bodies pushing against him from all sides. As he wades through the crowd, he sees a charred body at the side of the road. The form is carbonized. He cannot tell if it is a man or a woman. What might have been an arm points upward, a black branch emerging from a charcoal trunk.

A few feet beyond the first corpse, another lies on the ground. Half of the man's face is smashed, stoned to death. An eye stares out at Romulus from its hollowed cavity, blood pooling out from the deep wound staining the broken cement of the road. Romulus winces. *Poor devil*, he thinks.

Romulus's run has slowed to a fast walk as he navigates the debris in the roads as best he can, avoiding the waves of demonstrators emptying from the houses of the *bidonville* and spilling out into the street. His mind reels at the thought of what has been going on outside the jail walls all this time. He has been safer in there than out here, he realizes, and wonders if there is anything to return to, any home left standing, if his sister is still alive.

"Romulus!" he hears his name called. He continues, thinking the voice is in his head. After all, hasn't he gone mad? He keeps on.

"Romeo!" the voice calls again, more insistent, distinct. It is a man's voice and Romulus realizes then that it is coming from beyond him, from the direction he has just left.

He tries to keep on but as his feet move forward, his head turns back. He walks forward like an ostrich, his feet moving, his long neck peering over his shoulder, his eyes too curious to stay on course.

In the moment of turning his head, Romulus has the sensation of energy slipping away from his being. The feeling is like a small wave washing over him. It leaves a tingling in its wake and a sense of foreboding, of loss. But Romulus cannot fathom what it is that he could be losing, though he knows it has everything to do with this moment of turning around, with the need to hear his name called out more pronounced than his desire for freedom.

"Romeo," the voice says again, using his stage name to good effect. Romulus sees the lips of a square-jawed face mouthing his name. The man's high cheekbones seem to be holding up great folds of skin that embrace his chin in a swath of thickness. The folds stretch and tremble as he speaks. "Romeo, brotherman, where are you going?"

Romulus thinks about his sister's house out in the country cradled by those of neighbors they have known all of their lives who had practically raised them both out of the crib. He looks at the man who towers over him, thick and elongated cords of muscle binding his arms and legs. Romulus recognizes the man from the meeting in Miami that had led him home and then to prison. He remembers that the others had called him Marc or Marco. Romulus had never considered that he would run into him again.

Marc advances toward him, all muscled power. Romulus regrets having stopped. Marc is bad news. Romulus knows he is going to be swept away into something beyond his control and yet he stands still, refuses to turn away. He should keep on walking but he is used to being swept up. It has become a way of life. Romulus tries to think of the fact that Marc knows him only as a first-class junkie, not as the person he has become in the prison: swept clean, penniless, with only the shirt on his back to show for wealth. He has to maintain the coolness of intent he had had in that meeting in Miami when he had been wearing a designer suit and worn dark glasses to cover up the fact that he had been high even as he had made a deal with people he had never been involved with in his life as a musician, people who were far below him in the food chain of Haitian life.

Marc's face does nothing to promote trust, with the jagged scar that runs down the length of his left cheek, as if thunder had visited him there and felt his flesh wanting.

Still, Romulus moves toward the man as if he might present salvation. The truth is simply that the fear of returning to a place he can no longer legitimately call home has taken stronger root than the desire to continue running toward the place his youth remembers. He does not realize yet that he is running, nonetheless, from one hell to another. Sometimes, one hell was sufficiently different from another to seem like a worthwhile reprieve.

"*Sa k pase?*" Romulus asks, forgetting without truly forgetting the chaos surrounding them, the burning pyres of car tires, the crowd emptying into the streets chanting, *Libète, libète*—a rallying cry not heard for years.

The mantra of the dispossessed had escaped ready defi-
nition over the years as the times changed: leaders fleeing
and returning while the masses remained prisoners to a land
once rich, a land rich still with the echoes of their ancestors'
knowledge, their murmurs sounding out in the barren hills,
imitating the cries of children at their births. Some of them
had no intention of ever leaving. They watched those who
left and returned with mirth, sometimes with condescension.
Journalists mistook the hard glints in their eyes for murderous
envy while their anger festered for expression. Most of them
simply wanted their piece of land, their corner of the universe beneath the benighted stars promised to them after the
Revolution. They were frustrated by the constant denial. This
time, it was for their children that they abandoned shacks and
stands, some of the wealthy at long last joining them in solidarity to announce that the future might be different—that
the next generations might not have to survive in misery. It
was a wonder, really, Romulus thinks, that the masses had any
energy left at all.

"*Ki bagay sa a! Yo lage kò ou nan la ri a? Ou pa gen limouzin
ou?*" Marc laughs a wide laugh, baring red-gummed teeth, and
sweeps a large hand through the air as if to show an invisible
limousine. His head tips backward, forcing the muscles of his
wide neck into half-moon arcs that form an elongated v-shape
emanating from the clavicles of his collarbone and ending just
below each ear on both sides of his jaw. His laughter ripples
out in waves, making passersby heading out to join the dem-
onstration frown in wonder at this merriment. These are difficult times, after all.

Romulus feels only shame rising up from his solar plexus
like bitter bile, shame for the loss of his past fortune, shame
for the loss of the meaning of his family name. He keeps to

himself that he had been heading to his sister's home.

He walks toward Marc and feels, suddenly, for no reason at all, as if he might be letting go of his past forever. It is a feeling not unlike the snap and spin in his head when he flirts on the edge of an OD, a hair's breadth away from the black abyss of non-return.

He should never have turned around.

Romulus had known moments like this before, moments in which the past seemed to recede and the future seemed like a wide, open pit before him in which, without a care, he could fall headfirst. He had learned that the feeling was deceptive. There was nothing but the present with which to contend. Yet, he knew that what one decided to do could alter one's life so irrevocably that one would want to go back and undo each of those moments as if they were knots on a string. Sometimes, he'd made decisions that altered not only his own life but the lives of those for whom he cared—his wives, his children, his bandmates.

Romulus was an expert at leaving things and people behind as he moved forward. He was like the children in the fable of Hansel and Gretel, leaving houses and cars in his wake as the children had left morsels of bread when they walked through the forest. For Romulus, waiting at the end of the path, in the blistering heat of the witch's oven, was the anger and disappointment he engendered in others and would do everything to avoid. It never occurred to him that others did not see him as an innocent in a hostile world, but as the witch herself, hidden in the woods, waiting to strike. Deep down, as destructive as he was to himself and to others, he sought to be found. It was this yearning that delivered him to Marc, even though Marc's smile was no more convincing than a scorpion's.

"Ou ta prale?" Marc asks with false caring.

Romulus feigns ignorance of his motives and smiles sheepishly. Marc wraps a thick, seemingly protective arm around Romulus's diminished frame.

"E ou menm?" he asks Marc while he thinks of the last time someone had put an arm around him. His thoughts vaguely drift to Brigitte, his third and last wife, the only one who had looked nothing like the woman who appeared in his dreams, who persisted her haunting in his hallucinations.

It had been Brigitte who had prompted Romulus's illegal return to Haiti by locking him out of his own house. If it hadn't been for that, Romulus would *never* have agreed to become a carrier. He would *never* have seen Marc standing in the darkness of a room that contained some of the key figures involved in drug trafficking across Haiti's borders. He *never* would have found himself, now, with this fiend's thick arm around his shoulders. It wasn't his fault.

"Ou pral wè," Marc says as the two are encircled by a group of young men Romulus has mistakenly assumed to be on their way to the march, heading toward the square in front of the Presidential Palace where the statue of the unknown slave stands blowing his eternal bronze conch shell as if mocking them.

Freedom. Emancipation. These were words that had lost their meaning.

Romulus no longer knows the country well enough anymore to identify the group ferrying him along under the protection of Marc's heavy dark arm. He feels suddenly like a child, captive and subservient, afraid of what might happen if he chooses to break away, running, again, toward home or what was left of home. In Miami, he had heard about the paramilitaries dressed from head to toe in futuristic-looking black gear that seemed so anachronistic in a Haiti that still appeared almost medieval. As a child he had resented this more than anything. He had wanted to be a part of the modern world he saw advertised in the French press and on the news beamed in from the outside world. He yearned for the pleasures recounted by uncles who floated in and out of the country with unceasing levity, thick gold rings and bracelets shackled to their fingers and arms like spoils of war. These were uncles who fell beyond the circle of his mother's approval. Romulus had to seek them out on his own, surreptitiously. They were dangerous men, men who had links to the government, if one could call it that, men who talked of themselves as existing beyond the laws of any land and seemed successful in doing so. Romulus had wanted to be one of the anointed, not dangerous per se, but certainly beyond the law. He had learned that wealth was the key to obtaining this sort of dubious freedom. For him, music had been the way.

They walk against the flow of the crowd, lost in it for long stretches, and then they are suddenly alone, heading up into the hills above the capital where the houses of the rich gleam like white and pink shells rising fresh from the ocean bed. Romulus begins to feel nervous. He knew these homes well once. He had even owned one. There were relatives and friends of his father's who lived there still. What did these men want? He had heard of the *chimères* spreading panic in their wake. He had heard of the kidnappings and ransoms demanded of the wealthy or *dyasporas* like himself. Returning *dyaspos* were always surprised by such events. They did not realize that what was survival elsewhere constituted wealth here, that for those on the ground they had become part of the elite, however Black they might be.

Romulus wonders again what he has gotten himself into.

This is a rare thought for him, one that surely stems from his sobered state. For the first time, Romulus begins to understand the root of his addiction: his fear of being forgotten. He craves recognition of any kind. This is what has brought him within the fold of this unlikely group, men clad in discarded Nike-wear from the factories, brightly colored short-sleeved shirts and baseball hats advertising Canadian baseball teams. He has been brought amongst them by his fear of refusal at his sister's door. But as he feels his legs grow leaden while they make their way in convoy to the upper reaches of Lalue, it is a new fear that grips him, the fear of harming, in full consciousness, one of his own.

Romulus wonders if he is imagining the heaviness growing from Marc's encompassing arm dropping into his body like poisonous lead. He wonders when and where the journey will end. Some of the men are speaking in low whispers to each other while they look ahead, determination outlined in their posture and in the straight-ahead doggedness of their heads, eyes fixed on the goal lying before them, in those hills that still sing with green bursts of color, unlike so many of the bare mountain ranges that ring the city.

They pass tall wall after tall wall, some topped with coils of barbed wire, others with the more colonial lines of jagged broken bottles: green, amber, and clear, cemented to the top of the walls. Romulus recognizes his old house and cringes as they pass it. He does not own it any longer and doesn't know who lives there now. They pass the UNICEF headquarters and its half-mooned entrance filled with a line of high-end jeeps. It is surprising, even to someone of Romulus's background, to note how well-equipped their saviors are. The men point at the jeeps and comment. There is laughter in the ranks for the first time. And then, a few houses later, Marc's arm stops propelling Romulus forward and falls away. It is the moment that Romulus has been waiting for, to breathe again, but his stomach is clenched. They are in front of a house he knows all too well.

Marc smiles upon seeing the light of recognition of Romulus's eyes and the men move forward in unison. Unlike the other houses, the portal to this one has been left unlocked. The men move one by one in an organized single file past the gates and stumble into the yard. There is a familiarity in their movement. Romulus feels as if he is experiencing his own, disturbing *déjà vu*.

Romulus feels his hand on the vined gates as he follows Marc and the other men into the yard. His hand has performed this action before, pushed the gate open confidently and ushered himself into another world, a world so unlike the broken and sullen streets that greeted him daily like so much useless ash. He has walked down the flat white slabs shaping a snake-like path to the front door, through the lush flowers of the manicured front garden, his leather school bag bouncing up and down the length of his right thigh. He had come all the way from the private school for boys he attended in the city, brought to the hills in a tap-tap, when such service had been available and reliable, the streets not so far gone as to need American technology to be tackled. Now, there are no black-speckled orange lilies craning their necks toward the path, nor the pink leaves of fallen bougainvillea strewn across the stones, making a scratchy, papery noise as the wind lifts them away, nor are there roses in full bloom, their heady perfumes letting him know that more treasures lay ahead behind the heavy oak door of the house.

If Romulus had paused to think about love over the years,

in the absence of his mother's arms, and in the silence that enveloped his father's occasional appearances in his life after he had left home at sixteen, he would have remembered his times in this house as defined by such a thing. But since love had so far eluded him, like a glass vase kept out of grasping hands on a high shelf in his grandmother's house, he could not attach the word to the place. He could, though, feel warmth enveloping his chest as he moved forward across the stones that had been reshaped by the many feet that had rubbed away their harshness and left behind grooves telling of movement and hospitality. The owner of the house was as retiring as she was welcoming and only the stones revealed how many guests had quietly and ceaselessly beaten a path to her door. Was this what the men before him were doing? Had done already, in another time? Romulus could only wonder. They seemed so out of place, so ungainly, so unrefined. The owner of the house is nothing if not refined.

If love is not the word that came to mind when Romulus thought about this house and its once lush gardens, it is another word that pronounces itself a close synonym to his mind and in his memory: *music*. It had been here, amongst the sound of the bougainvillea flowers scraping past his feet, the rosebushes, and the tall, wild grass, that he had begun to understand the meaning of the word *symphony* and the conjoining of sound and scent to create a language that only the spirit and heart might be able to decipher.

She had been his piano teacher, and for a time, in his adolescent years, the years before he had drifted away into the fog of chemically induced visions, his muse. She had been the first woman he had loved without recognizing the feeling as love, and left, never to see her again, as his mother had left him some forty years before, without a trace. It dawned on him fleetingly that he himself was the trace his mother had left behind: the thought gave hollow comfort.

Although it had been the murmur of something akin to love that Romulus had felt then for Tatie Ruth, the owner of this house, Romulus had had no designs on the woman to whom he would dedicate his first songs and empty pop lyrics. He barely took note of the fact that Tatie Ruth had been in her thirties when he had taken lessons from her, still a relatively young woman. He had taken no notice of the curvature of her bare legs shaped by long walks in the mountains when the air was clear and crisp, legs that spindled out from beneath her skirts like the long stems of the most hardy of flowers. She would adjust a thin sweater on her shoulders, push back her reading glasses, and peer over his head at the notations on the weathered sheet music she allowed him to take home so that he could continue to practice, either at the home of the uncle with a piano, or in the large hall at school where gatherings were held on holidays of the Catholic calendar. In those days, he had no knowledge or interest in the female form, or perhaps Tatie Ruth had simply seemed beyond the reach of his eleven years. He kept all of his energies for the music, as if he was an athlete in strict training, remembering only much later how inebriated and inspired he had been by the pollen of flowers in the garden, by the whiff of Tatie Ruth's thick French perfume.

It is this sensory memory that strikes him as he walks into the foyer, the tiles radiating cold, stunning him into his past, his beginnings, a time that had been so innocent and free of all the madness that followed on its heels.

"*Sa n ap fè la?*" he asks Marc. "*Ou konnen Tatie?*" he continues, a childish innocence punctuating his words.

Marc leaves the questions hanging in the air and gestures

to the others to take their positions. He sweeps Romulus back toward the front door.

"*Sa k gen la?*" a thin, reedy voice wafts in from the back of the house. Tatie Ruth. Even after all these years, Romulus recognizes her distinctive Creole. *Soigné.* Careful and peppered with French intonations. She would be in her late seventies by now, aging, skin and bones made heavy by the pull of gravity.

Marc signals Romulus to speak. The men are positioned in the darkness of the receding perimeter of the round foyer like foxes circling a chicken coop. He hesitates. Marc gestures more emphatically. This is no rehearsal. What has he gotten himself into?

"Tatie," Romulus begins, "Romulus *ki la, wi.*"

"Romulus!" she exclaims, voice quivering slightly, emotion audibly catching in her throat. He hears her moving hurriedly through the halls of her house to the foyer. "You came back."

He sees confusion in her face.

"Are you back at the house?" she asks, referring to his old house up the road, the one he had once lived in with Ellen. He had hardly seen Ruth during the two years he had lived there, trying unsuccessfully to end the drug habit that eventually destroyed the marriage.

Romulus has no answer for her. He becomes suddenly self-conscious of his attire, of the soft layers of dust clinging to his perspiring skin. The heat is suffocating. He feels tired, wan. What can he be doing here? Why this, the gathering place? He has the impulse to tell her to run back, run back, to keep out of sight, but he knows it is too late. He is always too late.

"They let you out?" she asks, her voice weak.

"*Wi*," he says finally, because there is nothing else he can say. How did she know? Did everyone know? "Yes. They let me out. I'm out."

She emerges on one of the arcs leading from the foyer to the rest of the house. There are three such arcs. She stands in the hollow of the farthest to his right, the men forming a half-circle in the dark. She is still slightly too far away to see them all gathered there, foxes in the den.

Go back, back, Romulus thinks, hoping she will turn and ask him to follow her to another part of the house, perhaps to the back kitchen for a strong cup of *café.* Then he could tell her about Marc and the men and the need to find shelter in her yard, or elsewhere.

But she stands there like a ghost, waiting for him to speak, and Romulus realizes that she has been waiting for a long while, although he is not so sure that she has been waiting for him in particular. Does she already know what is about to happen? She must have heard about the jails being opened by the rebels.

"I'm sorry," she says, "It's just that . . ."

"*Je sais,*" he responds, feeling the rush of shame travel up the length of his neck.

She has lost nothing of her mystique with her wide robes and flower-print dresses. She is stooped slightly and grasps her back with one hand against the pain radiating there to her right hip. Her hair is held back in a tight bun and though they stand some fifteen feet and years apart, he can smell her perfume more strongly than ever, making him wonder at the clarity of his pre-addict memories. They are both like ghosts standing before each other, each remembering the other as they had been in another life, incredulous over the changes that time has wrought. Still, they cannot see each other clearly.

The foyer is dimly illuminated by light streaming in from the arcs. There are no windows here. Romulus can make out a table in the center of the room, a walnut table with a sturdy clubfooted stand. A thick plastic sheet seems to cover the surface of the table.

He would think later that this was an odd detail to note at the time—the thick plastic covering nothing like the delicate embroidery that usually graced Tatie Ruth's tabletops, embroidery she taught the young girls who were hired help in the neighborhood to make, so they would have some kind of a trade. He sees the photographs beneath the plastic, his much younger face staring up at him, as if looking at a stranger. What a failure he must be in her eyes, Romulus thinks, forgetting for the moment the men hidden in the shadows. What a failure.

Then, simultaneously, as if propelled by an invisible shift in gravitational pull, they advance toward each other. Romulus stands closer to the table with its plastic covering. He can see now that the plastic keeps a series of photographs locked in place beneath its weight. Tatie Ruth advances into the circle of awaiting men. He thinks that he sees her smile at them in recognition, a smile quickly dissolving into apprehension.

Their eyes catch and Romulus senses that he is being forgiven his betrayal. Tatie Ruth smiles again quietly, sadly, and then makes a small circular gesture of hand tight against her waist as if to say to them, *Come, come, I have been waiting for you.*

Later, only minutes later, minutes that seem to stretch into an unbearable knowledge of infinity, Romulus falls into a black hole of amnesia, a temporary blackout that will help him to survive the day as he has survived so many others. This time, however, he is sober and he still cannot believe the sight before his eyes: was it she who had fallen, or he? Was it Marc who had used the machete or one of the skinny young men in the troupe too impatient to wait to be led through the house's many halls to a treasure they must have assumed lay beyond? Was it their feet he heard running back up the path, leaving the front door wide open so that light inundated the dark foyer suddenly, like a blast of thunder in a storm, or was it he himself fleeing the scene? Had it been his fourteen-year-old face that he saw looking expectantly up from a jaggedly trimmed black-and-white photograph beneath a now blood-streaked clear, plastic tablecloth, he standing amidst the bougainvillea in the garden in his Sunday best, sheet music in his hand? Was that his smile as a twenty-four-year-old, cut from a newspaper and placed next to a picture of a young woman who eerily resembled his visitor in prison, that peaked face hovering above him on the walls? Picture upon picture: brown, yellow, peach-complexioned faces—a map of Tatie Ruth's inner world laid out as if she was afraid that she would forget them all, or that the disappearance of the actual people from her hall meant they would never return. There, too, was a photograph of an unsmiling Marc in short pants, exposing knobby knees, skinny fingers poised over piano keys.

In this way, she kept them captive to the echoes of another world that reverberated with music and laughter, sounds she hardly heard anymore, sounds replaced with the ringing of bullets and cries of despair and a silence all the more piercing for its meaning: the absence of love.

Blood speckles the bright faces and white teeth. *Was it hers or his?* There is a wild rush of sound in his ears, making a small whoosh as the liquid particles hit the solid surfaces in random syncopation. He's heard the sound before, usually before landing on the ground after a particularly bad hit. This time, he has to remember his sobered state. It is difficult to mark a difference. He wonders if he has ventured close to death. *His own? Hers?*

The pictures beneath the plastic look up at him, furiously, as if he could have stopped the chaos. It is vertiginous to peer down at so many faces and to feel the sensation of falling toward some unknown depth.

As Romulus's body convulses in a cold sweat against the clamminess of the linoleum floor, he hears some of the men walk through the house under Marc's supervision. They seem unable to uncover the treasure they have sought.

He hears them scramble and swear beneath their breaths. *We shouldn't have killed her so fast,* one of them says. He hears them curse him as they step over his body on their way to other parts of the house. Romulus cannot open his eyes. He cannot move. For a moment, he thinks he hears her call out his name. He thinks he can see her in his mind's eye, but he cannot move toward her, cannot embrace her. It is too late. All he wants to do is lie there and let life seep out of him. He is a coward too, not wanting to see what has already been done to Ruth. He cannot think ahead to what might happen to him if he is found there, in a house turned upside down with bitterness, a woman's dead body lying not far from him. His body aches; his mind feels on fire. He cannot move. He could be dying. He lets his mind drift away from his body, from the house, from the other men. He thinks about his childhood, his absent mother and brooding father. He wonders how it could all have been different.

He dares not open his eyes. He does not want to see the sight of blood, his own or another's. He does not want to see the ghost's face mocking him for his cowardice or Ruth's frozen in disbelief at what he has become.

The only thing Romulus can be sure of as he feels his body run cold and slick with sweat, before his head comes in contact with the ground, rendering him unconscious, is that he had not heard her scream her surrender or her pain. All he hears as he falls is a throbbing silence in the house and the muted sound of field crickets emanating from somewhere beyond.

THINGS I KNOW ABOUT FAIRY TALES

BY ROXANE GAY

Cité Soleil

(Originally published in 2011)

When I was very young, my mother told me she didn't believe in fairy tales. They were, she liked to say, lessons dressed in fancy clothes. She preferred to excise the princesses and villains and instead concerned herself with the moral of the story.

Once upon a time, not long ago, I was kidnapped and held captive for thirteen days. Shortly after I was freed, my mother told me there was nothing to be learned from what had happened to me. She told me to forget the entire *incident* because there was no moral to the story.

Little Red Riding Hood didn't see the danger she was facing until it was too late. She thought she was safe. She trusted. And then, she wasn't safe at all.

My husband Michael and I, while visiting my parents in Port-au-Prince, decided to take our son to the beach for the afternoon. As we backed out of their long, narrow driveway, three black Land Cruisers surrounded us. In the end, the details of the *incident* were largely irrelevant. What was done could not be undone.

On that day, Michael and I looked at each other. We knew what was happening. Kidnapping is all anyone with any kind of money talks about in Haiti, everyone in a fragile frenzied state wondering when it will be their time. It was a relief, in a sense, to know that my time was up—to know that this was the day I would be taken.

Two men with dark, angry faces broke the car windows with the butts of their rifles. The man on my side reached through the broken glass, unlocked my door, and pulled me out of our car. He sneered at me, called me *dyaspora* with the resentment that those Haitians who cannot leave hold for those of us who did. His skin was slick with sweat. There was no place for traction. When I tried to grab onto the car door, he slammed the butt of his gun against my fingers. The man on Michael's side hit him in the face and he slumped forward, his forehead pressed against the horn. They put a burlap sack over my head and shoved me into the backseat of one of the waiting cars. They told me, in broken English, to do as they said and I would be back with my family soon. I sat very still. The air was stifling. All I heard was their cruel laughter, my son crying, and the fading wail of the car horn.

My father is fond of saying that a woman's greatest asset is her beauty. Snow White had her beauty, and her beauty was her curse until it became her greatest asset.

Before the *incident* my mother and I often had frank conversations about being kidnapped. She was always very concerned with the logistics of the thing because she's a woman of manners and grace. It's the kind of quotidian conversation you have in a place where nothing makes sense and there is no respect for life. She told me she wouldn't be able to survive the indignity. I told her she would have to do whatever was necessary to get through it because we needed her. As I sat between two angry men, being jostled as we sped over the broken streets of Port-au-Prince, I remembered that conversation. I realized my arrogance.

Sleeping Beauty was cursed by her birthright, by her very name. In one telling, her fate was sealed by Maleficent before she ever had a chance. Even hidden away, she could not escape the curse placed upon her.

I couldn't take it personally, being kidnapped. That is what I told myself. It was a business transaction, one that would require intense negotiation and, eventually, compromise. One of the accountants who worked for my father, Gilbèrt, was kidnapped the previous year. His kidnappers originally asked for $125,000, but everyone knew it was simply a starting number, an initial conversation. Eventually, with professional assistance and proof of life, his family paid $53,850 for Gilbèrt. My negotiations would be somewhat more complex and far more costly. A good family name comes at a high price.

After the first days of my abduction, when negotiations began in earnest, I understood that the money my family would pay for my safe return was not for me. It was for the daughter, wife, mother they had last seen. I had become a different person entirely. It seemed, somehow, unfair for them to not get what they were paying for.

After the *incident*, when Michael and I returned to the States, a throng of reporters greeted us, waiting just past the crowded, suffocating Customs area in the Miami airport. Reporters lined the street where we lived. They followed us for weeks until a white woman went missing and then my story no longer mattered.

The thing about Rapunzel was that she had the means to her own salvation all along. If she had only known that, she would have never been cast out by the enchantress and been forced to wait to enjoy her ever-after with her prince.

My family hired an American firm that specializes in negotiating for US citizens who have been abducted abroad. They were efficient. Within twenty-four hours, they had demanded proof of life. I was able to call my husband from a disposable cell phone. I said hello. At first, it was a relief to hear his voice, to remember his smile, the softness of his lower lip, the way he always wanted to hold my hand. But then he started blathering about how I was going to be okay and that he was going to do everything in his power to get me back. I hung up because he was lying and he didn't know it.

Although my kidnapping was a business transaction, my captors enjoyed mixing in pleasure at my expense. I fought, but I also begged them to use condoms. I did what I had to do. Worse things could have happened. I was not broken. That's what I tell myself now, when I close my eyes and see their white teeth leering at me. It's what I tell myself when I smell their stink and their sweat or remember the weight of their thin, sinewy bodies on top of mine, taking things that weren't theirs to take. It's what I tell my husband when he thinks he wants to know what *really* happened. It is mostly true.

My parents' friend, Corinne LeBlanche, was kidnapped not long before I was taken. She and her husband and four children lived in Haiti year round. She always swore, to anyone who would listen, that if she were ever kidnapped, her husband Simon best meet her at the airport with her passport and children once she was returned because she would never spend another night in the country. Simon was a fat, happy, prominent businessman who owned a chain of restaurants and gas stations that did quite well. He laughed when Corinne made such declarations. He didn't yet understand that these things went differently for women. She and the children now live in Miami. She called me when Michael and I returned to the States. Even though we said very little, we spoke for a long time.

My kidnappers took me to a small two-story house without air-conditioning in a cramped neighborhood on the outskirts of Cité Soleil. They kept me in a back room furnished with a small cot and a green paint bucket filled with brackish water. Throughout the day, I could hear children playing on the street below, music from a house nearby, a car now and again, the occasional gunshot. I didn't scream or try to escape. There would be no point. Anyone I might run to would just as soon take me for themselves rather than rescue me, because compassion wasn't as valuable as *une dyaspora*.

Two years ago, the matriarch of the Gilles family was kidnapped. She was eighty-one. The kidnappers knew the family had more money than God. They failed to realize she was frail and diabetic. She died soon after she was abducted. Everyone who knew her was thankful that her suffering was abbreviated, until the kidnappers, having learned the lesson that the elderly are bad for business, kidnapped her grandson, who at thirty-seven promised to be a far more lucrative investment.

At least Cinderella had her work to keep her busy—the familiarity of sweeping floors and washing windows and cooking the daily bread. If nothing else, because she had truly suffered she could appreciate her ever-after.

What you cannot possibly know about kidnapping until it happens to you is the sheer boredom of being kept mostly alone, in a small, stifling room. You start to welcome the occasional interruption that comes with a meal or a bottle of water or a drunken captor climbing atop you to transact some pleasure against your will. You hate yourself for it, but you crave the stranger's unwanted touch because the fight left in you is a reminder that you haven't been broken. You haven't been broken.

Beauty learned to love the Beast. She forced herself to see

past the horror of his appearance, past his behavior, past the circumstance of how they came to know one another.

On the tenth night, Ti Pierre lies next to me, staring at the ceiling. He tells me his name, after he's had his pleasure and I've had my fight. His skin is caked beneath my fingernails and my body is stiff. A bruise is forming along my jaw. I cling to the edge of the bed, trying to create as much distance as possible between our bodies until I regain the energy to fight, to remind myself that I am not broken. Ti Pierre talks to me about his life, his young son, how he wants to be a nightclub deejay because he loves American hip-hop music. "We could be friends, maybe," he says, "We are close in age." I roll onto my side and bite my knuckles. He rests a tender hand on my back and I cringe, repulsed. It is the closest I will come to crying. These are the things I will never tell anyone.

At a dinner party once, with some of my colleagues and some of Michael's and lots of wine and music and excellent food and pretentious but engaging conversation, talk turned to Haiti. Everyone leaned forward in their seats, earnest in their desire to be genuine in their understanding of the world. One of my colleagues mentioned a magazine article he read about how Haiti had surpassed Colombia as the kidnapping capital of the world. Another colleague told us about a recent feature in a national magazine. Soon everyone was offering up their own desperate piece of information, conjuring a place that does not exist.

On the fourth day of my captivity, I thought about that silly evening, and the new bits and pieces my friends were adding to their portrait. Three years later, I would overhear one of these colleagues, trying to be charming at a cocktail party, telling a precocious graduate student that he knew someone who had been kidnapped in one of *those* third world countries.

When I walked by, he wouldn't have a strong enough sense of shame to look away. Instead, he would tip his wine glass in my direction before taking a long sip and continuing to regale his audience with the few lurid details he knew.

My kidnappers and my family's negotiators finally came to an agreement on the thirteenth day. My kidnappers shared the news gleefully. I could hear them in the next room, talking about all the things they were going to do with their money. Their plans were modest, really, which made it all so much worse. They wielded cartel-like precision, and for a long while the only sound I could hear was the bills sliding against each other as they were counted into $1,000 stacks. This is what my worth sounds like, I thought. How lucky I am.

A Cuban friend once told me of a popular lullaby from her country, about a mother with thirteen children. The mother kills one child to feed twelve, and so on and forth, until she is left with one child, whom she also slaughters. Finally, she returns to the middle of a cornfield where she slaughtered the other children, and slits her own throat because she cannot bear the burden of having done what needed to be done. After telling me this story, my Cuban friend said, "A West Indian woman always faces such choices."

When my kidnappers were satisfied that I had been properly bought and paid for, I was cleaned up, shoved into the back of the Land Cruiser, and dropped off in the center of an open market in Pètionville. I stood there in what remained of my shirt and my filthy jeans, my feet bare, my hair a mess. My hands were in my pockets, my fingers clenched into tight fists. I stood there and waited. I tried to breathe. I was not broken. I remember these details more than any others. Around me, men and women haggled over chicken and vegetables and water and corn flakes and radios. I was invisible, until

I wasn't—until I heard my husband shout my name and run toward me with a group of men I didn't recognize. As Michael moved to embrace me, I stepped back. His expression, in that moment, I also remember. "You're safe now," he told me, as if he understood the meaning of the word.

Alice had choices in Wonderland. Eat me, drink me, enjoy tea with a Mad Hatter, entertain the Queen of Hearts, down, down the rabbit hole.

I didn't speak for hours, not when I saw my parents or my child, who patted my cheeks with his chubby, wide-open hands. I took a long shower. I washed my hair and tried to scrub away the stink and sweat that comes with being trapped in a dark, hot place with strange angry men. Michael came into the bathroom to check on me, and when he saw the bruises, the weight I had lost, the bowed frame of my body, he gasped. I wrapped my arms around my body. "Get out," I hissed. "I'm not broken."

Afterward, I took my soiled clothes to the fire pit behind my parents' house and smoked cigarette after cigarette while I watched the clothes burn. For years, I had hidden my smoking from my parents, told them I'd quit, but this lie no longer seemed necessary. We ate dinner together that evening, as a family, acid burning my throat with each bite. Everyone watched me intently. I smiled politely, tried to give them what they needed.

In bed that night, Michael lay on his side, watching me as I sat on the edge of the bed. "When you're ready to talk, I'm ready to listen," he said. His tone was so kind it made me nauseous. I wanted to tell him that I wasn't the woman he married, that I knew things now. Instead, I nodded and kissed his shoulder. After he fell asleep, I slipped next door into the room where Christophe slept. I picked him up, inhaled the scent of soft skin, and sat on the floor, watching as his lower lip quivered and his tiny chest rose and fell with his rapid baby breaths.

My husband found me the next morning, asleep on the floor holding our son. "You don't have to be so strong. You can cry," he said over breakfast, as if I were waiting for his permission. I didn't know how to tell him that I felt nothing at all. I held myself together until three days later, after we said good-bye to my parents under the watchful eye of their new security detail and boarded our flight to Miami. The plane took off. My chest tightened because I knew I would never really get away from that place. "Are you okay?" Michael asked, brushing his fingers across my cheek. I shook my head, got up, and locked myself in the first class bathroom. After I threw up, I stared at the stranger in the mirror. I imagined going down, down the rabbit hole of my own happily-ever-after.

ABOUT THE CONTRIBUTORS

Gérald Bloncourt

JACQUES-STEPHEN ALEXIS (1922–1961) was a novelist and political activist. He founded the People's Consensus Party in 1959, which struggled against the Duvalierism of the time and forced Alexis's exile. Upon his return to Haiti in 1961, he and his supporters were captured and killed by Duvalierists. His works include the novels *Compère Général Soleil* (1955), *Les arbres musiciens* (1957), and *L'espace d'un cillement* (1959), as well as the short story collection *Romancero aux étoiles* (1960).

Thomas C. Spear

GEORGES ANGLADE (1944–2010) authored over thirty works of fiction and nonfiction. He was a professor of social geography at l'Université du Québec à Montreal from 1969 until his retirement in 2002. His works include *Les blancs de mémoire* (1999), *Et si Haïti déclarait la guerre aux USA?* (2004), *Rire haïtien/Haitian Laughter, Recueil bilingue de 90 lodyans de Georges Anglade* (2006), and the essay collections *L'espace haitien* and *Mon pays d'Haiti*. He died in the earthquake of January 12, 2010.

Eddie Harris

MYRIAM J.A. CHANCY, born in Port-au-Prince, is the author of *The Loneliness of Angels*, winner of the 2011 Guyana Prize Caribbean Award, Best Fiction 2010; *The Scorpion's Claw; Spirit of Haiti*, short-listed, Best First Book Category, Canada/Caribbean region, Commonwealth Prize 2004; *Framing Silence: Revolutionary Novels by Haitian Women;* and *Searching for Safe Spaces: Afro-Caribbean Women Writers in Exile*, Choice OAB Award, 1998.

Jill Krementz

EDWIDGE DANTICAT was born in Haiti and moved to the United States when she was twelve. She is the editor of *Haiti Noir*, and author of *Claire of the Sea Light, Breath, Eyes, Memory, Krik? Krak!, The Farming of Bones*, and *The Dew Breaker*, among others. Her memoir, *Brother, I'm Dying*, was a 2007 finalist for the National Book Award and winner of the National Book Critics Circle Award for autobiography. She now lives in Miami.

ÈZILI DANTÒ is an award-winning playwright, performance poet, author, and human rights attorney. Born in Port-au-Prince and raised in the US, she is president of the Haitian Lawyers Leadership Network (HLLN). She regularly publishes in the *Black Agenda Report, San Francisco Bay View, LA Progressive*, the *Progressive, Open Salon*, and has essays in several anthologies. *Vodun Woman* is a published collection of her Vodun Jazzoetry performance poetry.

Louise Leblanc

JAN J. DOMINIQUE is a former journalist and director of Radio Haiti, a station founded by her father, Jean Dominique. After her father's assassination in 2000, she continued working at the radio station until it was forced to close in 2003, when she left Haiti and moved to Montreal. Her works include the novels *Mémoire d'une amnésique*, which received Haiti's Prix Deschamps when it was published in 1984, and *La Célestine*.

Jean Faubert

IDA FAUBERT (1882–1969) was the only daughter of Haitian president Lysius Salomon and lived between Haiti and France throughout her life. Her early poems were some of the first published by a Haitian woman, and she played a key role in the Haitian literary revival of the early twentieth century. She received the 1939 Prix Jacques Normand for her poetry collection *Coeur des îles*. In 2007, Memoire d'encrier in Montreal published her collected works, *Anthologie secrète*.

Thorne Anderson

BEN FOUNTAIN is the author of the story collection *Brief Encounters with Che Guevara* and a novel, *Billy Lynn's Long Halftime Walk*, both published by Ecco/HarperCollins. His work has received the PEN/Hemingway Award, a Whiting Writers' Award, a *Los Angeles Times* Book Prize, and the National Book Critics Circle Award, and has been short-listed for the National Book Award. He lives in Texas.

Priscilla Harmel

DANIELLE LEGROS GEORGES is a writer and educator, and the author of a book of poems, *Maroon*. Her essays, interviews, poems, and reviews have appeared in publications including *Agni*, the *Boston Globe*, *Callaloo*, and the *Women's Review of Books*. Her poems have been widely anthologized. She recently completed translating into English from the French the poems of early-twentieth-century Haitian writer Ida Faubert. She is an associate professor at Lesley University.

Roxane Gay

ROXANE GAY'S writing has appeared in *Best American Short Stories 2012*, *Oxford American*, *American Short Fiction*, *Virginia Quarterly Review*, the *New York Times Book Review*, and more. Her novel *An Untamed State*, which grew out of the story appearing in this anthology, will be published by Grove/Atlantic in 2014. That same year, her essay collection, *Bad Feminist*, will be published by Harper Perennial.

Thomas C. Spear

DANY LAFERRIÈRE was born in Haiti in 1953. He is the author of several novels, including *Vers le sud* (made into a feature film by Laurent Cantet), *L'énigme du retour* (winner of the Prix Médicis), *Le goût des jeunes filles*, *Comment faire l'amour avec un nègre sans se fatiguer*, and *Tout bouge autour de moi*. He is also the author of a book for children, *Je suis fou de Vava*.

MARIE-HÉLÈNE LAFOREST, author of the short story collection *Foreign Shores*, grew up between New York City and San Juan, Puerto Rico. She currently makes her home in Italy where she is a professor of postcolonial literature at the University of Naples. Her writing has appeared in numerous periodicals and anthologies. She holds an MA in creative writing, has won a James Michener Fellowship, and was a semifinalist for the 1993 Iowa John Simmons Short Fiction Award.

Kendy Vérilus

PAULETTE POUJOL ORIOL (1926–2011) was a teacher, actress, author, and feminist activist. She founded Haiti's Piccolo Teatro, a theater company dedicated to teaching theater arts to children. From 1997 until 2011, she served as the president of the Women's League for Social Action in Haiti. She received the Prix Henri Deschamps 1980 for her first novel, *Le creuset*, and in 2001 she was awarded the Prix Gouverneur de la Rosée du Livre et de la Littérature.

Roderick Phipps-Kettlewell

MARILÈNE PHIPPS-KETTLEWELL is a poet, painter, and short story writer. She has held fellowships at the Guggenheim Foundation and at Harvard's W.E.B. Du Bois Institute. Her collection *Crossroads and Unholy Water* won the Crab Orchard Poetry Prize; and her collection *The Company of Heaven* won the 2010 Iowa Short Fiction Award. She is the editor of the Library of America's *Jack Kerouac: Collected Poems*.

Homère Cardichon

EMMELIE PROPHÈTE was born in Port-au-Prince. She is a poet, novelist, and short story writer. She is currently the head of Haiti's copyright bureau and has been the editor of the culture section of one of the most important newspapers in the country. Her poetry collections include *Des marges à remplir* and *Sur parure d'ombre*. In 2007, she was awarded the Association of French Language Writers' Prize for her novel *Le testament des solitudes*. Her most recent novel is *Impasse dignité*.

JACQUES ROUMAIN (1907–1944) was an author and political activist. His opposition to the United States' occupation of Haiti, combined with his role in founding the Haitian Communist Party in 1934, led to his exile. He attended Columbia University and worked with many African American poets, including Langston Hughes. He returned to Haiti in 1941 and founded the Haitian Bureau of Ethnology. His most well-known work was his groundbreaking novel *Masters of the Dew*.

NICK STONE was born in Cambridge, England, in 1966, to a Haitian mother. He spent the next three and a half years of his life in Haiti, where he learned to walk and talk. His first novel, *Mr. Clarinet*, set in Haiti in 1996, won the CWA Ian Fleming Steel Dagger Award, an International Thriller Writers Award, a Macavity Award, and the French SNCF Prix du Polar. Stone's other novels include *King of Swords* and *90 Miles*. His new novel, *The Verdict*, will be published in 2014.

LYONEL TROUILLOT writes poetry, fiction, and nonfiction. He cofounded the journal *Lakansyèl, Tèm et Langaj*, and is a member of the collective of the journal *Cahiers du Vendredi*, as well as a Chevalier de l'Ordre des Arts et des Lettres. His novel *Yanvalou pour Charlie* received the 2009 Prix Wepler, and his 2011 novel *La belle amour humaine* received the Grand Prix du Roman Métis, the Prix du Salon du livre de Genève, and the Prix Gitanjali.

MICHÈLE VOLTAIRE MARCELIN is a writer, actress, and painter. She was born in Port-au-Prince and has lived in Haiti, Chile, and the US. Voltaire Marcelin writes in three languages; she is the author of *La Désenchantée, Amours et Bagatelles*, and *Lost and Found*. Her work is included in the poetry anthologies *Terre de Femmes*, RAL'M's *Cahier Haiti, Revue Intranqu'illités*, and *Anthologie secrète Magloire St. Aude*.